From: Delphi@oracle.org
To: C_Evans@athena.edu
Re: FBI, Katie Rush

Christine,

Thank you for the update on the recent kidnappings at Athena Academy. I know you and your Athena Force won't rest until you've safely returned the girls to their families. I have just the person for quickly finding your missing students: FBI agent Katie Rush.

Failure is not an option for Agent Rush, and she's got the experience to bring down the abductors discreetly, with few—if any—casualties. She's the woman you want for the job.

You most likely have her contact info, since she's a friend of your local police lieutenant, Kayla Ryan. Knowing you, you've probably already put her on the case. If you need her cell number, or if there is anything else I can do to assist in this tragedy, let me know.

D.

Dear Reader,

Being asked to write for the exciting universe of Athena Force has been a great honor, as well as a great opportunity. This wonderful, popular series has a rich and colorful landscape of international settings, diverse characters and amazing stories. It has been challenging and rewarding to be a part of the Athena Force team.

I hope you enjoy *Line of Sight*—book one in the new Athena Force adventure—as much as I enjoyed writing it.

Best wishes,

Rachel Caine

Rachel Caine

LINE OF SIGHT

ATHENA FORCE

Published by Silhouette Books

America's Publisher of Contemporary Romance

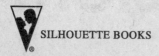

SILHOUETTE BOOKS

ISBN-13: 978-0-373-38972-8
ISBN-10:   0-373-38972-8

LINE OF SIGHT

Visit Athena Force at www.eHarlequin.com

Printed in U.S.A.

RACHEL CAINE

is the author of two previous novels for Silhouette Bombshell: *Devil's Bargain* and *Devil's Due*. She also currently has six novels in her popular Weather Warden series: *Ill Wind, Heat Stroke, Chill Factor, Windfall, Firestorm* and the soon-to-be-released *Thin Air*. In addition she has a bestselling young adult series, The Morganville Vampires, with two novels currently available: *Glass Houses* and *The Dead Girls' Dance*. The third book, *Midnight Alley,* will be released in August 2007.

Visit her Web site at www.rachelcaine.com.

To the fierce, fabulous authors, editors and readers
of the Bombshell line, and especially to
Natashya Wilson, for her faith and support.
What an honor to be part of the family!

Chapter 1

Until she chose to die, Katie Rush wasn't completely sure she had the guts. Sure, she'd considered it, she'd trained for it, but in the end there was always a doubt: Did she have what it took to trade her life for someone else's?

In that chaotic, oddly crystalline moment, it was very simple. She saw the gunman, she was out of rounds and there was a civilian being targeted. The calculations rose effortlessly in her brain: Given the angle of incidence, there was a seventy-five percent chance that the shooter would go for center mass, the safe shot. His ammunition wasn't armor-piercing. Of course, there were still decent odds that he'd choose the head shot instead, which was an almost certain kill at this distance.

It didn't even require a conscious decision. Her body just moved. She took a stunning blow to her chest, an impact that knocked her off balance and drove the breath from her lungs. She used the force in her favor, letting her weight fall against the boy who'd been in the line of fire and pushing him behind a parked car to safety.

"Agent down!" she heard someone yell, probably Special Agent in Charge Craig Evangelista; he was the one with the best vantage point of her position. She tried to take a breath but it was driven out of her by a second impact right over her solar plexus. Panic tried to smother her, but she grimly held on to her training, rolling on her side toward cover and ejecting the spent magazine of her Beretta as she did. Her right hand fumbled for the spares clipped to her belt and yanked one free, slapped it home with a precision built of hours of dry-fire drills, and completed her roll into a shooter's prone position, elbows braced. She acquired the target in a matter of a microsecond—which was good, because he had already acquired *her* again—and got off the first shot.

One was all she needed. She ignored the odds and went for the head shot.

The boy lying next to her was wailing and shaking. Katie felt calm, which she expected was the inevitable adrenaline shock as much as any real self-possession. She scanned the landscape for additional threats as the rest of the team swarmed in to apprehend any kidnappers who'd survived the firefight. There had been four of them—a large crew, unusually so for such a risky crime—and they'd been more than willing to go out in a blaze of glory. Katie could only see one man alive and responding to the agents' shouts and commands. It wasn't the one she'd shot. He wouldn't be moving on his own again.

She slowly got to her knees. The pain hadn't yet registered, but she had no doubt that later tonight her body was going to hurt like hell. She'd never taken a round before, but she'd seen the deeply colored bruises on other agents who had. Bulletproof vests saved lives. There was no promise that they'd do it painlessly.

At least she could breathe again, though not deeply enough to speak. She put her arm around the boy—Samuel Kaltoff, thirteen-year-old son of a prominent Russian politician—and tried to smile reassuringly. The kid was a mess, but then, he'd been through a hellish ordeal. Three days in the hands of captors who'd shown no signs of humanity or compassion. *We could have gotten him back faster*, Katie thought miserably. Samuel's dirty-pale skin showed so much bruising it looked as if he'd been tie-dyed, and that was only a hint of what had been done to him. *We should have had him yesterday.* Katie knew that logically they'd pushed the investigation as fast and as far as it was possible to do, but at moments like this, looking at the human wreckage left behind when law and chaos crashed, she never felt that it was enough.

The paramedics, who'd had to wait for the all-clear signal, suddenly dashed in. One peeled off toward her, but she waved him toward Samuel. Nothing they could do for bruises, and if that hot, glassy feeling in her side was a cracked rib, well, it wasn't going anywhere.

"Katie," said SAC Evangelista. He holstered his

weapon as he approached and wiped sweat from his forehead—it was a hot day, and the vests and FBI jackets weren't exactly summer-weight. He crouched down beside her, examining her with clinical thoroughness. He was middle-aged, on the heavy side of fit, with a bullet-bald head and big brown eyes that could look warm and sympathetic when he chose. It wasn't necessary with her. "You trying to give me a heart attack?"

"Sorry, sir, but I didn't see any alternative."

He waved that away. "Not how I would have handled it, but you got the right result. Understand, the only reason we're having this conversation now, and I'm not going to be writing the condolence letter to your folks tonight, is that you were lucky. The government has invested a hell of a lot in your training, Agent Rush. Letting some Russian mob moron shoot you ain't exactly the return on investment they're looking for."

"Live and fight another day," she said. "I know, Craig. Thanks. Believe me, I won't make a habit out of it."

"Good. Now, you go to the hospital, get checked out. Once you're green lighted, you can come back to the office and start paperwork." He hesitated, then looked away. "You saved that kid's life, Katie. One hell of a good day."

From Evangelista, that was effusive praise. He put his heavy, warm hand on her shoulder for one very short second before rising and striding off to oversee the mop-up.

This time, when the paramedics moved toward her, she didn't object. She was starting to ache now, and tremble with reaction. Being poked and prodded would give her time to get herself together again.

Katie was watching two equally heartwarming events—Samuel Kaltoff's weeping parents embracing him, and the sole surviving kidnapper getting handcuffed to a gurney—when her cell phone rang. She grabbed it from her jacket pocket before the paramedics took it away from her. "Hey, could you wait a second while I answer this?"

The paramedic undressing her shook his head and tugged open the Velcro straps of the vest. The sudden rush of air on her sweat-soaked skin was like being doused in cool water. He pulled the heavy armor over her head and set it aside. Katie ignored him as he lifted up the damp fabric of her shirt and probed the bruising beneath.

She flipped open the cell phone. "Rush," she said, a simple declaration of name as well as an instruction. She expected it would be a call from the field office asking for details, but instead she glanced at the number and saw that it was from out of state.

Arizona.

"Katie?" A young girl's voice. It sounded high and uneven. "Katie, it's Jazz. I need help. We need help!"

Jazz? Katie's mind froze for a second, then smoothly shifted gears. Jazz was Kayla Ryan's daughter. The voice had sounded unlike her, but now Katie recognized that it was probably due to stress. "Yes, I'm here. What's wrong, honey?" As far as Katie knew, Jazz was at the safest place on earth—at the Athena Academy, a secluded campus just outside of Glendale, Arizona. "Jazz, is your mother all right?"

There was a brief sound of shuffling, and then Kayla's no-nonsense voice said, "I'm right here. We've got a situation here, and I don't think the local resources are enough to handle it. We need you, Katie." Kayla was a cop, a good one, besides being a fellow Athena graduate and friend. Not a close friend, exactly—Katie didn't seem to attract many of those—but more of a sister. Athena alumni were all sisters. It was an implicit responsibility they all took very seriously. They'd suffered losses these past few years that had hurt them all. At least Jazz was safe. That was something.

"What happened?"

"I'll let Jazz tell you."

Another handoff, and Jazz's higher voice came back on the line. "It's Teal and Lena—Teal Arnett and Lena Poole. They're at the Academy with me. They're my friends. They were taken."

"Taken," Katie repeated. Her fingers tightened on the phone, and she forced them to relax. She'd seen the tragic aftermath of too many stories that began just this way, but none of them had involved girls from the Athena Academy—her own very extended family. If all of the Athena Force women were sisters, then all the girls at the Academy were nieces. "How did it happen?"

The very slight hesitation before Jazz answered raised a red flag in Katie's mind. *Need to get her away from her mother and get the full story,* she thought.

Even though Kayla was a cop, and Athena Force, that didn't mean mothers and daughters should or could share everything. Daughters had secrets, and in cases like this, secrets cost lives. "We were going to the movies," Jazz said. "Off the school grounds, in town. But they were waiting for us, I don't know how. It was a coordinated attack. Teal and Lena gave me time to get away, they told me to run. I didn't want to leave them, I swear I didn't!"

"I know you didn't. Jazz, tell me what you saw. Exactly what you saw."

Jazz took a deep breath. "We were walking on the sidewalk, talking, and a van pulled up to the curb ahead of us. It was a blue cargo van, and the license plates were muddy. I couldn't see any letters or numbers. There was dark tinting on the windows. I think it was a Ford van, probably about eight years old. Oh, and there was a fresh scratch on the passenger side, like somebody had keyed it in a parking lot."

Katie raised a commanding finger to the paramedic to back off when he tried to speak to her. He did, finally taking the look in her eyes seriously. "And?"

"The side door slid open, and two men jumped out. They were both tall, but one was bigger than the other one—I think they were about six feet and six feet four inches."

"What did they look like?"

"I couldn't tell," Jazz said unhappily. "They were wearing these mesh masks and bodysuits. I guess that was to keep from leaving trace evidence. They didn't say anything at all, and they were really fast and strong. Lena almost got away, but they caught her."

Sometime during Jazz's recital, Katie had closed her eyes, painting the picture in her mind. A cloudless Arizona day, clear and sunny. The van pulling to a smooth stop at the curb so as not to alarm the girls into flight. A blitz attack, scientifically calculated. Two abductors, plus a third to drive the van. They'd cut their losses once they'd realized they'd lost the initiative and Jazz was beyond their control…. More impulsive predators would have gone after her, allowed Teal and Lena space to act. Instead, these men had disengaged to minimize their exposure.

Dangerously competent. And the fact that they'd succeeded at all meant that they'd known what they'd be dealing with.

"Tell me about the girls," she said. "Teal and Lena."

"Teal's the oldest, she's seventeen. She's really fast— the fastest runner in the school. She looks a little bit like you in the face, and she's tall, too—she has lighter hair, and her eyes are more green." Jazz took a breath. "Lena's fifteen. You can't miss her. She's got purple streaks in her hair, it's cut all different lengths, you know? She was wearing a purple skirt and a hot-pink top." Jazz's voice wavered. "They're my friends, Katie. *Really* my friends. I should have stayed with them. I let them down."

Jazz was small, but she was a dynamo, like her mother. Self-possessed. A fiercer friend Katie couldn't imagine. Jazz was someone who wouldn't take failure easily in a situation like this. Athena Academy instilled that quality in those who hadn't come in the doors gifted with it, but in Jazz tenacity was a purely natural talent.

"Jazz, it's going to be all right. We're going to find them. Now, put your mom on the line, will you?" Jazz did. Katie dropped the warm-and-fuzzy from her voice. "I'm heading for the airport now," she said and slid off of the tail end of the ambulance. "I'll take a cab to the crime scene. What are the cross streets?"

Kayla gave them to her, relief evident in her voice. "Thanks for agreeing to help. I know you're the best at this, Katie, and I have the feeling we need to find these girls quickly. This wasn't random. No way was it random."

Kayla was being careful, not saying things that they were both thinking.

"Did they have enhancements?" Katie asked. She would have asked straight out, *psychic abilities,* but Kayla knew what she meant, knew exactly what made many of the girls fostered by the Athena Academy special. She and Kayla were included in that number, most definitely, although Katie herself had tried her best to downplay it throughout her career.

Kayla confirmed her worst fears. "Yes. Definitely…enhanced abilities."

"What about Teal and Lena's parents? Has somebody talked to them?"

"We're handling notifications through the school. I've already talked to Ms. Evans." Christine Evans, the principal of the Athena Academy—as tough as they came, even by Katie's admittedly high standards. So

tough, cops and FBI agents still automatically called her
Ms. Evans years after graduation. "I'll book you a seat
on the first available flight. I'll wait for you at the scene."

"Soon as I can," Katie promised, and was about to hang
up when she hesitated. "Kayla? Is Jazz okay? Physically?"

"As far as I can tell." Her friend's voice was tight. "I
want to take her to the hospital. Just to be sure."

It was what Katie would have advised, but she was
glad she didn't have to. Kayla had enough on her mind.

"Do that. I'm on my way," she promised and flipped
the phone closed.

The paramedic, frowning, rushed into the silence.
"Agent, you can't go anywhere before those ribs are
X-rayed," he said. "They might be broken."

"They're not broken," she said and pulled on her
jacket after tucking the FBI identification flap back into
its Velcro pocket. "You got forms for me to sign?
Because you have one minute to get them in front of me
before I'm gone."

She didn't wait for him; he could damn well catch up.
She strode off, looking for Evangelista, and found him
talking with two other agents. They all nodded to her.

"I need a minute," she said. Evangelista gave the other
two a crisp dismissal and turned to her with his full attention. "Two girls have been abducted in Phoenix. One
other girl got away, she's the kid of a friend of mine. I
need some personal time, okay? E-mail the paperwork
to my Web account. I'll get it completed tonight."

"Katie, you sure that's a good idea? You took a
couple of hard hits. Paramedics released you?"

"Sure." She lied like the professional she was. "Good to go?"

"Can I stop you?" He shrugged. "I'll need you to make yourself available tomorrow sometime for a recorded statement. If you need me to make a call to the Phoenix field office, let me know."

He extended his hand. She shook it briskly, not letting the pain in her ribs show. "No heroics, Rush," he reminded her.

"No, sir. No heroics."

That was it. He turned away and was immediately lost in the wash of detail and documentation that was the bane of every investigator's existence.

"Sign here," said the paramedic, appearing at her shoulder with a metal clipboard and pen. He pointed to a line, and she scribbled her name. "Agent, seriously, get yourself checked out wherever you're going. Those ribs don't look good."

"I'm fine," she said, and remembered to smile at him. "Thank you for taking care of me."

"My job." He nodded. No smile back. She supposed she was screwing up his ability to do his work. It occurred to her, a little late, that he was pretty cute—her type, too, with big dark eyes and nice shoulders. Ah well. She didn't have time for romance, anyway. She never did.

She retrieved her car, parked three blocks away, and drove to the airport without stopping for anything.

Chapter 2

The girl leaning over the table was wearing the tiniest orange bikini he'd ever seen. Stefan was a connoisseur of bikinis—some people watched birds or butterflies; he watched girls in outrageously small scraps of fabric. Today was a spectacular day for it, in fact—a cloudless deep-blue sky, a cool ocean breeze, a bright summer sun. Venice Beach at its finest, and the girls were in full bloom.

Life, he reflected, was very good to him. A great profession, a great place to live, stimulation of all kinds. Yeah, not bad. Not bad at all.

He didn't look at the deck of cards he was shuffling, just smiled at the girl in the orange bikini and the other girls crowded around his table. An invisibly fast motion of his little finger, and a card slid out of the deck he was manipulating and spun across the smooth marble surface of the café table toward the orange bikini. The girl squealed in excitement, grabbed the card and held it up for the admiring oohs and aahs of her friends. Four friends, to be exact, and every one a sculpted marvel. Not natural, of course. Venice Beach had more girls with breast implants than it did grains of sand on the beach, or at least it seemed that way these days. Not that Stefan minded, really. Nature was wonderful, but the human race had always been inclined to decorate.

And these girls…well, they were very, very decorative.

He gave them a charming smile, and they all smiled back, crowding closer. His hands were still moving on their own, shuffling, fanning, dazzling. It was a nervous habit now, something he did without even thinking about it. Illusion wasn't his main source of income, but it was his passion, and it kept him on the streets, where he belonged.

"Oh my God, that's amazing!" the girl in the orange bikini—Heather?—said, and showed him the queen of hearts he'd flipped her. "Stefan, do it again! Please?"

"Put it back in the deck. Anywhere." He didn't look, and his hands never stopped. She slid the card in, and he did the trick again, faster this time. The cool slap of the cards on his fingers was soothing. Relaxing. It was a kind of meditation for him, card tricks, and of course, it got the girls to lean closer. That was never a bad thing.

When the queen of hearts spun out this time, flipping in midair to land faceup, they all squealed. He followed it with the rest of the suit, in order, never looking down. It was his own trick, invented on long,

lonely nights when he hadn't felt like company. He
didn't sleep much, never had. He'd been up at dawn
this morning, down on the beach with a cup of Star-
bucks' finest, watching the sun gild the waves in
rolling gold.

"Wow," Heather breathed and looked up, delight shin-
ing in her eyes. That was what he loved about magic…. It
really *did* magical things, even if it was only illusion. It
made people feel a sense of wonder, and that could never
be underestimated. "Stefan, you are *amazing!*"

He winked at her. "Better save your praise. We just
met. I could get better, you know."

They all laughed, breathless and excited. He couldn't
understand what his attraction was for women; he
couldn't really see it when he looked in the mirror. He
was a collection of flaws: not tall enough, a little broad
in the shoulders, gypsy-dark skin at least three shades
off the golden glow that Californians seemed to crave.
His hair curled, and he'd given up styling it; it just
cascaded wild and black around his face and down past
his collar. His nose was too large, his eyes so dark brown
they looked black. No, he was hardly the California
ideal, and he was overdressed for the nearly naked dress
code of Venice Beach in loose low-slung jeans and a
roomy black cotton shirt over a red sleeveless undershirt.

And yet, he was surrounded by girls so hot that he
was surprised the wooden floor didn't catch fire around
them. Ah well. His cross to bear, he supposed.

Heather slid onto the bench beside him, and a girl in
a blue thong bikini slipped in on the other side. "Ladies,"

he said. "Are you trying to distract me? Or learn my secrets? I promise, there's nothing up my sleeves."

Heather leaned over, and her tongue touched his earlobe, a gentle wet caress that made him pause in his shuffling and close his eyes to control a deep, satisfying shudder. Oh, yes. He liked Venice Beach. "How about here?" she asked, and her hand moved on his leg under the table.

"Naughty," he said, and actually jumped when the girl on his other side moved, too. "Okay, that's—naughtier."

They giggled. Stefan started shuffling again, fumbling one or two cards, trying to think how to get himself out of this gracefully. Or at least how to retain as much of his mystery and dignity as possible while succumbing. After all, if it was beyond his control, who could blame him....

Over one of the girls' bronzed shoulders a TV was soundlessly playing on a twenty-four-hour news channel. He fixed on it, trying to take his mind off the girls while still enjoying what they were doing, and read the text crawling at the bottom of the screen. BREAKING NEWS, it read. DUAL ABDUCTION IN PHOENIX...

It hit him in a rush of light and color and sickening sensation. *Cold. Cold metal floor. Vibrations. Light leaking in through tinted, curtained windows. Fingers going numb, tied too tight. Sharp pain in bound ankles. Knees, too. Wet gag in his mouth, on the verge of choking him. No way to spit it out. The cool, gritty feeling of tear tracks on his face. Grim anger and fear, a trace of panic held down with difficulty.*

*A girl was lying across from him on the van floor,
similarly bound, her purple-streaked blond hair falling
over her face but not quite concealing her frantic eyes.
There was a bruise on her face, dark even in the dimness.*

*Two men sat on benches, one on each side. Couldn't
make out their features in the darkness. One was
smoking, the stink of it filling the van and making it even
harder to breathe around the gag....*

He jerked back into himself, gasping, and dropped
the cards. A strange sound sawed at his ears, and after
a couple of seconds he realized it was the girls, giggling.
He was still in the coffee shop, in Venice Beach. He was
safe. His heart was racing, his palms sweating, and he
couldn't get away from the feeling of fear and foreboding
and claustrophobia in the vision.

He stood up, gathered the cards and jammed them
into his pocket. "Sorry," he said, and pushed through the
crowd of girls to achieve the open air outside. He stood
there, breathing deeply, trying to slow his pulse. Blue
sky, warm sun, pounding surf. Laughing people. Weight
lifters on the beach, displaying their oiled muscles and
as much skin as legally possible. Skating, scantily clad
girls. Jugglers. Sidewalk artists. Musicians. Normal life,
by the community standards. Stefan stood there shaking,
struggling to put himself back in his own body. He
was unable to forget the bleak terror the girl was feeling.

DUAL ABDUCTION IN PHOENIX.

They were in a van, and they were in terrible danger.
He needed to tell someone.

He sat down on a bench facing the ocean and dialed his cell phone slowly, thinking hard about what to do. In the end, he did what he always did.

He called home.

"It's about time," his mother said. No hello because she already knew it was him—she always knew. "Are you all right, Stefan? I had a dream."

"Did you?" He closed his eyes and smiled. "What about?"

"You, obviously. You were somewhere dark, and you were in danger. Where are you, my dear?"

"Not in the dark," he said. "And not in danger. I think you had an echo of what I just had, Mom."

"Ah. Vision?" She was businesslike about it, but then, she would be: it *was* her business. Rose Blackman, psychic to the stars and Hollywood nobility. A genuine talent. She'd taught him all about showmanship, too. "Tell me about it, peanut."

"Mom, *please* don't call me that."

"Just tell me."

He did, in as much detail as he could remember. Unlike some of his other visions, this one wasn't fading like a nightmare—it remained immediate and frightening in its vividness. "Mom, I think it's the girls who were on the news. In Phoenix. I think I should call the cops."

"The cops? Oh, no. That's the worst thing you can do. Believe me, I've been down that road before. Even in L.A., the police don't believe in psychics, and you're talking about Arizona? Pffft. You might as well claim to be from outer space."

"What about the FBI?"

"What about them? Do you have any real information, Stefan? Anything that could really help those girls right now?"

He thought it over. The impressions had been immediate, but limited to the van, the pain, the fear. He couldn't describe the exterior of the van, or even the faces of the abductors.

His heart sank, and he bent over to rest his aching forehead on the heel of one hand. "Then what do I do?"

"Whatever you do, son, it will be the right thing. I know this, because I know you." Rose Blackman's voice had softened, as if she could sense his distress. Maybe she could, even at this distance. It had been a source of annoyance and comfort to him all his life, that he couldn't hide anything from his mother or—to a lesser extent— his father. They always knew, somehow, what he felt, if not what he was thinking. "Are you working today?"

"No. I'm supposed to have some production meetings later this week, but I'm at the beach." He didn't consider street performing to be working so much as playing, although he couldn't say she agreed with him. "Why?"

"Maybe you'll get more information," she said. "When you do, you can decide what to do. And where to go. But, peanut—"

"Mom!"

"—I had the dream. So watch yourself." There was a voice in the background, and Rose dropped her own voice to a lower volume. "I have to go. My morning's very full."

"Anything exciting?"

"Oh, you know, the usual. Should I take this job or that one? What about this guy I'm dating? Movie stars aren't really any different from everyone else when it comes to insecurities. Except that you can't keep them waiting. I love you, son."

"Love to you and Dad," he said and hung up. He rubbed the plastic of the phone case for a few long seconds, thinking, and then stood up to walk toward the stand of yellow taxis nearby.

"Stefan?" His gaggle of beach beauties stepped into his path, led by Heather in the orange bikini. She pressed against him, arms around his neck. Warm and so very tempting. "You're not leaving us, are you?" He'd be a fool, that much was clear.

And of course, he *was* a fool.

"Want to see another trick?" he asked, and they all agreed they did.

It was a disappearing act.

His.

Chapter 3

Katie had been lucky on flights. After grabbing an overnight bag—she always kept one in her car, packed and ready—she'd been the last passenger boarded on the MD-80 out of St. Louis, and spent the flight refreshing her memories of Phoenix, Glendale and the surrounding area. According to her maps, Teal and Lena had been grabbed several miles from the school, which was odd; why hadn't the girls caught a ride to the movies, or a bus or a cab? It was a long walk. She jotted down questions for Jazz and Kayla, then filled a second page with questions for Christine Evans. Made herself a note to contact the Phoenix field office on landing to make sure they knew she was involved. She might end up needing an intercession from SAC Evangelista, if the local bureaucracy was going to be difficult about things; then again, she expected at least one Athena grad in a position of authority would make some phone calls, and that would straighten out the tangle quickly.

Sitting strapped down made Katie's bruises and cracked ribs ache fiercely. She swallowed some non-prescription painkillers and tried to nap, since she'd been short on sleep for days. She couldn't. Her mind kept replaying the visuals she'd constructed from Jazz's verbal account.

The blue van, easing in at the curb ahead of the three unsuspecting girls. The blitz attack, fast and overwhelming—as if the attackers had known to anticipate considerable resistance. Which implied that they'd done their homework on the girls, and also implied an uncomfortable amount of knowledge about the Athena Academy and its students. Almost certainly not targets of opportunity, these girls, or they'd have managed to surprise their abductors and fight their way free.

Still. It was possible that she was reading too much into it. Maybe this was a simple case of sexual predators cruising for prey…which was never simple. Her mind veered off in unwelcome directions. Too many cases that had ended horribly, too many trials, too many autopsies. She'd seen and heard things that wouldn't leave her in moments like these, even with all her mental discipline and training. What if it was that rarest of breeds, the team of sexual predators—one to drive, two to abduct? That kind of organization was associated with the most frightening of offenders, the ones capable of the most excessive and calculated cruelty.

Given all that, sleep stayed a distant wish.

Katie opened her eyes as the plane approached the runway and got everything ready. She had one small bag, no purse, and she was fast off the starting blocks once the plane had taxied to a halt. She walked quickly down the Jetway ramp and breathed a sigh of relief when she achieved the open space of the terminal— room to breathe, finally.

As Katie made her way toward the transportation, the traffic congestion increased. It was prime West Coast arrival time, and the flight from LAX had just disgorged a flood of tanned beach-bunny types, along with some business travelers in the dreary uniform of the breed. She could fit in with them, really; she'd worn black slacks today, and sensible shoes, a white-collared linen shirt and black jacket. No jewelry. All she'd done was rinse off the worst of her sweat in the airport bathroom in St. Louis. Crime scenes weren't fashion runways.

She cut diagonally through the milling crowd, trying to move faster, and collided with someone who had the same idea. "My fault, sorry," Katie muttered and automatically backed off to steer around. So did he, and for a second she froze, staring, because he was…well, worthy of a good stare. Of a height with her, with a carefree tumble of raven-black curling hair. Big, dark, gentle eyes. Dark golden skin that could have come from half a dozen different ethnic heritages, a clever, handsome face and a devastating smile that he probably didn't even realize he was using on her.

"No, that was definitely my fault," he said. He had a

great voice, too. She wondered why she was noticing him so intently, and why *now,* and then it occurred to her: he was noticing *her.* She wasn't used to that kind of scrutiny, so blatant and yet nonintrusive. He didn't leer, he just…appreciated. "I don't think I can say I'm sorry about it, though. Nice to meet you."

Realities crashed in. She didn't have time for flirting; she had a crime scene to visit. The clock was ticking on two young girls, and she'd just wasted at least fifteen seconds of it on ephemera.

Katie took it out on him with a cool "Excuse me, I'm in a hurry," then brushed by him, walked even faster and didn't look back.

Stefan Blackman looked after the woman for a long moment, until she vanished into the crowd, and wondered what had possessed him to do a thing like that. There had been some kind of connection between them; he'd felt it, and he could have sworn she had, too. It hadn't been a vision, not the way his mother received them, or even the way he usually did; it certainly lacked the power and definition of the images he'd received from the girl in the van.

Still. Something there. The woman was gorgeous. Obviously, not in the way he was used to; he couldn't imagine her in an orange bikini, in-line skating around Venice Beach, for example. No, this one seemed cool and quiet and utterly self-confident, with just a hint of vulnerability in those dark eyes. Professional.

She was also armed. He'd felt it when they'd col-

lided—a pancake holster under her plain black jacket—
and his instant thought had been *air marshal,* but then
he'd revised that. She seemed to be on her way somewhere in a hurry, and not just spending her days in
airports. No, maybe a cop. FBI. Something like that. He
didn't imagine too many people other than those would
be eligible to carry firearms on planes these days.

He'd never really had much to do with cops, other
than the ones he ran into on the streets. Once or twice,
one of his less-than-savory clients had brought about a
visit from detectives, but usually it was perfunctory at
most. He'd certainly never seen a cop like *her.*

Too bad he was on a mission. He was tempted to
follow her, wherever she was going, although she'd
probably have arrested him for it.

Hmm. Handcuffs.

He entertained himself with mental handcuff escapes
as he shouldered his bag and strolled for the exits. He
still wasn't sure he'd done the right thing in hopping the
last-minute flight, but something had told him not to
delay. His mother had been correct—the police weren't
about to put any trust in what he had to say, and he
didn't yet have enough specifics to convince them. He
needed more detail, and to get that, he needed to start at
the beginning.

All he had to do was find the place where the girls had
been abducted. Stefan hitched his backpack to a more
comfortable position, thinking about the problem, and
then strolled over to the nearest bank of phones. He flipped
through the directory to find the number for the television

station whose call letters he'd seen on the TV earlier, then programmed the main number into his cell phone.

He always did like the press. They were all show people at heart.

The cab stand outside the terminal was a zoo, every cab already claimed and being loaded. Katie growled in frustration and paced, watching as vacationers and business travelers loaded bags and laptops and kids into the available transportation. Come on, she thought. All I need is a damn cab.

One pulled up at the far end of the row, and Katie dashed for it. Out of the corner of her eye she saw someone else heading there, moving fast, and he was closer. His hand touched the door of the cab before she made it, and she pulled up short, fuming, as he pulled on the handle.

It was the man from the California flight, the one she'd bumped into. He'd been gorgeous in the terminal, but out here in the sun he glowed, his skin an impossible shade of light bronze, his deep black hair picking up blue highlights.

His smile was as warm as the sun.

"Okay, this time I do apologize," he said and stepped back from the door to offer her the cab. "You look like you're in even more of a hurry than I am. How about we share? You get dropped off first."

She wrenched her stare away from that smile to some less dangerous territory. Not his eyes. His eyes were definitely, lethally beautiful.

"No," she said.

"No?" He hung on to the smile. "You mean, no, you don't want to share the cab, or no, you're not taking the cab?"

Yes, she thought. He was rattling her, and that was strange and very distracting in its own right. She never let guys get to her. She'd seen all kinds—gorgeous charmers included—and she was definitely inoculated against their particular gifts. She'd seen the wreckage they left behind.

But this one...well. He was a challenge.

"I'll take the next one," she said. "You take this one." She didn't need a distraction, and he was the Las Vegas of distractions, neon and glitter and flashing arrows.

He frowned a little, and started to say something she was sure was going to be an argument, but then she heard someone behind her call, "Agent Rush?"

She turned. There was a police cruiser parked at the curb farther down, lights flashing, with two uniformed officers standing next to it. Katie waved.

"I think I already have a ride," she said.

She walked away, resisting the urge to look back. After a few seconds she heard the click of the cab door shutting, and breathed a sigh of relief as the yellow sedan rolled by. She kept her focus on the police cruiser, and the two officers beside it, as she walked.

Okay, *one* glance at the taxi. He wouldn't still be looking....

He was. She looked away, furious with herself, as he waved.

"Agent Rush, welcome to the lovely city of Phoenix. Detective Ryan sent you chauffeurs. Hope you don't mind riding in our special visitor's seats."

The male officer was already opening up the back door of the cruiser. She ducked inside and found it depressingly familiar; she'd ridden in a lot of police cars around the country, and it always seemed to be the same damn car, over and over. Different colored wipe-down vinyl upholstery, and the heavy grillwork separating her from the front seat. There were no handles on the inside of the doors, of course. The whole thing smelled of the body odor and vomit of the last transport, overlaid with the astringent wipe-down they'd given it to make it presentable for her.

"Nice," she said. "So I'm getting the royal treatment."

"You know us locals, anything for our cousins from the FBI. Watch your head."

Their names, according to the name tags, were officers Samson and Gilhoulie—one black, one white, one thin, one plump, one female, one male. The differences didn't matter much, as far as Katie could tell; they seemed used to each other, in the way of partners or old married couples. Aware of each other at all times, but comfortable.

Samson was the driver of the two, apparently. He got behind the wheel and steered the cruiser into traffic, lights still flashing. Katie looked out the freshly cleaned window—it still smelled of the cleaning product they'd used to give it a streak-free shine—to get her bearings in the city again. In a sense, they really had rolled out the red carpet. Most cop shops would have assumed she could take care of her own transportation.

Phoenix never looked lush, but the weak winter sunlight gave it a wan quality that mirrored Katie's mood. She remembered the city very well, but it wasn't a homecoming, not given the circumstances.

"So," Officer Gilhoulie said and twisted around to look at her. She was a height-challenged redhead with fair Irish skin and blue eyes that seemed pleasant, but had that inner distance all cops everywhere shared. "How long have you known Detective Ryan, ma'am?"

The *ma'am* was reflexive. All beat cops were courteous to a fault, until they weren't. Part of their charm.

"Detective Ryan and I went to school together," Katie said. That usually derailed the conversation because there was nothing more boring than old school-days reminiscences; nobody wanted to hear high school stories except people from your high school. Sure enough, Gilhoulie turned back to face forward.

But, to Katie's surprise, she continued asking questions.

"You originally from Phoenix, then?"

"Pennsylvania. Philly, actually. I'm just assigned out of the Kansas City field office right now."

"They move you around in the FBI, huh?"

"Every two years," Katie said. "Until you get to a certain service level. I've probably got one rotation to go before they let me choose a permanent duty station. Doesn't matter, though. I work all over the country."

Chitchat, nothing Katie had to focus her attention on

beyond the bare minimum. Gilhoulie's partner, Samson, drove without saying much; he was constantly scanning the streets and sidewalks. Gilhoulie seemed to think it was her duty to entertain the guest, for some reason. "So," the officer asked, "do you have some kind of specialty, or…?"

"Missing persons," Katie said. "I specialize in missing persons cases."

"No wonder Ryan called you," Gilhoulie said. "So, what kind of school was it? Some kind of prep school, right? I heard it's exclusive."

Time to change the subject. "You get a lot of these kinds of abductions in Phoenix these days?"

"No, ma'am," Samson said immediately. "Mostly the usual, you know, custody disputes. Sometimes we get a kid or woman snatched by predators, though. It happens here same as anywhere else."

"Did you work the scene of today's abduction?"

"Just perimeter stuff," he said, shrugging. "Sorry. Can't tell you much, except that Detective Ryan's been a rock. If it was my kid nearly got snatched, I can tell you, I don't think I'd hold up so well."

Gilhoulie nodded soberly in agreement. "I always knew she was, you know, pretty good, but she's been all over this thing today. Her kid's been terrific, too."

"Real trooper," Samson added. He hit the blinker and turned the car onto a side street. "Right up ahead, Agent Rush. You'll find Detective Ryan in the middle of it."

He kept driving, passed through a police barricade and parked inside the perimeter, safely away from the crowd of bystanders and press. "Forensics is still processing," Samson added, although he didn't really need to; Katie knew from experience how long that could take, for a really complicated crime scene. "Probably got a couple more hours to go before they wrap it up."

"Got it. Thanks to you both," she said as Gilhoulie opened up the back door for her.

"Not a problem. Do us a favor. Find the girls, huh?"

"I'll do my best." Once upon a time, she'd have said, *I will,* but she knew that wasn't always the case. "I appreciate the ride, guys."

The air was cool outside, especially after the closed-in fug of the police cruiser; Katie took a deep breath, shouldered her bag and headed for the nearest on-duty cop she could spot. Her FBI badge got her instant directions to Kayla Ryan, who was half a block away in a huddle with other police.

There was something indefinable about seeing a fellow Athena Force member—a kind of recognition and simple comfort that went beyond just spotting an old friend. Katie saw Kayla step out of the impromptu meeting going on and head her way.

"Katie," Kayla said and smiled. They shook hands in a brisk, businesslike fashion rather than hugged—purely for any cameras that happened to be pointed in their direction. "I can't thank you enough for this. Let's go someplace more private to talk."

She led the way with quick strides. They'd always been the same height, but Katie recognized even more similarities. She and Kayla both moved with authority and confidence, thanks to their training both at the Academy and through their careers. Kayla's skin was shades darker, and she'd let her long dark hair grow. Her brown eyes still looked disarmingly warm. That probably served her very well in interrogations—Katie knew that intimidation, for all its dramatic presentation, was generally less useful than empathy in soliciting information.

In short, Kayla looked great, if strained at the moment. As they walked toward a row of high hedges, backs to the cameras, she caught Kayla exchanging a look with a tall, good-looking detective standing nearby. A *look*. You didn't have to be an investigator to read his regard for her, and to see it was something more than just professional courtesy.

"So I guess the press is all over this one," Katie said and winced as she adjusted her bag on her shoulder. Her ribs were making their protests felt. Again. "Why the cloak and dagger?"

"Parabolic microphones. Some of the more enterprising news reporters have them around here. They can't air the footage, unless they want to lose any cooperation in the future from the department, but they can still use the information they get in other ways." Kayla shook her head. "Lots of 'unnamed sources' come from surveillance. I'm not willing to take the chance. Besides, guess who's here as our special media guest?"

"60 Minutes?"

"I just wish. No, Shannon Connor."

"Shannon!" Katie blurted, shocked. Not that she

couldn't have foreseen it happening, of course. Shannon Connor had been a promising student at the Athena Academy—in Kayla's group, the Graces, in fact—but she'd shown a dark side, and had made history as the first girl ever expelled from the Academy. Not that she wasn't bright, but she was ambitious and bitter. Since getting thrown out of the school, she'd gone on to a relatively successful career in broadcast journalism…but she was always looking for dirt on the Academy and its graduates. "She'd better be looking to help, not just digging for trouble."

"You know Shannon. She's looking for any angle that will make us look…" Kayla shrugged.

"I can't believe she'd stoop that low. Not with kids at stake."

"She's a reporter. Of course she'd stoop that low." Which might have been ungenerous, but Katie wasn't much inclined to grant Shannon Connor any benefit of the doubt, either.

The hedges had a gate, which Kayla swung open and motioned her through. The other side was cool and green and open—a community garden, pretty and peaceful, xeriscaped with desert plants. Secluded.

A young lady slumped, hands folded, on a concrete park bench under the skeletal branches of a large tree. She looked up as Kayla and Katie approached, and got to her feet quickly.

Kayla's daughter, Jazz, looked taller than Katie remembered, but that was the way with kids.… They grew while you weren't watching. Jazz looked much more mature, though. She'd always been self-possessed, but the time at the Athena Academy had given her even more of that. Except for a hint of nervousness in the quick way she glanced at her mother, she looked as cool as ice.

She was dressed in blue jeans and a pink top, long-sleeved and hooded. Warm enough for a walk, but not for sitting on a cold bench. She was shivering.

"Officer," Katie called and got an instant response from one of the uniformed cops near the gate. "Can you lend me your jacket?"

He slid it off and handed it over; Katie draped the police-issue jacket around Jazz's thin shoulders. "There," she said. "Better?"

"Yeah," Jazz agreed softly. "Thanks. Hi, Katie."

"Hi, honey. So, bad day, huh?"

"Pretty bad." Jazz swallowed hard and glanced again at her mother, who was watching her with so much love and concern it made Katie's heart turn over. "They almost got me, but Teal and Lena, they made sure I got away. I didn't want to leave them, Katie. I didn't!"

"I know you didn't. Here. Sit with me." She took a seat on the cold concrete bench and patted the empty spot next to her. "Maybe your mom can get you something to drink? Some water?"

It was a pretext, but a necessary one; she couldn't just tell Kayla to leave, and Kayla needed an excuse to go. When Jazz nodded gratefully, the two women exchanged a quick glance, and Kayla reached down to hug her daughter before walking off in search of refreshments.

Katie waited until she was sure Kayla was out of earshot.

"You don't have to be brave with me," she said, and Jazz crumbled, sobbing against her. Katie put her arms around her, wincing as Jazz hugged back, but she bit her lip and stood the pain. She stroked the girl's soft, silky hair with slow movements. "You've been brave all day, haven't you?"

"I had to." Jazz gulped. Her voice was more like a little girl's now, shaking and high-pitched. "Everybody was counting on me. I had to remember, and tell people, and—"

"And you did that, you did. But you were scared, too, and that's okay. It's okay, you understand?"

Jazz pulled back, eyes swollen and streaming tears. She gave Katie a pleading look. "Mom never is."

"Your mom is scared a lot, but she tries not to let it show." Katie gave the girl a smile, a small one, appropriate to the mood. "Like me. But you need to break down sometimes to be stronger later. You understand that? I'll bet your mom cries later."

"She—" Jazz gulped air and looked more thoughtful. "Sometimes, I guess. She closes the door. I hear her crying, but only when things were really bad at work or something."

"Well, today, they're really bad at work *and* she's afraid for you, too. So give her a break. Let her take care of you, okay?"

Jazz nodded. Her body language was slowly uncoiling from the wire-tight posture it had been, and Katie breathed a cautious sigh of relief. The last thing the kid needed was to bottle all this up. It was traumatic, and Jazz was—like all Athena students—advanced for her age. A recipe for emotional disaster.

"You feel like telling me the story now? One last time?"

Jazz bent her head and sat up again, hands braced on either side on the cold concrete bench. Her voice was soft, and still a little unsteady, but Katie heard every word. "We decided to go to the movies. It was—we had the day off."

"Why didn't you ask for transportation? Call a cab?"

Jazz didn't look up. "We wanted to walk. It was a nice day."

Girls her age didn't want to walk, they wanted to get where they were going fast, and have fun even faster.

"Jazz, if you lie to me, you're putting Teal and Lena in danger. You know that, don't you?"

Jazz's head jerked up in outright astonishment. Katie raised an eyebrow and waited as Jazz found words. "I didn't lie!"

"I'm afraid you did. And you lied to your mother, and to the police, and now you think you can't change your story. But you can, Jazz. Nobody thinks you're at fault here."

"But—"

Katie let a little hardness creep into her voice. "You weren't going to the movies. You didn't take the school transportation service because you didn't want anybody to know where you were going, and you didn't take a cab because you didn't want any record. Right?"

Jazz looked as bewildered as if Katie had just pulled a rabbit out of her ear. "How—?" She swallowed the question and flushed pale pink under her matte-tan skin. "I didn't lie. We would have gone to the movies. We were planning to do it late afternoon."

"So where were you going in the morning?"

"It's supposed to be a secret. Teal made me promise."

"*Teal* made you promise."

Jazz nodded slowly. "There was someone from the school in trouble. She needed help. Teal and Lena promised to meet her. I wasn't really supposed to go along, but I followed them and caught up after I overheard. Besides, I wanted to go to the movies."

Precocious didn't half cover it, Katie thought. She wondered if she'd been so difficult at Jazz's age, thought back and decided that it was entirely possible. "Where were you going? And who were you meeting?"

"We were going to the mall. It's only a couple of blocks away. I don't know who we were meeting, it was a secret. Teal and Lena didn't want to talk about it."

This didn't sound nearly as innocent as Jazz probably thought it did. "Could it have been boys? Somebody they met in town, maybe?"

"I— No. No, they told me it was somebody from the school."

"There are men working at the school."

Jazz shook her head. "They said *she*."

It couldn't be an accident that Teal and Lena had been off-campus and picked off so neatly; somebody had set it up. Somebody had set a place and a time for them to be, and they'd walked right into it. Jazz had been an unexpected ride-along. No wonder they'd allowed her to escape.

"Okay, walk me through what happened. You were walking—"

Kayla returned midway through the recitation of the facts, but that was all right. The secret had been revealed, and Katie could see from the kid's body language that she had nothing more to conceal. She'd told everything she knew.

Nevertheless, just for clarity, Katie walked Jazz through the rest of the story, start to finish, stopping her for details that seemed unimportant but might be vital later on. She made illegible scribbles in her own fluid abbreviations and listened for any false notes.

Nothing.

When silence fell, Katie checked her watch. It was sliding toward evening, and the chill was getting sharper in the air. The desert didn't hold in the heat poured over it during the day, and it was going to get bone-shaking cold tonight. "Right," she said. "I think that's it, Jazz. You've been wonderful. I'll check in on you when I can, okay?"

"Wait." Jazz caught her hand. "You're going to find them, right? You promise?"

Katie Rush never promised. It was unprofessional; it was hurtful and it added complications the job didn't need. She'd learned that hard, and she never broke the rule.

She did now. "Yes," she said. "I promise. They're coming back safe."

She walked off a little distance with Kayla, who was anxious and trying hard not to look it. "Anything?" Kayla asked.

Katie didn't answer directly. "I need to go up to the school. Can someone give me a ride?"

"Of course. I'll take you—"

"No, you need to take your daughter home. I'll keep you fully briefed on what I find out—if anything. Be with Jazz right now." She remembered the tall detective they'd passed, who'd looked at Kayla with such outright concern and longing. "And…anybody else you might need to see."

Kayla flushed, just like her daughter. "It's my case, I can't just drop it!"

"It's not your case," Katie said and turned to face her. Cold air blew over them, reminding them that night was falling, that darkness was coming. "Your daughter was an assault victim. Two of her friends are missing. Nobody in their right mind is going to keep you in charge of this case, you know that. Phoenix PD is going to follow their own course. But me, I'm independent. I can follow leads they can't, especially leads that come up inside of the Academy. Let me do this for you."

Katie stared her down. It took a long time, but then Kayla always had been strong-willed, tough-minded and determined.

But she knew when to quit.

"All right," she said. "But you keep me in the loop. Daily. Hourly, if there's breaking news."

"Of course. Now go home."

"Not before I get you a car."

It took more than that, of course, but it wasn't more than fifteen minutes before Katie had her ride—a plain white Ford, police issue, complete with radio, siren, dashboard light and the lingering smell of old coffee.

Katie backed her new wheels out of the police barricades and through a tunnel of people that the uniformed officers kept open for her. As she applied the brakes, prior to turning around, her headlights swept across the faces of the reporters, the cops, the bystanders—fewer now than before, of course, but still a respectably sized crowd.

One stood out. She jammed the brakes harder, bringing the car to a full halt, and then slowly allowed the car to roll forward until she stopped next to the man on whom she'd focused.

He leaned down to rest his forearms on the frame of the open window and cocked his curly dark head. His eyes were as bright and curious as a raven's.

"Agent Rush," he said pleasantly. She didn't smile.

"Are you following me?" Because he was, unquestionably, the man from the airport. The man from the cab.

"No."

"You just ended up here by accident."

He had the good grace to look uncomfortable. "Not—exactly, look, can I get in the car and talk to you? I—"

"No," she said flatly. "I appreciate that you're persistent, but you need to stop now. Following a federal agent is a risky business, do you understand me? So please. Look for a date at your hotel bar."

He straightened up, obviously surprised and maybe a little bit angry; there was something in his eyes that flashed like lightning. But she hit the accelerator and left him behind, just a dim and distant figure that disappeared into the falling night.

Weird, she thought. He must have had the cab follow her from the airport, and then he'd spent the entire afternoon just…waiting. That was more extreme than she liked, no matter how attractive he was.

She impatiently shook off the memory of his eyes, his smile, and followed the road to Glendale, and the Athena Academy.

Chapter 4

Stefan Blackman stared after the glaring red taillights of Agent Rush's car, temporarily stunned into stillness. He'd expected skepticism, but not outright dismissal—especially *that* kind of dismissal. Frankly, he wasn't used to rejection. It stung. And it made him angry, too, because he had something to say, didn't he? Something useful.

Something not at all about how lovely she was.

"Great." He sighed and shook his head. Stuck in Phoenix, no transportation, no way to get the attention of anybody who would listen. He'd already tried to find a sympathetic officer to get to the good-looking brunette detective with the kid, but no go…. They'd taken his name and probably his photo, but they wouldn't let him near her. Or anyone. And he wasn't sure it was a good time to cause a scene—it would only make him look crazier.

What, then? Back to the airport? Back home? It was starting to have a powerful allure, getting the hell out of here and back to the warm, familiar cocoon of his life. He didn't like how all this was making him feel, not at all.

Yes, that was what he was going to do. Clearly, the police didn't need him; they had a massive presence here, and with the FBI descending, as well, surely they had more than enough leads without the admittedly not-very-specific visions of a psychic. Cops usually liked to resort to that sort of thing last, not first. And hell, there were phones, right? He could always call.

Maybe he could catch the red-eye back home....

The vision hit him with sudden, wrenching force, sending him sagging against the wooden police barricade and grabbing for support. He sensed all that distantly because this vision was even more visceral and immediate than the previous.

Still in the van. Driving. The girl was feeling the vibration through her body, facedown on the floor of the van. Muscles aching, hands and feet numbed from the tight bonds. Fear slowly receding, simply because she couldn't continue to be afraid forever...

The girl next to her, the blonde with punk-purple streaks, had mastered her own terror and was doing something with her fingers. She was slowly, clumsily signing letters....

Stefan felt the girl try to sign back.

A hand reached down from somewhere above in the darkness and grabbed the first girl's hair, yanking it painfully up and pulling her to her knees. She was breathing hard through her nose and trying not to cry. If her nose clogged up, she'd smother. The duct tape on her mouth wasn't giving, no matter how she tried to work her jaw to loosen it.

"Hey," said a rough male voice. "I told you not to move, get it? Don't move. I can always drug you if you give me trouble. You want to avoid that, you stay still. We need one of you, not both. Either one of you gets cute, you get to watch the other one get hurt. Bad. Understood? Nod."

The girl nodded, breathing hard. On the floor, the blonde nodded, too, eyes leaking furious tears.

The pressure on the girl's hair released, and she overbalanced and fell hard, banging into the floor face-first. The impact stunned her, and she tasted blood, coppery and hot....

Stefan jerked out of the vision, swallowed, and could still taste the blood. He felt like vomiting. Whoever the girl was, she was controlling her fear, but it was real and immediate. *Either one of you gets cute, you get to watch the other one get hurt.* He hadn't been able to sense her thoughts at all, only visuals and sensations, but that was enough. More than enough.

He still didn't know where she was, or even if the visions were real time; it could have been something that happened hours ago, or would happen an hour into the future. No time sense to any of it. The van was dark in the interior, and the girl hadn't been able to see....

Wait.

He realized he was still hunched over, clutching the

police barricade in both hands, and forced himself to let go and straighten up. He felt sweat trickling down his face, despite the cool night breeze, and wiped his forehead with shaking hands.

As her abductor had jerked the girl up to her knees by the hair, she'd been able to get a brief glimpse out of the front window. The headlights had spilled over a dark empty road, a brilliant yellow line…

…and a road sign.

"She's on Highway 347," he said to himself. "She's there *now.*" Because the view had still been washed with a faint tint of sunset, the far horizon not yet completely dark.

He needed to tell somebody. Anybody.

Stefan pushed through the crowd of bored reporters to the edge of the crime scene, where the uniformed officers were looking even more bored. Forensics was packing up, and the floodlights were going off. They were leaving.

No sign of the brunette detective and her girl; long gone, he guessed. Out the other side, where there were fewer reporters.

"Sir," he said, and then louder, "Officer!"

The nearest cop, who'd been speaking with two others, turned to look at him with a dead-eyed stare. "Stay behind the tape, sir," he said.

"I *am* behind the tape. I have—"

"You're leaning over."

"This is important, I know where they are! The girls!"

He had all their attention now, an uncomfortable weight of it. "How do you know that, sir?"

"I saw them."

"Where, sir?"

"In a van, traveling on Highway 347. I don't know if they're going north or south…"

"Back up, sir. How exactly did you see inside the van?"

Oh boy. "I just know, okay? I know. You need to look for them on Highway 347, and *hurry.* They probably won't be there long, and those girls are in danger. They're going to get hurt."

He didn't have to be a psychic to get the sense that the cops were not pleased with his explanation, although they dutifully took down all his contact information— home address, cell phone, everything but his brand of underwear. The male cop stepped forward and looked at Stefan from a height well above six feet. "You just know," he said. "As in, what? You had a dream?"

"A vision, actually," he said. "Look, I need to talk to the detectives. I can help!"

The cop nodded, but his face had shut down into an ex- pressionless mask. "I see. I've got your name and contact information, sir. I'll make sure it gets to the detectives."

"Highway 347—"

"Yes, sir. We'll follow that up."

The cop was humoring him. No question about it. Stefan felt a hot burn of rage, but it wouldn't do any good to let it out; he'd get to talk to the detectives, all right, in handcuffs. Not so much a talk as an interroga- tion, probably.

He needed to talk to Agent Rush.

"Fine," Stefan said and held up his hands in surrender. "Just check Highway 347. You know how to find me if you need more information."

Not that he had any more information, really. The glimpse of the road sign had been a pure gift of luck. It wasn't exactly breaking news that the girl was terrified, or that she was in a van. Or that her friend had purple-streaked hair.

Or that they were in real trouble.

Stefan moved away, furious and frustrated, and tried to decide on his next move. He had no idea where Agent Rush had gone, and had no way to track her down. And he needed to talk to her, he just sensed it. She would listen to what he had to say, if he could just get past that thick defensive shell.

And to do that, she had to *want* to talk to him.

"Cops giving you a hard time?" asked a cool female voice at his elbow. He turned and saw a petite blonde dressed from the waist up in an expensive silk shirt and tailored jacket, and from the waist down in blue jeans and flats. She looked styled and coiffed and per-fectly made-up.

Television reporter, beyond any doubt.

"A little," he said.

"I'm sorry, but I overheard what you said to him. You said you had information about the missing girls…? Something about Highway 347?"

He smiled at her. She smiled back. It was purely a professional exchange; there was something about her that put him on his guard, maybe the slightly harsh glitter in her eyes, or the ambition he sensed coming off her in waves. Not a bad person, he sensed, but a driven one. Compulsively needing to *win*.

He had no idea what game she was playing, but she clearly saw him as some kind of pawn.

"How do you know I'm not one of the kidnappers?" he asked. Her eyebrows rose, and those brown eyes sparkled even more.

"Are you? Because that would be one hell of a story." She hastily tamped down her excitement. "Provided the girls were returned unharmed, of course."

"Of course." He tried to keep the irony out of his voice. "I heard they're both students at a local girls' school."

"Private school," the reporter said. "What do you know about the Athena Academy?"

"Athena Academy?" he repeated blankly. He'd never heard of it. He knew about the goddess Athena, of course— "Nothing."

"You weren't called in? Maybe by one of the alumni to help with the investigation?" She seemed to be fishing for something, dangling bait, but he had no idea what she meant.

He shrugged. "I'm a private citizen. Not called in by anybody. How about you?"

She gave him a knowing smile. "I have my sources. I got a tip early in the investigation." Some of the light went out of her eyes. Too bad. They'd been quite pretty for a while, and now they were narrowing and hardening again. "But you're just a guy who listens to the police band and hangs around crime scenes? Wastes the time of the police with false leads?" She was in

pursuit of a completely different story now, one potentially damaging to him both personally and profession-
ally. He needed to establish credentials, quickly.

"No," he said and stepped forward, forcing her to
meet his eyes. "My name is Stefan Blackman, and I'm
a psychic well known in Los Angeles, and if you want
to put me on the air, I'll tell you everything I know
about the abduction of these girls. Including where the
van was as of five minutes ago."

Her eyes widened, and her lips parted, then smiled.
She held out her hand to him, and when he automatically took it, shook briskly. "Shannon Connor, ABS.
I've certainly heard of you, Mr. Blackman. Don't they
call you the Network Psychic?"

He hated that idiotic name, but he nodded. "I work
for the broadcast networks, but not as a psychic. What
I do for them really doesn't involve psychic ability," he
said. "I just read the concepts for the shows and pick the
ones I think will be most successful."

"But everybody says that your track record is extraordinary. Something like ninety-five percent, right?"

He shrugged. "That part's not visions. It's just
good sense."

"I like that. Save that for the camera, okay?" Shannon
turned and waved at someone in the crowd, then made
a pointing gesture toward a large panel van decorated
with the ABS logo. A broadcast van. Stefan recognized
the heavy extendable antenna mounted to the top of it.
"Ten minutes to get set up, then we can tape. I can't
promise when it will air, though. Probably in rotation

at the next news break. We're in luck that Tory Patton's off on maternity leave—I'm getting premium time, thanks to her getting knocked up. Next thing you know, I'll be the anchor." She winked, letting him know it was all in fun. Sort of. "Sound okay to you?"

He hadn't expected to land a full interview, not so quickly, but time was ticking away, and if he didn't attract the attention of that cool, dismissive FBI agent soon, it would—he knew—be too late.

"Ready when you are," he said and gave her a full, charming smile to seal the deal.

Chapter 5

Coming back to the Athena Academy was like coming home for Katie—but a home that had new occupants. The buildings all looked gracious and eternal, but there were signs of subtle changes: different paint on the trim of the outbuildings, new trees here and there. Hardy, drought-resistant native plants where she remembered an English herb garden. And had the driveway always been this *long?*

Her headlights swept a new building, adorned with a brass plaque, and she remembered that a new science wing had been dedicated to Rainy Miller. She hadn't been able to attend the ceremony, but Kayla had told her about it.

There were a few older students outside, dressed in casual clothes since the school day was over. Casual clothes far more fashionable than those Katie had worn during her school days. Or wore now, for that matter. Most were studying, nodding their heads in time with the music on their iPods, but a few were talking. One group was playing soccer in the fading light, squealing and laughing. If you didn't know what the Athena Academy was, you wouldn't have much of a clue to look at the scene. Maybe, if you were very observant, she thought, you'd notice the advanced nature of the texts the girls were studying. Or the fluid speed and grace of the ones playing soccer.

Even as she thought it, one girl slid feetfirst across the grass and executed a devastating sideways kick. The goalie deflected the shot, but it rebounded with force, hit a tree and caromed into Katie's unmarked police car as she pulled it to a stop.

"Sorry!" the goalie yelled, and jogged over to grab the ball and send it back into play. Katie watched her with a strange mixture of affection and dread—the affection was for the girl; the dread was for herself. Dread that she wouldn't do what everyone expected from her—that she wouldn't be able to find the girls, or save them. It was a dread she always felt, every time, and she mastered it with a few moments of concentration. *Focus on the facts, Katie.* Facts and procedure were what got you through the tough emotional moments in a job like this. And she had no doubt that there would be a tough emotional moment coming soon; the women she was about to sit down with were formidable, to say the least, and it was entirely possible that she was going to have to suggest—maybe more than suggest—that someone they knew and most likely trusted was involved in the abduction of two students.

She delayed for only a minute or so, thinking over what she would say, and how, and then stepped out into the cool, thin air.

And into memories.

The steps. She remembered walking up these steps so many times, sometimes trudging in exhaustion, sometimes skipping up so lightly it felt as though she floated on air. Around her, the girls of her group—the Graces—had chatted and quarreled and generally acted like the closest of sisters. Which they'd been, and still were, although the relationships had matured along with their ages. All Athena Academy graduates were siblings, in a sense; some were just closer than others.

Some were closer than family.

As she entered the open front door, she saw a tall, straight-backed figure standing on the stairs with one elegant hand on the railing. The lights in the foyer were dimmed, but still bright enough to show Katie the grave, composed expression on Rebecca Claussen's face. Rebecca still looked just the same to Katie's eyes; maybe a bit more gray in the shoulder-length hair, a few more lines at the corners of her eyes. But a welcoming smile and an extended hand, nonetheless. "Katie," she said. "Thank you for coming. I know this wasn't easy for you, to drop everything and rush to our aid."

It wasn't anything more than any other Athena graduate would have done, Katie was tempted to say, but she only nodded and shook the strong, dry hand, then followed Rebecca up the wide, sweeping staircase to the second floor.

"Are their parents here?" Katie asked. Rebecca glanced over her shoulder at her and nodded. "May I speak with them?"

"Of course. But I don't think you'll find many leads there—Teal and Lena were exemplary students, and they had permission to leave campus."

"Permission? So someone knew where they were going?"

"We log in destinations for any student who leaves the campus grounds, Katie. Here. We'll discuss this in private." Rebecca swung open a set of double doors and revealed her office, a Spartan kind of place with a few mementos and photographs of her husband. He'd died, Katie remembered, about eight years ago. Rebecca still wore the wedding ring. "Please, have a seat." She closed the doors after Katie and, instead of taking the chair behind the large wooden desk, pulled up a smaller visitor's chair to sit almost knee to knee with Katie.

"Where were they going? According to the official record?" Katie asked.

Rebecca's dark eyebrows rose. "Official record? Why would there be any discrepancy?"

"Because they're teenage girls, and I have an idea from Jazz Ryan that they weren't exactly lying, but they weren't telling the whole truth, either. May I see the records?"

Rebecca reached for a folder on her desk and flipped it open before handing it over. Katie scanned it quickly. It was a simple log of students, time and date out, destination, time and date back in. Completely routine. Teal and Lena had signed out together, and Jazz had signed out just afterward, which supported Jazz's statement that she'd tagged along without an invitation. Destination for Teal and Lena was listed as "movies," and the address of the mall theater in Glendale. Jazz had copied the same information.

Katie handed it back and said, "Jazz told me that they were planning on going to the movies, but they had something else to do first. Has anybody made any reference to it? Any student?"

"No, Katie. We would have informed the police immediately if we'd had any additional information. All we know is that the girls left campus and didn't return." Rebecca's hazel eyes assessed her coolly. She was a tough woman, and she'd always been able to at least appear to see a student's innermost secrets with a single glance. But Katie wasn't a student anymore, and she held the stare without flinching. "You think there's some kind of information here at the school. Some lead."

Katie didn't deny it. "I'd like to speak with their parents, and then with the girls in Lena and Teal's group. If anybody here knows, they would." Both of them knew how close the bonds were within those groups, assigned during the girls' first year. "Can you make them available for interviews?"

"So long as either Ms. Evans or I can be present during the conversations."

"Of course." She'd rather not, actually, but it seemed unlikely she'd get that much cooperation. The women in charge of Athena Academy were protective of their students. "How many are available tonight?"

"All of them. Naturally, we understand the urgency and time pressures you face. We've already gathered the girls. Do you want to speak with them individually?"

"Together first," she said. In her experience, adults weren't great at hiding things from authority figures, but kids were even worse.

And she needed to save time. Individual interviews would take too long.

Rebecca nodded. "If you'll wait here a moment, I'll get the girls together in a common area." She moved quickly, with confidence, and Katie was left alone in her office. She rose and paced restlessly, thinking through what was coming and trying not to think about what might be happening to the missing girls.

"Katie."

A voice behind her. She turned, hands clasped behind her back, and saw Christine Evans standing in the doorway. Christine was a striking figure, just as Katie remembered her—maybe a little more silver in the short gray hair, but it didn't so much soften her as add another touch of metal. Christine was solid. Katie was an active woman, fit as an FBI agent generally had to be, but Christine had always looked exactly like what she was: a war veteran. Tough, competent and perfectly capable of sending a drill sergeant in full retreat when she cared to do so.

"Ms. Evans," Katie said, and then corrected herself before she could be reminded. "Christine."

"I'm so glad you were brought into this. I can't think of anyone I'd rather have looking for the girls." Christine crossed the room toward her, and if Katie hadn't been well aware that she was blind in her left eye—had been since anyone Katie's age knew her—she'd never have suspected that the slight gesture of Christine's left hand at her side was designed to warn her of any obstacles in her path. Christine offered her hand—a large, square, capable hand, with meticulously clean French manicured fingernails—and Katie shook it. She knew she had a strong grip, but Christine's was always an order of magnitude greater—not out of any desire to intimidate, just because that was Christine's level.

Katie couldn't forget how things had been when Marion Gracelyn, the founder of Athena Academy, had met her death. Things could have so easily fallen apart. It had taken a strong personality to step into that hurricane and make order from chaos…and a gentle one. The girls had needed comfort and a sense of security, and Christine had been the perfect one to do it.

Still, that didn't make the strength of Christine's handshake any less painful. Katie smiled and reclaimed her tingling fingers as fast as she could. "It's good to see you, ma'am."

Christine snorted. "Ma'am. The next thing you know, you'll be saluting, Katie. How have you been?"

"Fine." She had no idea how to make small talk with someone who loomed as large in her personal cosmology as Christine Evans.

"As I recall," Christine said, "you always were a

private person. I hope you've worked through that somewhat—I hear you are exceptional at your job, of course. But I know all too well that the type of work you've chosen isolates you. You're happy?"

"Very." She wasn't about to talk about her personal life—or lack of one, more accurately—with her old headmistress. "I heard that your great-nephew, William, was injured…?"

Nothing like turning the focus on the other person to cover your own inadequacies, Katie thought wryly. But she also knew that Christine worried about her family, and it was probably a justified sort of worry.

"I just heard from him," Christine said. "He's recovering well, and I expect they'll have him back in uniform soon. Not soon enough, most likely—he's bored, and that's never a good sign for someone like William. Or us, for that matter."

"I'm glad he's all right," Katie said. "If I could see Teal and Lena's parents—"

"Together or separately?"

"Separately, please, if it's no bother."

"None at all." Christine's one bright eye fixed on her. "I've been thinking that this doesn't look like a random snatch-and-grab kidnapping. It appears more planned than impulsive. That implies that someone must have provided information about where the girls were going—if not students, then staff or employees. I've taken the liberty of retrieving personnel files for you."

It never failed to surprise Katie just how ahead of the game Christine was, although she supposed she should have gotten used to it by now. "Thank you," she said. "I was wondering how to bring that up. I know that you feel very loyal to everyone here, but—"

"But it's possible for anyone to be deceived," Christine said briskly. "Yes. I have no illusions about such things, Katie. However, if one of my people betrayed these girls, I promise you, hell hath no fury to match Christine Evans."

That, Katie could fully believe. She grinned slightly and said, "Could I look over the files after I speak with the parents and the other girls?"

"They'll be ready." Christine met her eyes. "I know that you can't keep me fully informed, but I'd like to have what information you can provide without violating your oaths."

"You'll have it." She hesitated for a second and then said, "These girls. You know I need to ask…. Can you tell me something about them? About what kind of unusual traits they have, specifically? Things that I'm guessing might not be in the files."

For a second, she wasn't sure Christine was going to cooperate, but then the woman nodded slightly. "It might be important," she agreed. "If Teal and Lena were specifically targeted, then it might have been because of what they could do, that's certainly a possibility. Lena's very fast and very strong—in fact, she's one of the only girls in school capable of keeping up with Teal's physical abilities. Lena's certainly outgoing, and she's also civic-minded—she likes entertaining children, the elderly, anyone in need of a little miracle."

That, more than anything else, made Katie feel a stab of true fear for Lena. She's in need of her own miracle, she thought. "And Teal?"

"Teal's a different case," Christine said. "Fast and strong, as I mentioned, but there's more to her. We haven't been able to determine the exact nature of it, because her abilities seem to be developing, but she's certainly capable of some telepathic contact, though thus far only with those who have similar abilities. You understand, none of this is in the standard files."

"Of course," Katie said. "And it won't go in my files, either. But it could help."

Christine smiled. It transformed her from severe to glowing, and Katie found herself smiling back, despite the situation, despite the dire danger that two girls faced somewhere out in the night. "It's really good to have you on our side, Katie," Christine said. "Really good. The resources of the Academy and Athena Force are at your disposal."

No small promise there.

The worst part of any case like this was facing the parents, Katie had always found, and this was no different. Teal's mother was composed, pale and tense, and she answered questions in a flat monotone while her husband sat staring at his hands. He was angry, Katie sensed, but he wasn't going to let it out. Teal's mother, on the other hand, was almost completely consumed with fear.

It wasn't a productive interview.

It wasn't until Katie was getting ready to leave that

Mrs. Arnett suddenly stepped forward, grabbed her arm, and whispered, "You have to find her. She's special."

Katie knew that, all too well. She nodded, but Mrs. Arnett kept talking. There was a feverish light in her eyes.

"Teal—you have to understand, we tried and tried to have children, nothing worked, it was really a miracle. If it hadn't been for the fertility clinic she wouldn't be here at all. She's a miracle baby. Please. Help her."

Katie covered Mrs. Arnett's trembling hand with her own. "I will." Out of some obscure impulse, almost as an afterthought, she asked, "Which clinic?"

"What?" Mrs. Arnett blinked. "Oh. The Women's Fertility Center in Zuni, New Mexico. Is that important?"

"Probably not. I promise you, ma'am, I'm going to do everything I can. You should rest. We'll keep you informed when we have any information."

Katie walked from that room—a study room, warm and cozy, lined with reference books—to the empty classroom next door, where Lena Poole's mother waited. No father in evidence—traveling, Katie learned, in Asia. Mrs. Poole didn't know when he'd get back. Unlike Mrs. Arnett, this mother *was* angry—white-hot with it. Almost vibrating. It didn't matter to Katie; she'd dealt with every kind of reaction, and she knew when to use strength, when to use persuasion, when to use sympathy. Mrs. Poole responded to sympathy. Ultimately, beyond providing a good photograph of Lena, she had nothing to add—but Katie, on that same obscure impulse from before, asked about medical history. Not just Lena's—

Lena had been exceptionally healthy, which wasn't unusual for the enhanced girls who attended the Athena Academy—but Mrs. Poole's, as well.

Lena, it appeared, was also a product of fertility treatments.

And Mrs. Poole had received her treatments at the same clinic as Mrs. Arnett.

Katie left Mrs. Poole weeping quietly, comforted by another of the Athena Academy staff members, and stepped into the hall to make a phone call, this time to Kayla Ryan. "Quick question," she said when Kayla answered. "What do you know about the Women's Fertility Clinic in Zuni, New Mexico?"

"Nothing. Doesn't ring any bells. Why?"

"Look into it, would you? Let me know." She flipped the phone shut, tried to put that strange puzzle out of her mind, and moved on to the next challenge.

The girls.

Although the students were understandably upset and anxious—as was the staff—the mass interview was brief, as Katie's well-honed instincts dismissed girl after girl from consideration. She pared down the numbers to just two after half an hour: Melissa Princeman and Gabriella Sanchez. They were as different as could be. Melissa was small, delicate, almost elfin, and every emotion showed on her heart-shaped face. Gabriella was large, solid and muscular.

Melissa was radiating frantic guilt. Gabriella was *so* controlled that Katie couldn't help but think that there was something waiting behind it to be discovered.

They sat in one of the smaller classrooms, one Katie remembered well; she'd suffered through geology in this room, absolutely convinced that knowing about rocks would never help her in the least. She'd held that opinion right up until she'd discovered the fascinations of forensic science, and geology had opened up for her like a new horizon.

She shook herself out of the past and focused on the present as she paced. Christine Evans had taken the teacher's desk at the front, and Rebecca stood quietly at the back of the room. The two girls were rigid and unmoving in their student chairs.

"Melissa," Katie said, "what if I told you that somebody saw you with Teal today?"

It was a shot in the dark, but it struck home. Melissa visibly flinched, and her china-blue eyes welled up with tears.

"It wasn't my fault!" she blurted. "It was just a note, I didn't read it or anything. I don't even know if it was important! I just handed it to her!"

"And did she open it while you were standing there?"

Melissa nodded, gulping back sobs. "She showed it to Lena. They both looked worried."

"But you don't know what was in it?"

Melissa shook her head violently. Tears broke free and slid down her pale cheeks.

"Melissa." Katie slowly lowered herself into a crouch, one hand on the student desk for stability, and looked Melissa in the eyes. "Honey, you need to tell me who gave you the note."

Melissa looked stricken and anguished. "It couldn't have been the note. Honest, it couldn't."

"You still need to tell me. You don't want anything to happen to Lena and Teal, do you? We need to eliminate that note as being part of what happened."

"No, it *couldn't* have been anything bad—" Melissa couldn't finish. She looked away. "I can't tell you. I'm sorry."

From the front, Christine Evans said softly, "Melissa. You may have promised not to tell, but promises sometimes have to be broken for the greater good. Keeping your word at a time like this is nothing but a way to avoid responsibility."

Melissa swallowed, nodded and looked down at her intertwined fingers. "I see that. But—"

"It was me," Gabriella interrupted flatly. "I gave Melissa the note to give to Teal. Liss, there's no reason to protect me. I don't have anything to hide."

Melissa looked tremendously relieved. Gabriella sat back in her chair and crossed her arms—defensive body language. Her deep brown eyes were steady. She was Teal's age, Katie remembered. Nearly adult, and probably determined to act more than her age. Not a bad girl, but one who might have a lot to prove.

"Tell me about the note," Katie said and sat down in the student desk across from her, leaning forward. Open posture. "What was in it?"

"It wasn't mine," Gabriella said. "Somebody gave it to me. I only gave it to Liss because I knew she'd see Teal first. They had track together."

Katie controlled her frustration with an effort. "Gabriella, what was in the note?"

Gabriella's eyes widened just slightly, but her tone stayed completely neutral. "How would I know? You think I read it?"

Not a denial, Katie noted. "I know you did. What did it say?"

Gabriella finally showed an expression—a flicker of shame. She looked away. "It wasn't a message really. It just said, Blue Camaro, in front of Macy's, at 11:00 a.m."

"It was instructions to meet someone," Katie said. "Why didn't you come forward with this?"

"Because I—" Gabriella's lips tightened. "Look, we were just trying to do the right thing, okay? Somebody was in trouble, and we were trying to help out. Besides, their disappearance couldn't be about the note. Teal and Lena never even got to Macy's, right?"

"Right," Katie agreed grimly. "But all that means is that they were never meant to arrive. Somebody knew where they'd be going, and when. And I suppose, because you girls were cloak-and-dagger, that's why Teal and Lena didn't take a cab or catch a ride to the mall."

The two girls, so different and yet in this moment so alike, exchanged a quick look. "Yeah," Gabriella agreed. Suddenly, she didn't sound nearly so sure of herself. "But—it wasn't any big thing! Honest… It was just— Look, somebody was in trouble. We were trying to help."

"Help how?" Katie pressed. "Why were they meeting this person?"

Melissa said, "Teal was going to give the guy money."

Oh God. "How much money?"

"Not that much. A couple of hundred dollars," Gabriella said defensively. "I told you, it wasn't that big a deal!"

Katie cursed all the fates she could think of. She'd thought the kidnapping would turn out to be relatively simple, but the complications kept rolling in. The addition of this kind of money drop opened up all sorts of unwelcome possibilities, from blackmail to kidnapping to—although she couldn't believe it—drugs. All fraught with danger, all involving professional criminals of one type or another, which didn't ensure the girls' safety by any means. Only that the situation would be far less easy to resolve.

She took a deep breath. Time for the million-dollar question. "Where did the note come from? Who's the one in trouble?"

There was a brief, telling silence, and then Gabriella said, "Miss Prichard. Well, it's about her kid. It was to help. We all agreed."

"Miss Prichard?" That was from Rebecca, at the back of the room. Katie glanced at her in inquiry. "She's new this year on staff, in administration in my office. Sheila Prichard. I'll pull her file." Rebecca exited the room, and Katie heard the quick tap of her footsteps echoing through the hall.

"I need to talk to Miss Prichard," Katie said. "Get her here, now, if she isn't on campus."

Christine nodded. "It'll be done." She went after Rebecca.

Katie focused back on the girls. "What kind of trouble was Miss Prichard in?" she asked.

"It wasn't her," Melissa said earnestly. "Honest, it wasn't. She was the victim! These guys, they were going to put some kind of crap on the Internet about her son. She just wanted to pay them off to get them to stop. Her son, he's had some bad times. She was afraid it would really hurt him."

Miss Prichard, whoever she was, had understood these girls too well. Every one of them wanted to save the world, even this little bit of it…and they'd neglect their own safety to do it. Katie continued her questions, but really, neither of the girls had more information; just what Prichard had told them. They were too young not to fall for it—and far too idealistic. Like most predators, Prichard had tailored her attack to their one vulnerability: their desire to help.

Katie finally closed the interview. "Either of you have anything more you'd like to tell me?" she asked. "Melissa? Gabriella?"

They each shook their heads. Her internal emotional tuning fork told her that they were now pitch-perfect, no secrets held back. She jotted down notes in her investigation book while she waited for the two other women to return.

It took longer than she expected, and in fact Katie had gotten up to check when Rebecca appeared in the doorway, Christine close behind. Her normally composed expression had gone very tense.

"Trouble," she said. "Turns out Sheila Prichard was

out sick today, and I'm getting no answer at her home phone. Here's Prichard's personnel file."

"See if anybody else is missing," Katie said immediately. "Students, faculty, staff. Do a roll call. We can't afford to miss anything."

Christine and Rebecca moved to comply, and Katie pushed her own growing sense of frustration and fear aside to smile at the girls. The folder felt cool and heavy in her hand, and she set it down on the desk next to her notebook. "Thank you," she said sincerely to the two students. "You've really helped me tonight, and more importantly, you helped Lena and Teal. I know it wasn't easy. Please, go ahead and get some rest. If you think of anything else, or hear of anything else, let me know. Here's my card. It has my cell phone number on it." She handed them the FBI contact cards, and watched as the two young women left the room.

A staff member. It was what she'd been afraid of all along, that someone in a position of trust would have betrayed the girls.

Hell hath no fury.

For Sheila Prichard's sake, Katie hoped it was just a bad case of the flu, and that there was a reasonable explanation of how she'd come to set a chain of events in motion that had led to the abduction of two very special girls.

Katie read over Prichard's personnel file, noting down addresses, contacts, previous employers, and then went out toward Rebecca's office to find a landline to use, since her cell phone battery wasn't going to last through the hard use she was bound to put it through before this was done.

As she did, she passed one of the common rooms, where a television was playing on low volume in the corner. She glanced toward it, warned by some sense that she couldn't possibly explain, and saw that Shannon Connor was interviewing someone.

Television was kind to Shannon, although she was lovely no matter what setting; some people had a special aptitude for it, Katie had found. She wasn't one of them. She came across grim and embarrassed when interviewed. She always tried to put another, more telegenic FBI spokesperson out when possible.

The shot cut to Shannon's interviewee, and Katie's mouth dropped open. She took three quick steps into the room, grabbed the remote control from the table and turned the sound up. Around her, studying girls looked up in annoyance, noted her age and—presumably—authority, and went back to what they were doing.

The guy from the airport. From the crime scene.

He was talking to Shannon Connor, on the air.

Her first impression was that he was even more telegenic than Shannon; the camera loved him, loved his big dark eyes and curling hair and quirky smile. He leaned forward in his chair, demonstrating a command of body language that Katie thought was impressive, and said, "I didn't *want* to come here, Shannon, I *had* to come. It was a matter of duty, not choice."

"Duty," Shannon repeated. "Let's back up a moment, Mr. Blackman. You're not employed as a psychic, are you?"

"No," he said, with that cute, I'm-not-one-of-the-odd-people smile that somehow conveyed fondness for them at the same time. "I work in television. Behind the camera."

"In development."

"Consulting."

"And you're here in Phoenix because…" Shannon looked authentically skeptical.

"Because I had a psychic vision," Blackman said, with just the right matter-of-fact tone. He shrugged. "Didn't ask for it, didn't want it, never had one like this before and believe me, hope I never have one like it again."

"You predicted the girls' abduction?"

"No. I saw it on the news and something just connected. It was like I was seeing through one of the girls' eyes." He said it in the same tone, but Katie saw something shift in him, behind his controlled expression.

Teal. Teal can touch others with similar abilities.

Shannon must have seen it, too. "That sounds frightening."

"I'm not in any danger. But those girls are."

"So tell me what you saw."

Katie wasn't normally a believer in psychics, and the idea that this Blackman had suddenly turned up with visions at an opportune moment—well, she'd seen it before. Usually people with an attention-seeking disorder, or a con man looking to defraud the families. Which was he? Her money was on con man. But…still…Teal *could* have reached out to him.

She was about to mute the sound again when she heard him say, "—pink and purple streaks in her hair." He was describing Lena. Katie hesitated because those

were specifics, and con men and attention-seekers alike
avoided anything specific. "They're in a van, one either
without windows in the cargo area or with the windows
blacked out, and they're in the desert on Highway 347,
or they were half an hour ago. There are at least three
abductors in the van with the girls."

That was *far* too specific for a con. Katie hesitated,
weighing the remote in her hand. Watching Blackman,
who radiated nothing but a tense sincerity.

"I don't think it's sexual," he said. "It doesn't feel like
that. It's more like a kidnapping—money, politics, I
don't know. But it seems professional, the way these
people are acting."

The camera cut back to Shannon, who looked appro-
priately skeptical. "Mr. Blackman." It was a reproof,
perfectly delivered. "You flew out here from L.A. on the
strength of a vision, to tell us that two girls we already
knew were in danger are in danger? Don't you think
that's a little self-serving, at best? What proof can you
offer that you're not a fake or a con artist?"

Bravo, Katie thought. An on-point thrust.

Blackman parried without apparent effort. "I didn't
come here to get attention, and I didn't come to make
money," he said. "I came to help the police. If the police
won't talk to me, then I'll catch the red-eye back home
tomorrow. But I hope they will. I believe I can help, and
that's the important thing. Getting these girls back alive
and unharmed."

Somehow, Katie felt as if Blackman were talking
directly to *her.* As if he knew she'd hear. It even seemed

that his eyes were on hers through the television screen, although of course that was impossible.

Shannon maintained her skepticism as she turned back toward the camera. "That's the latest from the scene of the kidnapping of two young girls here in the Phoenix area, Charles. The police are shutting down the crime scene, and we'll have to wait for an official statement from the Glendale police, which should be coming in the next hour. Back to you."

They were still at the crime scene.

Katie muted the television and continued on to Rebecca's office, where she dialed Kayla Ryan's home phone number. Kayla answered on the second ring.

"I need another favor," Katie said.

"Well, I can't say I don't owe you a few, especially since you're here doing a big one for us."

"I need to have a uniformed officer pick up a guy at the crime scene and detain him until I get there. The guy's name is Blackman. He's with Shannon Connor right now." She gave his physical description, trying to keep any subjective judgments out of it.

"How long will you be?" Kayla asked. "Just so I can tell the cops who pick him up."

"Believe me," Katie answered, "I'll hurry."

Chapter 6

Playing keep-away with bikini girls on Venice Beach was nothing compared to playing intellectual keep-away with Shannon Connor. She wasn't just some stringer for ABS, Stefan realized almost immediately; she was ambitious, she was sharp and she was *good*. Good enough to engage him on a level he hadn't felt in a long time. Part of it was her aura—she gave off a complicated, heady energy that was two parts cleverness and one part bitterness.

If he hadn't been empathic, and hadn't been able to tell what she *wanted* him to say, she'd have manipulated him halfway back to Los Angeles without him being any the wiser. He was glad to be done with the interview, glad to have, he thought, come off as considerably more sane than she wanted him to. Reporters liked the crazy. Especially television reporters.

Once the hot lights were off, Shannon turned off some of her intensity, too. She was beautiful, he thought, but not his type—too demanding, too focused on herself and not others. He sensed she had more in her, better things, but she'd spent a long time covering that up.

"So, Stefan," she said, and slipped her arm in his as she stepped down from the wide truck that served as her mobile studio. "Are you really just going to hang around here all night, waiting for someone from the police to take an interest? Because I can promise you, if they do, it'll be the wrong kind of interest. They're not trusting people."

"Do you have any other suggestions?" Reflexive flirting. He didn't mean it. He realized thankfully that neither did she.

"Well, I'd volunteer to show you around the town, but I'm a little busy with the kidnapping story." Shannon gave him a smile to show him that was a pity. "Really, you should go home. Nobody's going to take you seriously, not unless you come up with a viable suspect's name."

Two uniformed police officers ducked under the crime-scene tape. That wasn't unusual; the cops were packing up and dismantling equipment, getting ready to roll up the scene. It was a bit like watching a set being struck in Hollywood, Stefan thought.

What was unusual about *these* two cops was that they headed straight for the ABS remote van, walking with a purpose.

"Heads up," Shannon said. "Looks like you got what you wanted. Nice meeting you, Stefan."

She winked at him and walked away. He stayed

where he was, hands at his sides, as the cops approached. Something about cops always made him want to stick his hands in his pockets, but he'd long ago realized that it made them paranoid.

"Hi," he said as the two of them stopped just about two feet away. He extended his hand. They were both big men with identically hard eyes. Neither took his hand.

"Mr. Blackman?"

He nodded.

"Would you come with us, sir?" The spokesman for the two had a deep Barry White voice. "We've been asked to hold you for a while until the FBI can talk to you."

"Am I under arrest?"

"No, sir. Not under arrest. The agent would just like to speak with you. She'll be here as soon as possible."

Unexpectedly, the other officer smiled. "We've got coffee. It's almost fresh."

"Well," Stefan said, "why didn't you say so? Lead on."

He wasn't thinking of the coffee, though it did sound tempting. He was thinking that they'd said *FBI,* and they'd said *she.*

That gave him an unexpected feeling of pleasure.

The search of the Academy and its grounds turned up nothing. Sheila Prichard wasn't answering either her home or cell phones. Katie handed that part of the investigation over to the Glendale PD, and Kayla, and headed back out to the crime scene.

The only sign that it had been a crime scene was a few lingering news vans packing up for the night after their live shots. The cops had all gone, except for one police cruiser sitting parked at the curb, just about where Teal and Lena had been dragged into a van.

The police cruiser was empty. She looked around, and saw a small diner on the corner with a warm glow coming from its plate glass window. And clearly silhouetted inside, two uniformed police officers and Blackman.

She walked across the street and down the block, slowing as she approached. She wanted to observe her subject without being watched in turn. He wouldn't be able to see far into the dark, as bright as it was inside the diner. Whatever he and the two cops were talking about, it was clear they'd bonded; they were all smiling, animated. Blackman gestured like an Italian when he was engaged.

The diner's door chimed when she walked in, and the counter man looked up and nodded at her, unsmiling. She ordered a cup of coffee and went back to join the three in the booth.

"Officers," she said and nodded to them. They'd both gone back to the sober, blank masks she was used to seeing with street cops. "FBI Special Agent Katie Rush. Thank you for your courtesy."

"Ma'am." They slid out of the booth, one at a time. "He's all yours. Night, Stefan."

"Night, guys," he said, as casually as if the cops who'd detained him were old poker buddies. Strange. More than strange, that they'd been treating him with the same bonhomie. It wasn't natural, not for police.

Stefan nodded for her to take a seat. He was still

smiling, hands curled around his coffee cup on the laminate tabletop. Nice hands, she couldn't help but notice—not overly large, but graceful fingers. Funny how attractive men's hands could be.

Katie sat down and waited until the counter man delivered her own drink before she said, "Stefan Blackman."

"Hi again," he said and held out his hand. She shook it. "I'm not stalking you. Just wanted to make that clear."

She blinked. "That's comforting."

"I thought, given the circumstances, that I should get that out of the way," he said. "After all, it's a weird string of coincidences. Airport, crime scene, now this. Weird, right?"

"Weird," she confirmed. "Unless you planned it that way."

"Why on earth would I do that?"

She didn't answer. Sometimes silence was more effective than words in leading a subject to drop important clues. Not this time, though. Stefan seemed perfectly content to sip coffee and smile and study her with those big, dark, compelling eyes.

"Tell me about this vision you had," she said.

"That's good." Stefan sat back without breaking eye contact. "You managed to say that without sounding like you think it's total crap, even though you probably think it's total crap. And it's *visions,* not *vision.* I seem to be tuned in on this girl's frequency."

"Has that happened before?"

He finally looked away, out the window. She saw muscles tense in his jawline. "Believe me, *nothing* like this has ever happened to me before. As psychics go, I'm pretty low level. I can usually pick up blurry impressions and emotions, but this is the full-on sensory experience." He paused for long enough that she thought he might be finished, but then he went on. "I don't like it. I want it to be over. And for it to be over, you need to find these girls. So it's really selfish, you see."

Interesting. She couldn't quite imagine a con man presenting it that way—con men were all about adapting to the needs of the listener—and an attention-seeker wouldn't be looking for a quick end to anything.

"Tell me about your vision," she repeated. "The first one. How it happened, where, what you saw."

He repeated it, closing his eyes to bring it back. It seemed to disturb him; his face tightened, and so did his hands around his coffee cup. He deliberately relaxed when he was done, breathed deeply and took a long swallow from his cup as he told her all about it. She heard nothing exceptional, which was odd—generally, liars liked to throw in colorful, nonspecific details. His account was very tight, and very consistent with witness statements, including Jazz Ryan's.

Katie jotted a few things down in her notebook and said without looking up, "Tell me about the second vision."

"It was more intense. It was also worse," he said. His tenor voice, which had been velvet-soft, grew rougher. "The girls were trying to communicate with each other. I think they know sign language. But the abductors saw them, and—"

He stopped. Just…stopped. Stopped talking, stopped

breathing. Katie looked up, startled, and saw that he'd stopped *being there* behind his eyes. Some kind of petit mal seizure, she thought. Epilepsy. His hands were slightly trembling, growing tighter around the cup. Tighter. The porcelain rattled against the tabletop with a dull chatter. She reached over and put her hand on his wrist, and she could feel the convulsive energy flowing through his muscles.

He didn't respond to her touch.

"Mr. Blackman?" Nothing. She slid out of her side of the booth and leaned over him. "Stefan?"

A drop of sweat glided down the side of his face and splashed on his blue jeans, and suddenly, he gulped in a huge lungful of air, spasmed, and sent his coffee cup flying in a wobbling circle toward the other side of the table as his hands slipped free. Katie reached out and caught it, lightning-fast, and set it back upright, ignoring the spilled coffee.

"You okay?" she asked and crouched down to look into his face. He looked dazed, but *there* again. Shaken. "What happened?"

"I—" His voice caught, rusty in his throat. He tried again. "It was another vision. In the van. They stopped for gas." He was shaking, and he didn't look good. Katie eased back into the bench seat opposite him, frowning. "My God, that was—it was different. Stronger. Look, one of the girls—the one I'm in contact with—tried to get away. She didn't get far. The thing is, the attendant at the gas station—" He stopped again and ran his hands over his eyes as if trying to scrub away the memory of what he'd seen. "He's dead. He saw her and he tried to help, and they killed him."

That was very specific. Utterly, incontrovertibly subject to fact-check. She sat frozen, staring at him. Of all the things she'd expected, she hadn't expected this.

She found her voice. "How did they kill him?" Another thing that was incontrovertible.

"Shot him." Stefan squeezed his eyes shut again. "They shot him in the head. He went down...."

"Stefan, look at me." Katie kept her tone soft and low, and leaned forward toward him. He opened his eyes and focused on her. She felt a shock run through her, a desire that had nothing to do with attraction or lust and everything to do with a need to *help*. He seemed so vulnerable just now. So...*surprised*. "Did you get any sense of the time this happened?"

"*Now.* Just now. It's—well, it feels like real time."

Over his shoulder was a big retro diner clock, hands sweeping silently through seconds; Katie focused on it and noted the time.

"Do you know where?"

"Interstate 8, the off-ramp to Smurr. I keep *telling* you people—" He stopped, swallowed and visibly composed himself. "Sorry. That wasn't—pleasant."

No kidding. If he was delusional, if he'd had a mini-seizure, that wasn't pleasant, either, but at least he'd given her something to check. Something concrete. "Wait here," she said and slid out of the booth. The two police officers were still sitting in their cruiser across the street, watching the two of them;

somehow, she'd expected that. The slightly taller one leaned out of the driver's-side window as she approached.

"I need you to dispatch the Highway Patrol out to a gas station on Interstate 8, at the exit to Smurr," she said.

The officer blinked. "Ma'am?"

"Please."

He gave her one of those you're-crazy-but-you're-a-fed-and-it's-no-skin-off-my-nose looks—she knew those well—and got on the radio.

"Tell them to call my cell phone when they get there," she said, and gave him the number. His partner jotted it down and nodded. "I'll be in there." She pointed back at the diner, then turned and jogged back to the diner. Stefan hadn't moved. He was staring down into his coffee cup as if it were the open pit to hell.

She'd seen that look before. She slowed as she approached, studying him. Whether he was delusional or not was still an open question, but whatever he was, he wasn't a liar. She knew that look far too well, and she'd seen it on the faces of victims and witnesses to violence.

Con men wouldn't bother to fake it.

Katie put her hand on his shoulder. Stefan looked up at her and forced a smile. "Sorry for the drama," he said. His voice was getting back to normal, but still a little uneven. "I'm not usually this weird, I swear."

There was still a possibility—however remote it seemed—that he was playing her. If he was a plant from the bad guys, they could have agreed on a time-table…but this murder, if actually true, sounded spur of the moment, not planned. Still. Better to be careful. Her grandmother had always said you catch more flies with honey…and Stefan was nothing if not sweet, tempting, golden honey.

She needed to be sure he stayed put, while the police checked out the scene. For lack of anything better to do, she began to clean up the spilled coffee on the table, then took out a menu from the holder. "Hungry?" she asked. She was—an unavoidable demand of a body pushed too far, for too long.

Stefan looked briefly sick, and shook his head. "I couldn't eat. Not after that."

"You'd be surprised," she said. "Besides, if you're really hooked into one of these girls and getting psychic impulses, I don't need you dropping because of low blood sugar."

"Look, I just saw somebody get shot in the head! I don't think I'm really up for a hamburger."

Put that way, it did sound revolting. "Then at least get a piece of pie and some milk. Milk will settle your stomach."

"I don't know—"

"Well, I do. Believe me. Special FBI training." She'd puked her guts out after her first real crime scene, as a trainee, and one of her instructors—Hibbard, she thought—had taken her to a place around the corner and forced pie and milk on her. It had worked.

"Well," Stefan said, "so long as it's government approved, I guess I'd better comply."

* * *

Stefan couldn't tell if this woman believed him. That was unusual. He could almost always read people instantly, but FBI Special Agent Katie Rush was a whole different thing. Too controlled, too interior, too cool. He felt a compassion buried deep inside her, at odds with her thousand-yard police-issue stare, but that didn't tell him what she really thought, especially about him.

She probably thought he was nuts, he concluded. He would have, in her shoes. He tried not to take it personally.

God, that last vision had been horrible. His pulse was still racing erratically, his heart pounding. He'd thought for a second that he'd been about to pass out, when he'd come hurtling back from that bloody, catastrophic vision, and it had only been Katie's voice calling his name that had held him upright.

That, and the humiliation of passing out in front of one of the most attractive women he'd ever seen, much less talked with. She looked fiercely capable; he doubted she'd be much impressed by him doing a face-plant on the table.

She looked up from her menu and gave him a little crook of her lips—could barely be called a smile, but somehow, it transformed her. It softened her face and made it luminous, almost angelic, and woke an appealingly wicked glint in her eyes. He fell in love with her eyes, and the one corner of her mouth that pulled higher than the other. And her skin. She had gorgeous matte-satin skin.

She'd said something. He blinked. "Sorry?"

"Pie. What kind of pie?" she asked.

He cleared his throat, retrieved a sticky plastic-laminated menu from the holder on the table and pretended to be interested in the choices. "Sharing food. Does that make this some kind of a date, Special Agent Rush?"

When he glanced up, she was still smiling, but it had changed slightly, a Mona Lisa echo he wasn't sure he could decipher. She focused on her menu while he was still wondering. It confused him. What was she waiting for? She didn't seem like the kind of person who would sit around for a leisurely dinner if she had hard information about where two abducted girls might be, or at least, had been recently.

Of course. She hadn't believed him, or at least, she was waiting for confirmation one way or the other. She'd gone out to ask the cops in the cruiser to dispatch someone to the gas station. So this was a stalling tactic. And she was charming him to disarm him, in case he might decide to get up and try to leave before she had hard facts as to his truthfulness. And/or sanity.

He had to admire her for her dedication.

Well, since they were being so polite, he might as well get a decent piece of pie out of it.

The tired-looking waitress wandered over, and Stefan ordered a slice of coconut meringue pie, and—as Katie suggested—milk. He expected Agent Rush to order a salad—it seemed to be de rigueur for women on dates, even pretend dates, these days—but then again, she was from the Midwest, not SoCal.

She went with a hamburger. Once the menus were

out of the way, she avoided his gaze, choosing to meticulously line up her hard-used tableware and inspect the interior of her coffee cup, from which all coffee had been safely extracted.

She was just—he hated to think it about someone as potentially, catastrophically dangerous as an FBI agent—*cute.*

And you're thinking like this to keep your mind off of other things, some traitor voice in his head reminded him, and just like that, the whole vision was back, vivid and violent.

Fear. Darkness, then pain as the girl was forced to her knees and then to her feet. She'd run, she'd gotten loose and run but her balance was off because of the bonds on her wrists, and she'd tripped and gone sprawling on the still-warm concrete, bathed in the harsh white lights of the gas station awning.

The attendant had ducked out of the booth and yelled, "Hey, you leave her alone!" She'd whimpered deep in her throat, unable to scream or warn him, and had to stand and watch, just watch, as one of the black-masked men slipped up from the side, extended his arm, and a sharp pop echoed through the desert.

Blood spattered the plate glass window as the attendant fell. No time for the horror because hands were dragging her, off balance, back to the van....

He jerked and pressed his hands flat against the table, furious with himself. He'd never had this problem. He'd become a street magician because it was fun, it was challenging and it required razor-sharp mental and physical control, and now he was reduced to a trembling wreck. Couldn't cut a deck one-handed to save his life.

"You all right?" the strict goddess across the table asked. He didn't look up.

"Fine," he said. "I'm fine. So what's the next step? What do you do now?"

"It's already being done," she said. "You've given us a lead. Once we verify it, we'll be moving quickly to seal off the area and isolate the van. We're trained for this. It's going to be okay."

"Only you don't believe me," he said, very quietly, and looked up to meet her eyes. "Right?"

Silence. Katie was good with silence; she used it as a tool. Growing up in the Blackman household had been an exercise in coping with controlled chaos, day in and day out. Silence…wasn't part of Stefan's life experience.

She finally said, "I want to believe you, Mr. Blackman. But I can't afford to blindly trust anyone. There are two girls' lives at stake."

It was, he had to admit, a valid point, but it was still irritating. In his entire life, Stefan had never *not* been trusted by a woman. Of course, he wasn't generally trusted by cops, and an FBI agent was a kind of white-collar cop, but still, it rankled. Women *liked* him.

Maybe he was losing his touch.

"If you'd just listen to me, we could do it faster," he said. "I could try to tell you exactly where the van was."

She looked intrigued. "How? Psychometry?"

"What's psychometry?"

"Touching an object that belongs to one of the girls."

The waitress came back to refill their cups; Stefan leaned back to avoid being splashed. "You know more than I do about it. Not my bag."

"So what exactly is your bag?" A cop's question, delivered casually but no less important for all that.

"Didn't you check me out already?"

"I know that you're from Los Angeles—"

"Venice Beach, actually. I just work in Los Angeles part of the time."

"—and that you're involved in film and television."

"As a consultant."

"And I know that you've had a couple of arrests for fraud," she said.

Ah. He'd been wondering when that would come snarling up out of the dark to bite him in the ass. She delivered it with perfect poker-faced impartiality, and waited for his reaction.

He nodded. "True," he said. "I have been. I work the streets in Venice Beach as a magician—not a psychic. But from time to time, really obnoxious people won't take no for an answer, they want me to be psychic on demand. Those guys deserve a first-class prognostication, don't you think? Something to tell them how to invest their money wisely? It's not my fault they buy some dog of a stock and get burned. Being wrong's not illegal. Besides, all of the charges were dismissed."

She thought it over. "If you don't bill yourself as a psychic, why do they seek you out for advice?"

"Because the Blackman name comes with baggage." He sighed. "My grandfather was a famous psychic. So was my grandmother. My mother is a psychic to the stars, she's got quite a reputation. Even my dad is a pet psychic. So I'm a psychic by association, and some people just won't take 'not interested' for an answer. When they get pushy, I sting. But it's not fraud. It's their own greed getting the better of them."

Which, he was well aware, was the basis of any con game, but he hoped she could see the difference. He couldn't tell. It unsettled him that she was so self-contained.

"Mr. Blackman—"

"Stefan."

She didn't blink. "Mr. Blackman, let's just say that regardless of how you explain it now, it doesn't exactly enhance your credibility. You see that, don't you?"

He gave up. "Yes." Luckily, he was saved from groveling by the arrival of her hamburger and his pie. Both looked surprisingly delicious, and he was shocked to feel a sudden wave of hunger, verging on starvation. They fell to eating without another word, except for a few subvocal moans of pleasure from Agent Rush, which made him forget a little bit about the horror show inside of his head and wonder what it might take to get her to moan like that over things other than food. A very diverting question.

He was tempted to moan over the pie, which was excellent, but he didn't want her to think he was easy.

They'd both taken the last bites when her cell phone rang. Stefan swallowed and sat back, tense and still, as Agent Rush flipped open her phone. "Rush."

Silence as she listened. He couldn't tell what was going on in her head, though he could read a confusing turmoil of feelings radiating like a fever. He wanted to touch her. Touching her would make things clearer. There might be other side benefits to it, too....

She said a terse thanks and hung up. Stared at him with those lovely, impenetrable eyes.

"Mr. Blackman," she said, "the Highway Patrol tell me that there is a dead man at a Conoco station at the Smurr exit. Shot in the head. They estimate he's only been dead half an hour, at most. I'm going to need you to come with me." She signaled the waitress for the check.

"And the van?" he asked.

"The Highway Patrol are working to close off all exits from the area. They know their job. We'll get them, but I may need your help."

"So you believe me."

"Let's just say that I don't see any other way you could possibly have known what you did, other than what you're telling me. That doesn't mean I completely buy into the whole psychic theory, just that I'm willing to listen to what you have to say."

He felt a surge of hope and adrenaline. Somehow, some way, this was a good thing. He was sure of it.

Chapter 7

They drove in silence, watching scenery flash by in the street-lit darkness. Next to Katie in the passenger seat, Stefan Blackman looked uncomfortable—justifiably so. This ride was probably a good reminder of how fast "material witness helping the police" could turn to "prime suspect."

Even with lights and sirens clearing the way, it took nearly an hour to get to the Smurr exit, but it was visible a long way off from the cluster of police cars, flashers lighting up the night. Stefan looked pale in the red-blue-red glow, and his throat was working nervously.

"You can stay in the car if you want," she said, and he looked over at her and smiled. It wasn't a very convincing smile.

"No, I can't," he said. "Look, maybe I can be of some help. I feel like I should at least try."

Katie pulled the sedan in with a metallic squeal of brakes and coasted to a stop just inches from a Highway Patrol vehicle.

"You don't have to," she said. The engine ticked as it burned off heat, and the entire car shook with a sudden gust of wind that blew a dry rattle of sand over the hood. "This isn't your job."

Stefan didn't look at her. He looked stone-faced, staring at the confusing blur of flashing lights, the busy knot of people behind the fluttering crime-scene tape.

"Guess it is now," he said and got out of the car.

The air was cooling fast, dry and thin as it stung sand in her face. Katie took a breath and turned toward the Highway Patrol officer who was approaching.

"FBI?" he asked, scanning her top to toe. She nodded and produced credentials without being asked. "You want to see the body?"

"First, tell me what you've done to find the van," she said.

"How'd you know it was a van?" he asked and doffed his hat to smooth back his thick, iron-gray hair. He had a face as creased and brown as a leather bag, and his name tag said MENCHACA. "We just found that out on the surveillance tape."

"I had some tips." She didn't look toward where Stefan was standing. He looked ill at ease enough without any help from her.

"Good for you. We don't have the plates, but we've

got the make and color from the camera. We've already set up stops—Hawkins! Get me a map!"

"Sir!" Another officer set off at a trot and returned about a minute later with an accordion-fold laminated map that he spread out over the hood of the cruiser.

"We set up stops here, here, here and here. Problem is, there's lots of farm roads, back roads, rough trails, though I wouldn't call that damn van any damn off-roader—they could go around us if they have half a brain. I don't have the manpower to cover every cow path from here to the border." Menchaca shook his head. "Kidnapping, huh? That's what the Glendale PD said."

"Two young girls," Katie verified. "At least one of them saw the shooting."

Another head shake, world-weary and grim. "A shame."

"Could I take a look—" she glanced quickly at his rank, indicated by the pins on his collar "—Captain Menchaca?"

"Sure. Forensic team's still en route, so don't touch and stay outside of the tape."

She shook hands and met Stefan's eyes, then indicated with a fast jerk of her head that he should follow her. Which he did, though not exactly willingly. She could almost hear the extra weight of dread in his footsteps.

She stopped at the fluttering yellow border. Behind her, Stefan took an audible breath and moved up to join her there.

Like all crime scenes, it looked oddly staged. Human brains just didn't like to compute things like this and kept returning it as false; the blood looked black where it was drying on the concrete, a muddy crimson nearer to the head. The smears and drips on the glass behind retained a backlit red tint.

The body was simply that—a body. Rubber, slack, utterly devoid of any sense that it had ever moved at all. The dead bothered Katie for different reasons than they did most of her colleagues; it wasn't the mess, or the smell. No, it was this pathetic sense of the body simply no longer being *human*. Of having been demoted to a colder, crueler status.

She cataloged the head wound, automatically figuring angles and trajectories and how far the shooter might have been when the bullet was fired. An inexact science without the caliber of bullet, but she thought she was pretty close.

Stefan hadn't made a sound. He was staring at the dead man—boy, really—with lightless, fixed eyes, and his skin had a tinge of dirty ash beneath the natural golden brown. He'd jammed his hands in his jeans pockets.

"Is it what you saw?" she asked, although it was a foregone conclusion. He nodded jerkily, and for the briefest second there was fury in his eyes, incandescent and startling.

"You're going to catch them," he said, low in his throat. "Right? You're going to catch them and make them pay for this."

"This, among other things," she said. "Let's do what we can to keep the list from getting any longer."

He nodded and closed his eyes. She waited, focused on him and nearly oblivious to the police milling around her, the radios crackling, the strobe lights flashing. His face was tense, and his eyes moved back and forth under the lids, as if searching....

He relaxed, after a full minute, and looked at her bleakly. "I'm not getting anything," he said. "Maybe she's asleep."

He was, she saw, hoping rather than knowing for certain. It had to be Teal he was seeing, she thought suddenly. He'd described Lena Poole, so his visions were coming through the eyes of Teal Arnett. Teal was the one with innate psychic abilities.

"You let me know the second you feel anything coming from her, right?"

He nodded. She spun away from him, walked away from the circuslike chaos and dialed a number on her cell phone.

"Athena Academy, Rebecca Claussen speaking," came the response after two short rings.

"It's Katie Rush," she said. "Our kidnapping's gone up to kidnapping and murder." As soon as she said it, she realized how it sounded, and hurried on to say, "It's neither one of the girls. A gas station attendant who saw Teal trying to escape got shot."

Rebecca muttered an obscenity that revealed a rich experience as a military wife, back in the day. Katie wholeheartedly agreed, although the FBI code of conduct didn't include airing that aloud.

"The Arizona Highway Patrol is working to cordon off the area, but they don't seem very confident that it's going to work," Katie said. "Any news on Sheila Prichard?"

"Well." Rebecca's voice went dry and cool. "Miss Prichard seems to be something more of a black box than we'd anticipated. Alex Forsythe has been here, and she's already turning up some dramatic inconsistencies—nothing that a general background check would have turned up, but enough to be very worrisome. For instance, her name was not originally Sheila Prichard."

Alex? Well, it made sense; Alex's grandfather Charles had helped found the Athena Academy in the first place, and Alex was, of course, an alumnus. Though Alex was a coworker, in a sense—also in the FBI—her path didn't cross Katie's much. Her specialty was forensics, which Katie supposed could also include data mining. Katie stopped pacing, listening with all her concentration. "If Prichard wasn't her original name, what was?"

"That, we don't yet know. Alex is digging. I'll keep you posted."

"Tell Alex to call me directly," Katie said. "I want to talk this over with her."

"Will do. What's your next step?"

Katie blew out a frustrated breath. "The thing I hate the most," she said. "I wait."

Her next call was to the FBI local field office. She knew the Resident Special Agent in Charge, or Resident SAIC; she'd worked with him on a couple of assignments, not closely but enough to establish a professional rapport. He'd already received a call from her boss back home, who'd paved the way for any special requests.

Hers was simple. "I need a better car," she said. It went

without saying that any car issued by the FBI would be reliable and durable—and the sedan she'd been issued was serviceable—but she needed the federal equivalent of a rental upgrade. "This investigation keeps hopscotching, and I need something with networking ability."

Within the hour, she had a freshly washed Lincoln, nondescript and scrupulously clean, with local Arizona plates and the necessary accessories, like an in-dash flasher and built-in siren, radio, GPS tracking uplinks. There were computer hookups, as well, and the whole car was a mobile Wi-Fi hot spot.

As an added bonus—and God only knew how it had happened, because no bureaucracy in the world, even the FBI, was about initiative—there was a laptop in the car, as well. A good one, loaded with everything she needed.

She thanked the agent who delivered it, and logged in on the laptop with her FBI identification codes. Surprisingly, the Wi-Fi connection was good even here. She began some digging in various databases, making and discarding search parameters as quickly as possible, chasing elusive bits of information and data through the system...

...and there it was. Alex Forsythe probably already had the trail, but Katie's job was tracing people, and she was better at it than most. Besides, she needed to keep busy.

In the end, she discovered that Sheila Prichard's original name was Sheila Richards Stanley. Which didn't ring any bells, but Katie put it through the system anyway, and forgot to breathe when she read the information that popped up on the screen.

Sheila Richards Stanley, twenty-six years old, was the

illegitimate daughter of East Coast drug kingpin Timmons Kent. Kent was as dirty and unprincipled as they came, even among drug lords…and from the looks of things, she was very much Daddy's little girl, or had been up until a few years ago, when overnight, she'd cleaned up her act, changed her name and set about acquiring just the right credentials to apply to Athena Academy.

It was perfect, Katie had to admit. Having too much responsibility at the school would trigger a next-level personnel review, but her cover would have just passed the lowest-level scrutiny for the school—which was still far better than anything that would have been administered for the average government desk job.

Sheila Prichard was a plant. She'd been sent inside with a specific mission, and, mission accomplished, was gone.

Gone with two students.

Katie slapped down the lid of the laptop and went in search of Stefan. She found him perched on the back bumper of a Highway Patrol cruiser, sipping coffee with two female officers. A blonde and a redhead.

She felt an inexplicable surge of irritation. "How much of that stuff do you drink in a day?" she snapped.

Stefan looked at her in surprise, then at the coffee cup. "As much as possible," he said. "Why? Is it a crime? Some kind of Breathalyzer test?"

Ought to be, she thought. "Time to go."

He didn't move. "Go where?"

"I'm going back to Glendale. Unless you'd rather stay here?"

He cut a quick glance right and left to the two female

officers. They were young, competent and cute, and they were smiling at him. The redhead shrugged.

"Sorry, Officers, duty calls," he said and started to toss his coffee cup into the nearest trash can.

Duty?

"Freeze!" Katie snapped. "It's a crime scene. The last thing they need is to sort through more trash."

Stefan stopped in midgesture. "Oh. Sorry."

"Just bring it with you. Say your goodbyes, and hurry up. I can't wait for you."

She was irrationally angry, and she knew it. She didn't like waiting, although she was usually better at it than this. No, this was the fact that Sheila Prichard's new identity opened up a huge field of new possibilities, unpleasant ones. As dangerous as kidnapping for ransom or drug abductions might be, political kidnappings were far, far worse. But why these two girls? Sure, someone with enough knowledge might be able to link the Athena Academy to AA.gov, and Athena Force. There were plenty of bad people in the world who might want to put a stop to the training of Athena women, or curtail their activities by using pressure.

But why *these two girls?*

Somebody knew. Somebody knew about the abilities the girls were displaying, and that opened up whole unpleasant vistas of possibilities.

Katie got in the car and started it up. It felt good to be behind the wheel again, in control of her destination. Stefan got in on the passenger side without another word. She dialed her cell phone again as she accelerated out of the parking lot and onto the highway access road. This car was a huge improvement, no doubt about it…sleek, smooth-driving, powerful.

"Kayla? It's Katie. Have you got access to Sheila Prichard's apartment yet?"

"Warrant's in process," Kayla said. She sounded tired, but still focused. "I haven't got access yet, but I was pulling it together. Look, I can meet you there. Alex Forsythe is here with me, too. Is it okay if she—"

"Yes, absolutely, tell her hi for me," Katie said. "Address?"

She didn't need a notepad; her memory was more than sharp enough for streets and numbers. When she hung up, Stefan, who was looking out the window, said, "Who's Sheila Prichard?"

She debated telling him, but it was too soon; the jury was still out on Stefan Blackman and his true relationship to the crimes. "Someone who may have information about the kidnapping."

He let that sit in silence for a few seconds, then asked, "You keep saying *kidnapping*. Some of the other cops called it an abduction. What's the difference between an abduction and a kidnapping?"

It was a good question, one she'd asked herself early in her FBI training. "Kidnappers generally interact with the authorities or the families. They want something. Kidnapping is just a way to get what they want. That doesn't mean they're not dangerous and brutal, but at least they're more logical."

"And abductions?"

"Abductors already have what they want," she said and hooked a U-turn to get back on the freeway, heading back toward Phoenix. "And they don't need to interact with anybody but the victim."

"Interact," he echoed faintly, and looked out the window again. "You're not talking about conversation, are you?"

"Sometimes," she said. "Mostly, no. By the time they go far enough to risk prison like that, they're not usually satisfied with talk."

He was silent for a few seconds. "These guys haven't interacted with the families or the authorities."

"No."

"So you calling them kidnappers—"

"Wishful thinking," she said. "I'd like to think of them as kidnappers right now. Kidnappers have a standard operating procedure, a framework, and they do things in a logical manner. I can deal with kidnappers."

"Do I even want to know what you've seen?"

"You really don't," she said, and meant it. She liked that he was so shaken over a single dead body; that meant he had a soul. So many men she dealt with, week in and week out, had no souls left, or if they did, they were so irredeemably sick that it no longer mattered. That didn't just go for the villains, of course; the burnout rate in law enforcement was shocking. "Tell me about what you do."

"What *I* do?" He sounded shocked.

"Trust me, I'd rather not talk about my work." She was tired, she realized, tired and sick at heart, and a little scared, too. This situation was big, and she was working without her usual support. Granted, she had Stefan Blackman, but she wasn't exactly sure how to categorize that. Advantage? Burden? Annoyance? In any case, he wasn't trained in law enforcement, and they were on the trail of some very unpleasant people. Another good reason to be certain to turf the man when she picked up solid real-world leads.

"Most days, I do street magic in Venice Beach," he said. "You understand what that is?"

"Somewhere between David Blaine and three-card monty?"

For answer, he flipped his hand, and instantly a playing card appeared, held lightly between two elegant, relaxed fingers. "Depends on how you do it," he said. "Street magic is more fun than stage magic, at least for me. Up close and personal. You have to be better with your hands for it to work."

The playing card—it was the queen of hearts, she noticed—disappeared in the same graceful gesture. "You always carry cards up your sleeve to crime scenes, Mr. Blackman?"

"Stefan," he said, "and I don't keep them up my sleeve."

His voice had changed back to its more usual tones, she noticed—low, gentle, underlaid with some sly and private amusement. Very sexy.

Like the hands. Which he knew, of course. She had the feeling he knew exactly his effect on women.

"So, do street magicians have a union? Dental plan?"

"The fringe benefits are mostly—" He never finished whatever quip he'd been working on. He stopped dead, and when she looked over, his eyes were open, fixed and staring, and they were—once again—empty of presence. He was somewhere else, seeing something other than the road disappearing under the wheels of the car.

She didn't disturb him with questions. This didn't look like as violent a vision—or seizure—as the last one. He was gone a while, and signaled his return with a deep-inhaled breath. He lowered his head for a few seconds.

"Take your time," she said. "It's okay."

"Nothing specific this time," he said. "I think they must have knocked her out when she tried to escape, back at the gas station. She seemed confused, just waking up. That was the impression I got, anyway. She's alive, and so's the other girl."

"Lena," Katie supplied quietly. "Her name is Lena Poole, the one with blond streaked hair."

He nodded. "And the one who's showing me this?"

"Teal Arnett. She's seventeen."

"She seems—" He searched for words. "Good. Smart. Strong."

She was Athena Academy, Katie thought. Of course she was. But it was nice that he recognized it. It proved him to be slightly less of a jerk than most men she'd ever known. "How's she holding up?"

"Pretty well," he said. "I can't communicate with her exactly, but I get the feeling that she's thinking. Always thinking." He paused. "Did you speak to her family?"

"Yes, but just briefly. Hers and Lena's family, both."

"Do you think—do you think we can get these girls back safely?"

Katie recognized the tension along her shoulders and down her back, and tried to relax it. "I don't know," she said. "But I made a promise, and I intend to keep it. Now, show me a card trick."

Sheila Prichard's apartment complex was utterly nondescript; drug kingpins' children grew up surrounded by excessive wealth and a minimum of good taste, so the conservative boxy setting—conventional square two-story structures surrounded by parking lots—came as a surprise. Katie checked the address carefully, but no, this was it. A standard medium-rent place, nothing special in any way. Prichard's unit was toward the back, facing an empty lot overgrown with dry, desiccated weeds from last year's growing season.

Kayla Ryan, looking as tired as she'd sounded, stood near the stairs, and with her were two others, instantly recognizable to Katie. She felt her face relax into a welcoming smile. "Alex," she said, and stepped forward to give—and receive—a big hug. Alex looked as dramatic and gorgeous as ever, though she'd tied her thick red hair back into a ponytail for convenience. No makeup, but then, she didn't need it. "Fancy meeting you here."

"You knew I had to come," Alex said. "After all—" She didn't need to finish. Katie just nodded in acceptance. Standing behind her, arms folded, was Justin Cohen, Alex's fiancé. He smiled slightly at Katie, professional to professional. There was a large black tackle box, unmarked, sitting by his feet. Tools of Alex's trade, without a doubt. Both Alex and Justin were, like Katie, FBI, though none of them worked in the same area— Katie out of the Kansas City office, Alex out of Washington, Justin out of Quantico, in the basement, with the rest of the Behavioral Science Unit. But there was a shared culture between them, if nothing else, and genuine respect.

"It's so good to see you, Katie," Alex said and pulled back to frown at her. "Did I just feel you flinch? And by the way, are you bringing civilians with you on investigations these days?"

Katie stepped back. Trust Alex to dive right to the heart of things. "I had some trouble early this morning during a takedown," she said. "I'm fine, just some bruising, no big thing. This is Stefan Blackman. He's— it's complicated. Let's just say I'd like him to stick with me for a while." She was well aware that could be taken a multitude of ways, and Justin and Alex, at least, took it the most serious way, as a potential threat to safety. Their looks at Stefan were decidedly not friendly.

Kayla looked grim, too. She said, "You were at the abduction scene earlier today. You wanted to talk to a cop."

Stefan's dark eyes darted busily from one of them to the other, clearly curious. Clearly not realizing what kind of potential peril he was in. "I did talk to one. More than one, actually."

"Uh-huh. How did that go?" Kayla's tone was dry. Stefan gave her a wide, luminous smile.

"Some of the nicest cops I've ever met," he said, and

only at the very last of that did he throw a lightning-fast glance Katie's way.

Alex and Justin continued to stare at him, then looked at each other and did that invisible communication that the best couples seemed to share. Justin shrugged and took a key from his coat pocket.

"Shouldn't they have somebody here?" Stefan stage-whispered as Justin inserted the key into the dead bolt of the apartment door.

"Who?"

"The management company? An apartment manager?"

"You watch too much television," Katie said. "Trust me, the apartment manager is too busy right now worrying what made the FBI show up with a warrant. She's probably scanning the contracts, looking for a way to terminate Prichard's lease."

"That's terrifying," he said.

She snorted. "Not as terrifying as some of the things we actually find in apartments," Katie snapped back.

"So this is all you do? You just pick up a key and walk in? No wonder people are scared of the government."

Justin eased the door open. Alex was right beside him, sidearm drawn, and Katie had a flash of *something*—not a premonition, more of a subliminal recognition, and saw the same thing snap Alex's head around. Alex grabbed Justin by the collar and yanked him backward just as Katie bodychecked Stefan out of the way into the bushes and dived for the ground.

The world erupted in a wave of heat and pressure, and a split second later, an eardrum-rattling roar. Katie finished rolling for the cover of the stairs and felt debris hitting her. Some of it was on fire. She couldn't hear anything except a violent ringing in her ears, but she could see—razor-sharp detail etched by adrenaline. Stefan was lying on the ground, eyes open, staring upward in shock at the cloud of smoke rising into the night sky.

Katie scrambled up and lunged for Alex and Justin. Justin was on his side, lying half-across Alex, who was trying to get up. He looked as if he was out, but as Katie pressed her fingers to his throat his eyes fluttered open, dazed and unfocused.

A hand fell on her shoulder, and Katie looked up to see Kayla Ryan mouthing words.

…hear me?

Katie shook her head. Kayla spun away, grabbing a radio from her coat pocket. Calling for emergency services, certainly. It seemed, miraculously, that none of them would need the paramedics; even Justin, who'd been closest to the blast, was shaking it off and starting to look more angry than dazed. Alex lunged for the doorway, kicked open the bent, smoke-blackened metal, and leaned in. Justin grabbed her arm and held her back when she would have ventured inside, and he was right, Katie thought; whatever was in there, it wasn't worth Alex's life. Fire alarms were going off all over the apartment complex; she could hear them now, dimly, as if they—or she—were underwater. It wouldn't take long for the firefighters to arrive.

She reassured herself about Alex and Justin, then went to check on Stefan. He was still on the ground, lying very still, staring at the sky. She felt a pulse of alarm—had he been hit? Spinal injury of some kind?

"Holy shit," he said, or she thought he said. "That was much, much worse than on television."

She almost laughed, but somehow managed to control herself. Inappropriate humor: sometimes, it got you through the crisis. Stefan slowly levered himself up to a sitting position.

"You okay?" she asked him.

"Apart from almost getting blown up? What kind of a psychic am I, if I didn't see that coming!"

This time, she had to bite the inside of her lip to keep from bursting out into a full hysterical giggle.

"Stay down," she said. "I think you have a head injury."

"I don't think so. I'm pretty much always like this," he said, and rolled to his hands and knees, then up to his feet. "We'd better get people out of their apartments in case this wreck goes up."

He was right. She sent him to the left, and she took doors on the right while Alex and Justin went down to the next cluster of doors. By the time they'd evacuated the residents—and pets—the fire trucks were rolling up into the parking lot, sirens blaring and lights blazing. The police were only seconds behind.

"It's going to be a long night," Stefan said.

If that was a psychic prediction, he wasn't wrong.

Chapter 8

Two hours later, crime-scene technicians were allowed to begin sifting through the sodden mess of Sheila Prichard's apartment. Katie left it to them, Alex and Justin, and grabbed Stefan on the way back to the car.

"Where are we going?" he asked.

"We're not going anywhere, you are," she said. "This is turning dangerous. I want you out of here. Catch a plane, go back to California. Leave."

"Whoa, whoa, wait!" Stefan pulled free of her grasp and stopped. "I don't think that's exactly your choice. Or mine. So long as I'm hooked into Teal with these visions…"

"You haven't had one in the last couple of hours. Maybe she's cut the connection." Or something worse had happened. "It doesn't matter. Alex is right. I don't take civilians on investigations. It's not safe."

"I'm not going to sue." He sounded offended. They had to dodge out of the way for some passing firefighters, carrying hose, who were trudging back to their truck. "Come on, Agent Rush. Don't shut me out. Not now, when it's really starting to get interesting."

"Interesting? You call that interesting?"

"Well, it isn't boring."

"Look, Mr. Blackman—"

"Once you've been blown up together, you're on a first-name basis, don't you think? Call me Stefan."

Katie gritted her teeth. "*Stefan.* Fine. The point is, you are a civilian, and I am an FBI agent, and I can't endanger your life by keeping you involved in this investigation. Clearly, this is going places we never anticipated, and while I appreciate the help you've offered, I don't think—"

"It's not your choice!" Stefan gestured helplessly, anger flashing in his dark eyes like lightning in storm clouds. "I didn't ask for this, but I'm not turning my back on it, either. I can't. That girl out there, she reached out, and she reached out to *me.* If I back off now, I let her down. I'm not going to do that, Katie. I'll do whatever it takes. If I can do that with you, fine, but if I can't, then you'd better get used to seeing me in your rearview mirror because I'll be right behind until this is over and those girls are safe!"

She wasn't used to direct challenges, not like this; FBI agents typically commanded more respectful disagreement. But there was something insidiously wonderful about his passion, even misplaced as it was; she worked with witnesses every day, and she knew how few of them were capable of that kind of caring. She knew she was stretching the legal definition of *witness,* but hadn't he been a witness, really? As much of one as Jazz Ryan?

How many men do you know who wouldn't take the opportunity to bail out and leave this in the hands of others?

None who weren't already in law enforcement, she thought. Certainly none who were vagabond street magicians/psychics/television consultants.

He kept surprising her. She couldn't remember the last time someone who hadn't been in handcuffs had done that.

"Katie." He took a step forward, and they were suddenly close, very close, and she could see the scrape he'd gotten on his forehead when she'd pushed him out of the way of the explosion. "How did you know?"

"Know?" she echoed. "Know what?"

"About the bomb."

"Oh. I just—knew. So did Alex."

"But not the other guy. Justin."

She shrugged. "I guess so. Why?"

"Just curious." He gave her an odd, considering look. "Does that happen to you often? Sensing things ahead of others?"

This was going into territory she definitely did not want to cover, especially not with someone who was proving as insightful as Stefan Blackman. "No," she said shortly, and reached out to snag the arm of a passing patrol officer. "My friend here needs a ride to the airport. He's going back to California tonight."

"He's not," Stefan said flatly. "It's still a free country, I haven't violated any laws that I know of, and I'm not going home."

"Fine. Dump him at the nearest motel where they won't knife him for his jacket," she said. The officer looked as if he was tempted to smile, but too wise to succumb. He just nodded, stone faced, and turned to look at Stefan.

"Let's go, sir. You heard the lady." The officer gave the badge hanging around her neck a fast glance. "The agent."

"I heard," Stefan said, unmoving. "You're sure you want to do this, Katie?"

She felt a funny little kick start every time he said her name. And why had she let it get informal? This was way out of hand, and she had no idea why. She wasn't like this. She never let men walk into her life like this, especially not during cases.

"Yes, I'm sure I want to do this. I want you to go away," she said and met his eyes. "Call me if you get more information." She handed him her card, the one with her cell phone number penciled on the back. "I'm sorry."

"Are you?" He put the card in his pocket, glanced at the officer waiting at his side, and shook his head. "You'll come looking for me."

"Is that a prediction?" She couldn't keep the sarcasm out of her voice, and she saw it hurt him just a little.

"No," he said. "It's not a prediction. I'm not a prognosticator."

He turned and walked away. Katie watched him go, frowning.

I almost got him killed tonight.

Odd that he didn't seem to mind it much.

She dismissed the strange emptiness his departure left, and flipped open her cell phone to dial the Highway Patrol's Captain Menchaca for an update.

"Not good news," Alex Forsythe said as Katie dropped down on the gritty curb next to her. She had a bottle of chilled water and passed it over. Katie chugged three gulps and gave it back.

"Highway Patrol didn't find the van," Katie replied. "After this amount of time, they're not going to. Too many roads, too many variables. We're going to have to wait for another sighting."

"Wait for a lucky break, you mean," Alex agreed. "Where's your special friend? The gypsy prince?"

"Gone home, I hope. It was a mistake bringing him here."

"From the way he was looking at you, it was a mistake letting him go." Alex favored her with a smile, then reached in her pocket and pulled out a small silver PDA. "I need to beam you some info."

Katie pulled out her own matching device, watched as the screen registered a request and allowed the transfer. Data and photographs. She studied one, a mug shot, carefully. Sheila Richards Stanley, looking defiant and—unlike most people in mug shots—as if she'd been interrupted on her way to an important engagement. Perfect makeup, understated and elegant; perfect short blond hair, too. Big brown eyes. Her skin was a matte tan, and could have owed its shading either to dedicated worship at the altar of the tanning bed or her genetic heritage.

It was the latter, Katie saw, as she paged through the documentation. Sheila's father, Timmons Kent, had married a Venezuelan woman named Socorro Almeida—a model, who'd bequeathed beauty on her daughter as Timmons had handed down his blond hair and bad attitude.

Something in the data caught Katie's eye. "She's got a brother," she said. "Max."

"Good catch," Alex said. She unwrapped a protein bar and took a bite, then offered Katie a second; Katie shook her head. "Good old Max has a record. Petty stuff as a juvenile, escalating to aggravated assault, rape, armed robbery. He's twenty-eight now. You've got his file, too."

Katie changed documents and speed-scanned Max Stanley's résumé. He was as bad as he looked angelic, in his mug shots. A chip off the old block. Dad must have been proud.

Aggravated assault. Rape. This wasn't good. "Any location on Max?" she asked aloud.

"He hasn't been seen for about a week. He's got two louts he hangs around with, and they haven't been spotted, either."

"Three men," Katie repeated slowly. "Sheila on the inside, gaining the girls' trust. They had this planned down to the last detail. The only thing they couldn't anticipate were the girls' abilities."

Alex looked at her quizzically. "What abilities?"

"Besides being faster and stronger than most? I think Teal may be telepathic."

"You're kidding."

"The gypsy prince? He's getting messages from her. Visual, not thoughts. So maybe she's got more going on than anyone suspected, even at the school." Katie paged through documentation, speeding along faster. She was good at picking important details from piles of dross, but Max Stanley's life and sentences didn't seem significant, other than to reinforce yet again the danger that Lena and Teal were in. "I think these guys know exactly what they have. Clearly, they're not after ransom, or we'd have gotten some kind of message by now."

"You think the girls are being sold?" Alex asked. "Highest bidder, maybe? For their abilities?"

"If it's just random slavery, they were pretty stupid in their choice of victims. Hell hath no fury like Athena Force in defense of its children."

"Amen," Alex said. She looked thoughtful. "Your gypsy prince—can he help? Really?"

"I think he legitimately wants to help. Needs to, even." Katie sighed. "I just can't drag a civilian along on this. You understand."

"I do," Alex agreed. "I have a hard time involving Justin, and he's not exactly a stranger. But just having someone dropped on you, out of the blue…especially some shady street psychic…"

"You checked him out," Katie said and turned to stare at her in disbelief. "You did, didn't you? That fast?"

Alex's elegant eyebrows rose. "Didn't you?"

Well, yes, Katie had. But she'd had a good excuse. And now, obscurely, she felt she needed to defend the man. "He may not have the best background, but he's got a good heart, Alex. I can tell that much. He's not just making up these visions—there's too much cross-verification for detail."

"Unless he's working with them," Alex said, staring at the asphalt beneath her feet. "Unless they're feeding him the details."

Again, nothing she hadn't already worried over herself. Katie frowned. "How? He's not wearing an earpiece—"

"Got that close, did you?"

Katie rolled her eyes. "And he hasn't gotten any calls or messages."

"That you're aware of."

"Is there something you know that I should know?"

Alex shook her head. "I'm just trying to play devil's advocate. Actually, just from the few seconds I met the guy, I liked him. Of course, that always makes me suspicious."

Katie laughed out loud, and just for a second, things seemed a little lighter…a little more absurd, if nothing else. But then a police officer striding through the parking lot adjusted his course straight for her, and she felt a little sinking sensation. *Trouble.*

"Ma'am." It was one of the officers who'd been escorting Stefan off premises. "I think you'd better come with me."

Katie stood up, hardly aware she'd done it. "What's wrong?"

"Your friend," he said. "I think he's having some kind of a fit."

Something wrong.

He woke up suddenly, heart pounding, aching in every muscle. Sweating from the stifling heat inside the van.

Afraid.

Voices, indistinct, coming from the front part of the van. Argument. The van swerved, sending him thumping against the metal side, and he saw that Lena was awake, too, staring at him with wide eyes.

Not you, some part of Stefan insisted. This is her, not you. Not you.

But it felt like his skin, his bones, his flesh. Arranged differently, yes, but...

Fear. A sharp, hot surge of it, a spike through the back of his neck, and he froze. He could almost see, almost understand what she was thinking, but it was only emotion that came through clearly: fear, anger and frustration.

He looked through the back window of the van and saw headlights behind them. Police? No, there were no lights or sirens. But something about the car was making his—her!—captors nervous and edgy. Maybe it had been following for a while, or maybe they recognized it; either way, it was dangerous for whoever was in that car, trapped out here in the middle of nowhere on a deserted two-lane blacktop.

The van swerved again, and suddenly braked. The

car following fishtailed, burning rubber as it tried to stop. The van backed up and slammed into the car with shuddering force, sending Stefan—Teal—flying to collide with Lena, and the van kept growling, pushing the car back, back....

There was a rending crash. Stefan fought his way upright to catch a glimpse out the back window.

It was a maroon car, the color vivid in the glow of the backup lights. It had fallen over an embankment, and lay on its side, rocking slightly. There was a woman behind the wheel, bloody and unconscious, hanging from the safety straps.

Someone shoved him down, and one of the three masked figures stripped off its mask and smiled down at him.

A woman, pretty, blond. He felt a strong pulse of recognition and anger—this was someone Teal knew, then. Someone she'd trusted.

The woman flipped open a black leather case, took out a hypodermic, and slammed it home in his arm. A bright white-hot spark of pain, and then he was falling....

"Stefan!"

Someone was calling his name. It sounded like a long distance off, but as he blinked and pulled in a breath—the air in his lungs had gone sour and stale—he saw that Katie Rush was leaning over him. Her face was tense, worried and pale.

He managed a weak smile. "Found her," he said. His voice sounded strange and rusty. "There was a car catching up to them. Maroon. Woman behind the wheel, maybe one of yours, I don't know. They ran it off the road—"

"Slow down, Stefan. Here." Something cold pressed into his hand—a bottle of water, beaded with sweat. He twisted off the cap and chugged down several gulps before nodding.

He was sitting on the curb next to the police cruiser—he remembered getting in, remembered discussing things—that was the polite term—with the two cops Katie had assigned to take him away from her, but then...then...

Then Teal had connected again, and blown his mind like a circuit trying to channel too much current. She was getting stronger each time. And much better.

"You said something about a car?" Katie asked in that low, soothing voice he was sure she used for dealing with victims, and sometimes—maybe—suspects. "Can you describe it?"

He struggled to put impressions into words. Nothing felt right, inside or out. Definitely one of the more disconcerting experiences of his life... "Maroon, some kind of sedan. I didn't get a better look. There was a woman behind the wheel, like I said. I think she might have been hurt in the crash."

"Do you know where?"

He struggled to find anything in the vision to tell him where they'd been traveling, and finally shook his head.

Katie made a low, frustrated sound. "What kind of road? Highway? Freeway? Separated? Two-lane blacktop?"

"Two-lane blacktop," he said. "Not in very good

repair, I—Teal was feeling the roughness of the road."
He held up a finger as something flashed across his
mind, just a glimpse out of the corner of Teal's eye.
She'd been focused on the wreck, the woman behind the
wheel, but at the edge of her vision there had been a road
sign. Green and white. "There was a sign that said it was
sixty-two miles to Blythe—does that help?"

"Yeah," said one of the cops who had been listening.
"Narrows it down. We can send cars to every road within
that radius, see what we come up with."

"Do it," Katie said. She hadn't, and didn't, look away
from Stefan. "You all right?" Her voice had dropped
lower, almost a caress.

"Never better," he said, and she held out a hand to
him. He looked at it, at her, and then took it. She
hauled him to his feet. "Just another beautiful day on
Planet Psychic."

"I mean it. Are you okay?"

"I'm fine." Their eyes met, and Stefan felt something shift inside, shift and lock. I finally found you,
some part of him said—the hopeless romantic part.
Until I lose you, the cynic in him added. Which he
always was, in the end, not from any bitterness or anger
or frustration, but just because he wasn't really capable
of deep and abiding commitment.

He knew, to his marrow, that this was not a woman
he could have a pleasant, superficial love affair with.
It wasn't that she was a cop, or that she was so
capable. There was something inside her that just went
deeper than that.

Not, he reminded himself as she pulled her hand free of his, that she'd really let him get close enough to find out.

Whatever she'd felt in that moment, she was turning away now, facing the cops standing nearby. "I'm taking him with me," she said. "Get those units rolling on the roads toward Blythe."

"Where are we going?" he asked. It occurred to him, wryly, that this was getting to be a standard question with her.

"We're heading the same direction," she said. "Whenever that crash happened, that's our next crime scene." A tick of silence, and then she said, "If there is one." But it was a pro forma afterthought. She'd given up her skepticism; he could feel it.

It should have been a victory, but it felt hollow. He kept feeling the all-too-real pain Teal was experiencing, and seeing the dead gas station attendant, the woman slumped behind the wheel of the maroon car.

It might be a victory, but they weren't exactly *winning*.

Katie hadn't paused for long before leading Stefan to her new FBI-supplied transportation; she'd only stopped to grab Alex and Justin for a huddle, to update them on the information Stefan had provided. What Justin thought, she couldn't tell; he was carefully neutral. Alex accepted it, though Katie thought she detected a slightly wry twist to her lips.

"Katie," Alex said as she turned away. "I'm following up on our lovely Sheila. I'll get the info to you as soon as I can. You be careful." She meant that in a number of ways, not the least of which, Katie suspected, was *be careful of that gypsy prince, he's got you wrapped around his little finger.*

And Katie also suspected Alex might be right. It pissed her off, and it made her tone cooler than it should have been when she rejoined Stefan and headed for the car. "Let's go."

He didn't comment. In fact, he didn't comment as he got in the sedan, closed the door and strapped in. Nor as she backed up from the parking spot and headed for the apartment complex exit.

Eventually, she felt compelled to offer a conversational olive branch. "Blythe's only about two hours away on the freeway," she said and turned onto the street. It was late, verging on early morning, and traffic was light. She surprised herself by yawning. She hadn't realized she was that tired.

"But they'd only gotten halfway there," Stefan said. "If the sixty-two-mile sign was right. Why?"

"They're working hard to stay off our radar. We've got cops fanned out all over the state. Eventually they're bound to run into the net. It slows them down."

"Not that much. Where have they been since the gas station?"

It was a pretty decent question. She didn't have an answer. Stefan was concentrating on it, frowning, and then answered it himself. "The van."

"What about it?"

"You're looking for the wrong one."

Katie shook her head. "We have a good visual of it on the surveillance tape from the gas station."

"They've changed vans," he said. "I'm sure. It was different on the inside. And there were more windows on the sides. They ditched the first van and stole one, or had one waiting. It has to be."

It would make sense, especially as professional as these assholes seemed to be. They'd have a means to ditch the first compromised ride and get something clean, and they'd take their time doing it, knowing that the search was likely to widen outward, leaving them in relative safety.

Damn.

She hated smart criminals. It was a good thing they were so rare.

"Can you describe the new van at all?" she asked. "Color? Make? Anything?"

She'd known what the answer would be, but she still felt a surge of frustration when Stefan shook his head. What the hell use was having your own pet psychic if he couldn't describe the color of the getaway van?

"But at least you know where they are," he pointed out.

She reached for the radio and got a patch to Arizona Highway Patrol, where they put her through to Captain Menchaca. "FBI Special Agent Katie Rush," she identified herself.

"Go ahead." Menchaca sounded gruff, tired and distracted. She understood that. It hadn't been an easy day for anybody.

"Check in the Smurr area for any vans that have gone missing in the past couple of hours," she said. "Passen-

ger or cargo, with windows in the back and on the sides."
She raised her eyebrows at Stefan for confirmation, and
he nodded. "Maybe we'll get lucky."

"You think they switched?"

"We think so."

"I'll put my people on it," he promised. "Anything
else?"

"I'd ask for coffee, but I don't think you guys de-
liver," she said, and got a chuckle. "Rush, out."

Menchaca signed off. She put the handset back in its
cradle and settled back, foot pressing past the legal
speed limit, as the car headed for Blythe, California.

"This is wrong," Stefan said after a few minutes.
"They weren't on a major freeway like this. It was a
smaller road."

"We're making up time. When we hit just outside the
radius, I'll circle us around and see what we can pick
up," she said. "Don't get your hopes up. The chances of
us finding anything are one in a hundred, maybe. The
Highway Patrol will find the wreck first, if there is one."

A muscle fluttered in his jaw. "You say that like you
still have doubts."

"I'd be a fool if I didn't. Look, I'm acting on your
information. I'm committing resources to it, which is
career suicide if this doesn't work out, not to mention
potentially costing people their lives. I'm trusting you
the best I can. So back off."

He didn't answer directly. In fact, he was silent for
two or three miles before he said, "When did you stop
being a believer?"

"In what?"

"In anything."

He'd slipped under her guard, and that was a cold, strange surprise. Painfully intense. "I don't know what you mean." She did, though. And from the look he threw her, he knew that, too.

"You used to be a believer, Katie. You had faith, once upon a time. Something made you lose it, devote your life to what you can see and hear and prove in a forensic lab. I'm just curious about what that was."

A dozen responses ripped through her mind, starting with *It's none of your damn business,* and ending with *Curiosity killed the psychic,* but instead of choosing any of those she heard herself say, "I lost my mother."

"I'm sorry. When did she die?"

"She didn't. Or at least, if she did, I don't know when, where or how. When I say lost, I mean exactly that—misplaced. She left home one day when I was five, and she never came back."

Stefan thought about that for a long second, then asked, "Do you think she wanted to leave? Or did someone take her?"

It was exactly the question that had tormented Katie throughout her childhood, adolescence, angst-ridden teen years and into adulthood. Had her mother just gotten fed up with a life burdened by four children, a life that might have been too difficult for her to bear? Had she vanished deliberately, covered her tracks, changed her name, forgotten all about the husband and children she'd left broken behind her? It happened.

Or had it been different: a stranger—or someone she knew—forcing her into a car or van or truck, dragging her away to horror and degradation, death and burial in an unmarked grave? Katie had seen the scenario many times, and it never failed to raise that sick specter of familiarity. She always pictured her mother's face, eternally frozen at the age of thirty-two, when she unearthed those terribly betrayed women. She couldn't stop herself.

Stefan was still waiting for the answer. "I don't know," she finally said. "My father always thought she just…left. So do my brothers. But I don't know. It might not have been her choice."

"Is that why you got into this work? Finding people who go missing?"

"I'm good at it," she said. It was a deflection, mostly reflexive, and he accepted the signal without probing deeper. She checked the speedometer and decided to press a little faster. Not legal, but her reflexes were better than most people's; she knew that without ego or guilt. It didn't excuse the violation, and she wouldn't have done it for convenience, but this was turning into a special case on every possible front.

"Katie." Stefan turned toward her. It was breaking some law of physics, that black eyes should look so warm. "We may not find these girls. You know that."

"We will."

"It's just that I'm sensing—" He stopped and shrugged, helpless to articulate it. "Maybe I'm just tired."

She knew what he meant. The day was catching up

to her, in a big and ugly way, from the aching bruises she'd collected in the morning's shootout to the accumulated exhaustion trembling in her muscles. A bed would have been a miracle. She found herself fantasizing about it the way starving people fantasized about food…in a tactile way. She could almost feel the crisp, cool sheets on her bare skin, the soft pillow under her head, the warmth of…

She blinked. The car swerved a bit, but it hadn't been that she was on the edge of sleep—far from it. It was just that the image of Stefan's naked body curled next to hers in her fantasy had taken her utterly by surprise.

"Not happening," she muttered aloud. Stefan frowned.

"What isn't?"

"Never mind." She kept her eyes on the road because she was afraid that if she looked at him too long she'd start doing it again. Exhaustion didn't usually make her libido go nuts, but there was something about him, something about this day…

"If you're about to offer to drive, don't bother," she snapped, bitchy precisely because she was acutely aware of him, of his presence, his warmth, his leather-and-incense smell. In her peripheral vision she saw him open his mouth, then shut it without speaking. "I'm fine."

"Just field-testing the side of the road, making sure it's stable." He nodded. "Absolutely. It's commendable, how you federal agents keep track of things like that."

She refused to let him lighten her mood. "We *are* going to find these people, Stefan. By *we,* I don't mean you and me. I mean the team. The whole reason law enforcement works is that we're a team, we act in concert while the criminals operate as individuals."

"Don't knock individuals," he said. "They're the ones who have the original thoughts. Not teams. By the way, if you want to pull off the freeway for coffee—"

"I'm fine."

"I'm not." He made an elegant, embarrassed motion, spreading his hands wide. "Sorry. Pit stop. You did mention I drank too much of the stuff. Gotta off-load it sometime."

She controlled the impulse to growl—everybody had bladders, after all—and checked the road sign. The next exit had one of those gas-food-lodging truck stops. She couldn't have missed it, unless she'd been dead asleep; the lights looked either as if they'd arrived in Los Angeles hours ahead of time, or an alien mothership had landed.

The truck stop was pretty much the kind of place she'd expected, well used but still clean, catering to the long-haul crowd as well as passing tourists. Scrupulously fresh bathrooms, which was a relief. She emerged to find Stefan already browsing the coffee selections.

She leaned against the wall, waiting, and studied him. In fact, she was observing the women in the truck stop, too; several of them were checking him out, head to toe. It was a bit charming, how oblivious he was to it. Or at least, she assumed he was oblivious. Maybe he was just practiced at ignoring it until he wanted to take advantage of it.

He looked up, as if he'd suddenly felt her stare on him, and smiled.

The sweetest, most naive smile she'd ever seen. Heartbreaking.

Paired with the look in his eyes, which was as far from naive as it was possible to get…devastating.

Katie cleared her throat and went in search of something cold.

They were at the checkout counter when her cell phone rang, its no-nonsense, no-frills tone cutting through the noise of the music, the diner patrons' chatter and the big rigs rumbling out in the parking lot.

She was no psychic, but Katie felt a premonition as she reached in her pocket and touched the warm plastic. She hesitated for a bare second, then pulled it out and flipped it open. "Rush," she said.

"Captain Menchaca," came the response. He sounded flat and discouraged. "Found your maroon sedan on a farm-to-market road near Aguila, just outside of Wickenburg. One occupant, a female driver, off-duty cop. Looks like she spotted the van and was trying to call it in when they sideswiped her."

"Is she alive?"

"Wouldn't have been by morning, if we hadn't been looking for her. She had some head injuries, couple of broken bones. She's being airlifted to Prescott now." Menchaca paused, then asked, "How'd you know?"

"I told you, Captain. Tips."

He was silent. She heard the distant, agitated click of a pen.

"Any sign of the van?" she asked.

"You're not going to tell me."

"Need to know, Captain."

"Then no. No sign of the van. We're restarting the hub search using the wreck as a spoke point. Good news is, we can't be far behind them now, no more than a couple of hours at most. The bad news…"

"The bad news," Katie said for him, "is that they could have caught one of the interstates by now, and if so, they're over the border into California."

"Probably so, ma'am. Which means the amount of help I can offer you is pretty limited. I'm sorry."

She pulled in a deep breath, held it and let it out. Suddenly, all of her weariness came flooding back, and she almost staggered under the weight of it. "Nothing to apologize for, Captain, I know you did your best. At least we have a live cop to show for it. Do me a favor, will you? Keep somebody with her in case she comes to long enough to give us information. And copy me on any forensic information you get from the wreck."

"Can do. Oh, one fast fact I can tell you—the van's white."

"White? You're sure?"

"Standard white, nothing special about the paint, except that it was on the front bumper and door panels of the Saturn our cop was driving."

White. Well, that didn't exactly narrow it down, but of course that was the intention: they'd picked the best statistical choice of blending in, the bastards. On a busy freeway like I-10 or I-8, both of which headed west into California, it would be like a raindrop in a thunderstorm.

Unless it had visible damage.

She said that aloud, and Menchaca agreed. "We already thought of it," he said. "Got the California Highway Patrol as much detail as possible, so we're working it from both borders. Cross your fingers, Agent Rush."

She thanked him again and hung up, then walked away to look out the windows of the Quik Stop onto the vast parking lot, lit by orange sodium bulbs. Out on the freeway, traffic continued to move in a sea of lights.

A warm hand fell on her shoulder and squeezed with surprising strength. She turned her head. Stefan, un-smiling, held out a cardboard coffee cup. She took it, gulped without tasting anything but heat, and said, "I'm going to lose them. I promised Jazz, and now I'm going to lose these girls."

He could have lied to her, told her she wouldn't, that she was going to win despite the odds.

Instead Stefan said, "You might, but if you do, it won't be because you didn't give it your heart. Don't count yourself out yet, Katie. I can't think of anybody I'd want on my side more, if I were Teal or Lena."

She found it hard to swallow, suddenly. She put the coffee cup down and without thinking it through, clasped his hand in hers. Warm, strong fingers that inter-laced with hers as if born to do it.

They didn't speak for a few seconds, and then Stefan said blandly, "Are you going to shoot me if I make a sug-gestion?"

"Depends on the suggestion."

"First, you need food, and I'm not talking about—"

he consulted the package in her other hand "—Sno Balls. What the hell are Sno Balls, anyway?"

She sighed. "Chocolate cake with cream filling, covered in marshmallow and coconut."

"And they're bright pink because…"

"Don't ask."

"Right." He took the package from her as if it were an unexploded bomb and carefully set it aside. "I'm guessing that you're one of those women who just burn it all off in metabolism. Let's think about food that doesn't come in pink."

The diner didn't look as if it was serving anything much healthier, but she didn't argue. Instead, she met his eyes. "And two?"

"What?"

"You said, first…so there's got to be a second part to the statement."

His eyes widened, very slightly, and she could see he was debating something. Then he said, "You need sleep."

Her shields came up, full strength. "Forget it."

"Seriously, isn't there some kind of regulation about how long an FBI agent gets to stay awake and behind the wheel? Because I'm guessing your day didn't begin when you got off the plane in the airport."

He hadn't let go of her hand. She looked down at where their fingers intertwined, shook loose, and said, "Are you seriously propositioning me? You want to get a room while two girls are being driven off in a van by three men, one of whom probably has a conviction for rape? Because I thought better of you, Stefan."

When he spoke again, his voice had cooled off, gone soft and distant. "I was going to suggest I drive while you sleep," he said. "Or that we get separate rooms. Though hey, if you're up for it—"

"Don't be a bastard."

"I wasn't. You think I'm trying to delay you? Distract you? You think I'm working with the kidnappers, Katie?"

"No." She didn't, really. She'd seen too far into him, and there was nothing that wasn't truthful on that score.

"Look at me."

She did. He reached out to fit his palms around her face. It took her breath, froze her in place like some innocent virgin.

"Listen very carefully," Stefan said, with a scary, quiet intensity. "I am not trying to get you in bed. I do have some sense of propriety, and even though I find you very, very attractive, I know that there are more important things at work today."

If she thought she'd been intensely aware of him before, on a sexual level, she was now. Deeply. Her whole body hummed with it, and it was maddening, it was *stupid,* because he was right, there were more important things, and her body was betraying her principles in ways she'd never thought possible.

"I think I'm going to kiss you," Stefan said with that same blind intensity. "If you're going to shoot me, wait until I'm done, okay?"

His lips were warm and soft and full, and he tasted of coffee and sugar and cream. She licked at that taste, devoured it, craved it more. She was against him now, their bodies burning where they touched, and his hand slid around to cup the back of her head as his tongue touched her lips, stroked them open, explored.

As good a kisser as she knew she was, she was a novice compared to Stefan Blackman. Maybe he was a magician after all, not just an illusionist; he was transmuting her bones into light, making her glow from the inside out, and he hadn't done anything except…kiss her.

Stefan pulled back, breathing fast, and she opened her eyes to stare at him. She felt drunk on the residual energy he'd left inside of her, and if *that* wasn't magic…

"Wow," he said faintly. "That…never happens."

"What never happens?" Automatic question; she didn't care and was too busy watching the mesmerizing damp movements of his lips. Then his tongue, as he licked her taste from them.

"That. That thing. That thing that just…happened."

She knew what he meant, but sanity was starting to creep in again, and she grabbed it for a shield. "I don't know what they call it in California, but in Missouri we call it assault."

"Funny, I thought Missouri was the Show-Me State."

"It's not you-show-me-yours, I'll-show-you-mine." The sharp-edged attack was working, it was helping her clear the adrenaline out of her system and get her brain working again. "Fine. You've had your kiss. Try it again, and I'll handcuff you so fast you'll think you've died and gone to bondage heaven. Now *back off.*" She was desperate to get distance, too, and he must have seen that in her eyes; it wasn't because she was really offended. She was afraid that if he stayed that close to her, she was going to reach out and devour that sweet, hot mouth and sink into the completely animal world of sensation.

And she *couldn't*.

Stefan hesitated, then took a step back. A large one. And he picked up the fluorescent-pink Sno Balls from the counter, handed them over to her and walked away, toward the car.

Katie stood there, shaking, furious with him, even more furious with herself, and tried to control the blood pouring fast through her veins. She'd had plenty of practice at it, through firefights and face-offs with bad, dangerous men, and yet, somehow, this was more difficult.

She felt something squish in her right hand, and looked down to see that she'd destroyed the cupcake treats in their plastic package, reduced them to a fluorescent-pink misshapen mess leaking chocolate cake and cream filling.

Katie tossed them in the trash, picked up her coffee and followed Stefan.

Outside, the cold desert wind slapped some sense into her. Katie spotted Stefan ahead of her, heading purposefully for the car, and stretched her long legs into a jog to catch up.

She was still ten steps behind, or more, when she saw that there was someone in the shadows near the car. Stefan hadn't seen him, clearly; he was walking with his head down, lost in his own world. It was possible the lurker was

just a trucker out for a stroll, but few people felt comfortable standing in the shadows in a deserted early morning
parking lot, waiting in stillness without so much as a lit
cigarette or a cell phone to keep them company. Every
nerve in her body switched to alert mode, and she increased her speed, dug in with her elbows and knees, and
flew into Stefan, pushing him down to the ground just as
a muzzle flash exploded in the shadows. The sound of the
shot came an instant later as a hollow boom echoing off
the trucks. Stefan landed hard; Katie rolled away from
him and to one knee. She pulled her gun, thumbed the
safety back and fired in one smooth, practiced motion.

And watched, for the second time in a day, a man
drop dead at her hands.

Stefan squirmed next to her, panting and shaking.
"What the hell— What happened?"

She kept her gun barrel on the unmoving shadow
of their attacker and didn't blink as she said, "Offhand,
I think somebody thinks you're helping us a little too
effectively."

The problems went deeper than that, of course. It
wasn't just that somebody had come gunning for Stefan,
it was how they'd found him. How they knew to stake
out her entirely anonymous, and recently acquired,
sedan. Katie sat in the diner, thinking about all of those
things, after the Highway Patrol had come and gone.
They weren't cleared to leave, of course. That would
take extraordinary dispensation from Captain Menchaca, at the very least. And she imagined her own boss

back in Missouri might have a word or two for her when she came back. This was an off-the-books assignment, and that meant she hadn't really been supposed to do things like shoot bad guys.

But the bad guy had clearly been going to shoot Stefan, and she absolutely couldn't allow that.

She couldn't tell what Stefan was thinking, at this moment; his normal open expression was closed for business, his attention focused inside. Well, nearly getting killed twice in one day would do that. The tremor was back in his hands, too. He must have noticed it at the same time she did because he made a sound of disgust, stretched his fingers out and did some complicated limbering exercises that reminded her of piano studies, only without the piano.

"They know," Stefan said. "Right? They have to know. Why else come after me?"

"Let's not jump to that conclusion," Katie replied. "We don't know anything yet. Maybe it's a random bad guy looking to rip off wallets."

"He didn't ask for my wallet."

"Some of them find it easier just to take it off of your body later," she said, which was perfectly true. "We'll know more when his sheet comes back, and we know who we're dealing with."

Stefan looked up at her. "How did you know?"

"I saw him."

"But you *knew*. I heard you start running, you reacted so fast—that's the second time today I've seen you do that, Katie. Precognition."

"It's nothing but observation and reaction," she said,

shrugging. "Maybe it looks like magic at a distance. You should know, a lot of things do."

She surprised a smile from him, and for answer, he reached over, took the fork from the place setting on her right, and held it up for her inspection.

She frowned, puzzled.

Stefan drove the fork smoothly through the back of his left hand.

She let out a cry and reached out to grab him, coming half out of her chair, but he wasn't yelling in pain, and now he was showing her the fork, pristine and blood-free. And then his hand, unmarked. He turned it to show her both sides.

Katie sank back into the worn bench seat. "How?"

"Human perception is a flawed instrument. We learn to work the edges of it. Often, what the brain sees is really interpretation, filling in the holes with assumptions because it takes time to process the full picture. Street magic takes advantage of that with quick and dirty illusions, some improvised with surroundings." He put the fork back in its place. "But no amount of street magic could have gotten me there in time to save your life, and I'm fast. Very fast. What does that make you?"

"Someone who saved your life. Twice today. You could be more grateful."

He smiled. She wasn't building up an immunity to it, despite close and intense exposure. "Oh, believe me," he said. "I'm grateful. It's just that I'm naturally curious."

"Or naturally unlucky."

"Not until I bumped into you." An almost comical

look of horror crossed his face. "Not that I meant— you—meeting you was *not* unlucky—"

"I get your point." She sighed and took a bite of the salad she'd ordered. It was plain diner food, iceberg lettuce, slightly mealy tomatoes, fat-free Russian dressing. She contemplated wistfully the squashed Sno Balls she'd thrown in the trash. "You're sure nobody's out to kill you? Nobody, say, you taught a lesson to with the whole psychic investment scam?"

He didn't debate the word *scam,* as she'd thought he would. "I don't think so. They're mostly broke, and some are in jail, but none of them could have known I'd be here, with you." He poked around at his broiled chicken, but didn't eat. "But a lot of cops knew. FBI, too. Right?"

She didn't confirm or deny that; for one thing, it was obvious, and for another, she didn't want to go down that road unless she had to do it. She'd already acknowledged it silently, that someone in law enforcement could have sold her out, maybe even someone standing around at that last crime scene, and that possibility deeply angered her. This case kept growing roots, and the deeper they went, the more poisonous they were.

"Are you all right with this?" Stefan asked. "I mean, twice in one day—"

She went still and focused on him. "How did you know about the first shooting?"

"I—"

"I wasn't anywhere near Los Angeles or Phoenix. It hasn't been in the news reports."

"But—"

"And don't give me any crap about psychic abilities, Stefan. You said yourself you mostly get emotions and impressions, not current events!"

He leaned forward and captured her hands on either side of her plate, a liberty she resisted, then allowed because too much struggling would have coated them both with flying food.

"Katie," he said in a soft, level voice, "I was talking about the explosion. I didn't know you'd had another shooting today." He let go of her. "What happened?"

She reviewed the conversation at lightning speed in her head, and realized that she'd been guilty of an assumptive leap—something she'd warned him to avoid. Of *course* he'd been talking about the explosion. It had only been her own preconceptions that had made his reference seem sinister.

"There was a bad situation," she said after a long second. "Back home. We'd spent three days tracking the kidnappers. It came to a confrontation and I had to shoot a man."

"But it was necessary."

"He exchanged fire with federal agents, he was a kidnapping bastard who tortured a thirteen-year-old boy for information, and he was about to kill his hostage. What do you think?" Evangelista had been right, she thought; she hadn't processed all of the rage and pain and fear from this morning—yesterday morning—before she'd hopped the plane to take on this crisis. It was starting to snarl her up. That, and the accumulated heavy drag of exhaustion. One day without sleep she could manage—it was the

price of being good at her job—but she'd barely cat-
napped for the last forty-eight hours, and hadn't exactly
been rested before that. Her body might be tougher and
stronger than average, but her brain was tiring.

That was deadly.

Her cell phone rang before Stefan could think of
any reply; she answered as he chewed an apparently
unwanted bite of chicken and peas. "Rush." She listened
carefully, then thanked the officer on the other end and
hung up. "The shooter was one Paul Gallatin, local loser
out of Prescott. He's been up on assault and murder a
couple of times, but what he's mostly known for is drug
dealing. He's associated with Timmons Kent—also
known as Sheila Prichard's father."

"The one whose apartment blew up. Prichard, I
mean. Not her father."

"It was designed to blow up cops who came looking
for her. She wasn't there. Obviously, Timmons Kent is
looking out for his daughter, and that means he's
looking straight at us." The likelihood of a cop selling
them out was pegging near one hundred percent, she
thought. Kent had always had resources inside of law
enforcement. But still, dispatching a hired gun to take
out an FBI agent and a psychic—that was extreme.

She wondered why he'd bother. Did he really believe
in psychics?

"I think I can find them," Stefan said. He had a faraway
look in his eyes, but not the blankness that had so far indicated a vision. "I got the impression last time that Teal
was actually trying to reach me—that somehow she knows

I'm there. I don't know how much she can hear me. I can't hear clearly at all, although visuals come through fine."

"What about thoughts? Can you tell what she's thinking?"

Stefan shook his head. "Just emotions. They're strong, but it's not enough to really give any clues. But if I can create a strong link to her, without distractions, maybe I can keep it open long enough to give you a good fix on them. They can't be that far from here, can they?"

"They could be into Los Angeles, for all I know," she said. "We're not going to catch them this way. We have to get ahead of them, and for that, we don't just need location, we need direction and speed. Do you think you could get all that? From a link with her?"

He looked thoughtful. "Maybe. I could try, anyway, but like I said, I need a place without distractions."

"Would the car do?"

"Not really. Road noise, vibration—" He shrugged. "What about a room? If I can't do it in an hour, we can get in the car and keep trying."

"A room," she said.

"It's a motel. They do rent rooms here. Probably not the Hilton, but…"

"We don't have time." But they did, she realized. The police were still a little bit wary of her story, and it was the middle of the night, and she wasn't likely to be driving out of their immediate supervision any time in the next sixty minutes.

Stefan frowned. "You said yourself that we need to get ahead of them, and we need information. So we have time for it. Or I do, anyway. If you want to take off and send someone to get me…"

"No," she said. "No, I'll stay."

Something in his shoulders loosened, and she realized that he'd been tense.

"Good," he said. "I think…I think you can help."

Chapter 9

Stefan just wanted to sleep. His eyes felt grainy, his muscles tight and aching with the tension and exhaustion of the day. But he couldn't sleep, not if Katie was staying awake. But at least he'd bargained for a bed to lie down on, and if sleep came, well…it came.

Not that you don't want other things.

Oh, he did. It had been unwise, kissing her like that, but he'd wanted it, and he could resist anything except, well, temptation. And she'd been wonderfully receptive in ways that he'd never felt before, despite a pretty broad range of experience.

Something between them had resonated like a struck bell. He felt it tolling now, as he watched Katie book the room and take the clumsy orange triangular key holder. They were in number four.

"Not a word," she warned him, and pushed past him to lead the way down the hall. He closed his mouth and followed, exchanging a look with the woman at the counter. She winked at him. He winked back purely out of habit.

The hallway, like the rest of the truck stop, was clean and worn. The door opened on a Spartan room, with a plain white queen-size bed, a dark green blanket folded neatly at the foot. Two fluffed pillows. A small desk, a TV in the corner, a phone, a couple of lamps. No decor to speak of.

Katie excused herself to the bathroom, which Stefan thought looked like a continuation of the white theme. White tile, white shower curtain, white towels.

Well, he'd wanted a lack of distractions. This certainly qualified.

He sat down on the bed and took off his shoes, then settled back on the unbelievably soft feather pillow. Bliss. His exhausted body felt as if it were floating.

Stefan opened his eyes as he felt the blanket settling over him. Katie was bent over him, tucking him in, and they were close. Very close.

"You sure you want to do this?" she asked. "You're tired, and so am I. Maybe you should just rest."

"No. I want to do this, Katie. I *need* to do this."

He reached up to move a lock of hair back from her face. She smiled, but it looked sad.

"We can't, can we?" he asked. "Not now."

She hesitated, clearly torn, and then shook her head. "I don't think so, Stefan."

He nodded and closed his eyes.

The featherlight pressure of her lips on his surprised and stirred him, and he lifted into the kiss and reached out to stroke his fingers up her arms, bury them in the warm silky mass of her hair. The kiss deepened, sweetened. She opened her mouth and slowly, dreamily caressed his lips with her tongue. He felt her weight sink down on the bed next to him, as if her legs didn't want to support her, and that was good; it kept her from bolting away and ending this still, quiet, sunlit moment.

When she pulled back, he cleared his throat, trying to look as if that kind of kiss happened to him every day, trying not to betray exactly how compelling he'd found it. Only the fact that she'd spread a blanket over him was keeping him from instant confession on that score.

Katie brushed her fingertips across his forehead. Her eyes—gorgeous dark eyes, with hints of green shimmering in the depths—were wide and almost glowing, and the color in her face, the wet firmness of her lips... He knew when a woman was deeply aroused, and he was looking at one now.

So it was even more frustrating when she said, "Sixty minutes, remember? We're looking for location and direction, and any other information you can pick up."

He nodded, not trusting himself to speak, and closed his eyes. That was easier, not looking at her, though it only increased the frequency of the pictures flashing through his mind, most of which were speculation about how she would look when—to be honest, if—he managed to get her out of that suit and in bed.

She didn't speak again, and she didn't move. He forced his heart rate to slow, his breathing to regulate, and at long last put to use all those meditation techniques that his mother had insisted the entire family learn during her latest yoga craze. Someday, she'd told him, you're going to need to know how to shut out distractions, Stefan.

Well, Mom was right, as always.

The room was well insulated; he heard nothing but the slow ticking of a clock, the regular whisper of Katie's breathing. The silence pooled in the room, then filled him, flowing and lapping like water.

And then, with no transition, he was lying on the floor of a van, screaming into a gag.

Katie felt it happen; his whole body changed, relaxed in ways that it didn't when awake. At first, she thought he'd simply drifted off to sleep, and despite the driving urgency that never left her now, she couldn't really begrudge him that.

But he wasn't asleep. His eyes opened, and they were empty and dark.

He was with Teal.

It took a long time—twenty minutes, by the clock on the side of the bed—but as long as he was gone, she stayed completely still and waited. He breathed, occasionally blinked, but it was just the body remembering a need, not the mind.

Finally, he jerked; his chest rose and fell in a gulping gasp, and he turned on his side, away from her. She heard distress in the uneven rhythm of his breathing, and put her hand on his back.

"Stefan?"

"Give me a minute," he croaked, a parody of his usual velvet-soft voice. He was shaking all over, as if he'd been stranded in a freezer instead of lying in a comfortable bed, covered with a blanket. When she touched the back of her hand to his face, his skin felt ice cold. She bolted up, alarmed, and grabbed an extra blanket from the closet that she spread over him, then stripped off her jacket and the shoulder holster, kicked off her shoes, and crawled under the warm weight on the other side of the bed. She burrowed closer to his shivering body and pulled him in close.

His breath continued to fan warm across her neck, fast and unsteady, but he reached for her and held on like a drowning man in a flood.

"I'm here," Katie murmured. "Stefan, I'm right here. You're safe. Can you hear me?"

A convulsive nod of his head.

"Are they all right? The girls?"

Another nod, this one not quite as uncontrolled. Her presence, her warmth, was helping him reconnect.

"Has something happened to them?"

No nod this time. No reaction. She pulled back slightly and looked into his face, into his warm brown eyes.

"I can't keep doing this," he blurted, almost frantic. "Katie, I can't, it's too—it *hurts* now. I feel everything, everything—"

She felt a surge of true fear. "Stefan, did something happen to Teal?"

His throat worked as he swallowed, and then said, "She distracted one of them long enough for Lena to try to make a break for it at a stoplight. Didn't work, they caught up with Lena before she was out of the van, but they used Tasers, Katie, they used Tasers on both of them. They're just *kids* and they were—" His voice locked in his throat and she understood that words wouldn't convey the depth of horror he was feeling now. He'd reached that place—everyone who worked with missing kids felt it. The place where the bottom dropped out of the world, where you realized just how cruel and horrifying people could become.

Most cops reached that bottom after witnessing the aftermath, but Stefan—Stefan was *living* it. Sharing it with the victims.

"I can't do this," he said again. "I could feel it, and I can't—God, Katie, he was *touching* her."

"Touching her?"

"One of them... The other one made him stop, but—" Stefan shook his head. "She's just a *kid!*"

There was something sweet and sad about his innocence. Katie had been elbow deep in the swamp of filthy emotions and horrors for so long, she'd forgotten that people could still be shocked by it. She wanted to preserve that for him, that feeling that had radiated from him since the beginning that he was part of the world, and liked it.

"Shh," she whispered and rubbed warmth back into his arms, his hands. "She's smart, our girl. Right? Smart and strong. And obviously, they think Teal and

Lena are valuable, too valuable to really hurt. That'll keep them off of her. Greed is a pretty strong motivator. So's fear. If the others stopped him, they'll watch over Teal for us."

"*I* should be watching over her," Stefan said. "I want to. I pulled out, I had to, I couldn't keep—I'm just—God, Katie, it's—"

It was like being a captive, too, helpless to prevent whatever was coming. She understood that; she'd seen strong men reduced to shaking wrecks by it. For some men, witnessing violence done to someone they felt close to was worse than taking the punishment themselves.

Men like Stefan, who couldn't close himself off, who cared enough to come when Teal called and stay committed despite all the odds and disbelief.

It was, Katie realized, bravery. Sheer courage. She just hadn't seen it before because it was coming at her in a guise she hadn't seen before, wrapped in charm and outrageous claims.

But Stefan Blackman was, quite simply, brave.

"Did you get anything we can use?" she asked, very gently. "Direction? Location?"

"I saw a name, I don't know if it was a town or not—it was on a store. Calipatria."

It didn't ring any bells with her. "Anything else?"

"They're heading south right now. They left the interstate. Maybe they were getting boxed in by the Highway Patrol."

South. So they might be heading for San Diego, or they could go south and turn back west to avoid pursuit, and hit Los Angeles, where they'd be almost impossible to find. Either one was dangerous.

"Calipatria," she repeated. "You're sure?"

"It's the only thing I saw," he said. "I'm sorry." And then he pulled in a deep breath, closed his eyes and said, "I'll do better next time. But I need some time."

She knew, right then, that Stefan was the real thing. Not just a real psychic, but a real, living, courageous *man*, of the variety that she'd come across all too rarely in her travels. Someone who faced duty with commitment.

"Gypsy prince," she murmured.

"What?"

She kissed him. It went on for a long, hot, delicious while, and then he pulled back with a gasp. "Katie, I don't think this is a good idea if you don't want…"

"I do want," she said, and kissed him again.

He moaned, deep in his throat, and almost devoured her in his breathtaking response. His hands were wandering, but she didn't care; they trailed liquid fire where they ventured down her back, across her ribs, stroking flat across her fluttering stomach. Still not venturing into any territory that could be considered taboo. Even here, even now, it was nothing they couldn't have done standing up in public.

He was still in control, she realized. He was still letting her give him a signal, tell him *this far and no farther,* and that blew her mind in a big way.

If he wanted a signal…

She unbuttoned his shirt, running fingertips down the exposed skin beneath. He was still cool to the touch, but warming fast now. When she reached the waistband of his pants, she yanked the tail of the shirt out and finished unfastening the buttons, spread it wide to run her hands greedily up his flat stomach, up to the hard planes of his chest. He had chest hair, not a forest of it, but a satisfying amount that caressed her fingers as she explored his contours.

When she looked up into his eyes, they were huge, simmering with fire. "Careful," he said. Just that, nothing more; she knew exactly what he meant. *Be careful what you're asking for, Katie Rush. Be sure what you want before we start this.*

She was sure.

She'd never been more sure in her life.

She unbuttoned the first two fastenings on her shirt and guided his hand to the rest of the task. The cool bite of air on her skin made her tremble, and the heat of his touch gliding down the valley between her breasts and hooking fingers in the front of her bra… That made her shiver outright. She sat up to let the shirt slide off, folded it, and set it on the nightstand next to the jacket she'd discarded, with the gun concealed beneath.

He watched her with eyes so hungry it was as if he'd been starving for years.

"Come here," he said, and she settled into the warm circle of his arms for another damp, silken, urgent kiss. His fingers worked the clasp of her bra and eased it away from her body, leaving her naked from the waist up and pressed against his body as close as the clothing they'd both lost. It felt…perfect. She felt him heating beneath her touch, coming back to himself, coming back to the world, and although she wasn't doing this for therapy, it seemed to be helping him that way, too.

His smile, when he pulled back this time, was wicked and wholly his own.

"Thirty-two minutes," he said. She blinked. "You said we had sixty minutes. We're down to thirty-two. I just thought you should know before we pass the waistband of no return. Also, I have condoms, but they're in a suitcase in the car."

She laughed, and that felt good, felt healing. Heat pulsed through her like sunlight.

"Lucky you," she said. "I have some in my purse." Which was hanging over the back of the single wooden chair. Stefan reached out and snagged it, and she retrieved three foil packets from an interior pocket.

Stefan raised his eyebrows.

"Oh, relax," she said. "They sell them in three-packs. No pressure."

He cleared his throat. "And I think we're down to thirty minutes."

"Then you'd better get a move on," she said and rolled over on her back, smiling. She wasn't one for displaying herself, especially not on the first time, but he made her feel…safe. Protected. Clothed in something invisible and yet utterly modest.

For answer, Stefan bent over and ran his tongue down between her breasts in a long, wet caress that spiraled up to the right, then the left, and left her breathless and whimpering. She felt a tug at her waistband, and then the soft rasp of the zipper, and then cool air on her legs as he pulled her pants away.

Nothing left but the panties now. She was grateful that she'd worn good ones.

But Stefan had stopped, and the look on his face—"What?" she asked. "What's wrong?"

He spread a hand over her rib cage, and she looked down. Beneath the spread of his fingers, her skin was livid red, brown, black, blue, green…a rainbow of bruising. "My God," he said. "What happened?"

"I told you before. There was a firefight."

His head came up, quickly. "You were *shot?*"

"No, my bulletproof vest was shot. I got a couple of bruises."

"Katie, that's not a couple of bruises!" He looked, and sounded, appalled. "Did you go to the hospital?"

"I've had worse."

"That's not an answer!" He pressed slightly, and she winced. "Are you sure those aren't broken?"

"Stefan. They're not broken. They don't even hurt that much. It's just bruises. I'll live."

He gave her a look, then bestowed a light kiss in the dark center of the area, where it ached the most. "I think we should wait," he said. "That can't be comfortable for you—"

For answer, she grabbed him, threw him flat on the bed and straddled him. And smiled.

"Trust me," she said. "I'm tougher than I look."

"Oh," he said faintly. "Well, I'm not, so please warn me before you— But you can keep on doing that, I'm not going to be complaining...." His eyes drifted half-closed, looking up at her as she leaned forward, her weight moving in slow circles against him. "Katie—" he made her name a caress "—twenty-seven minutes."

She couldn't quite remember how his pants ended up on the floor—magic, probably—but she remembered, vividly, peeling down the fabric of his shorts, remembered the full, powerful burn of undisguised need in his eyes, remembered...

...oh, everything. Every nerve firing hot, every square inch of skin caressed, every damp kiss and silken slide of body on body. He fitted with her perfectly, and if he was using some mad psychic ability to read her emotions and tailor his lovemaking, she was entirely in favor, because it was utterly, completely mind-blowing.

She was lying spent and sweating on his chest, still trembling with aftershocks and idly tracing his lips with her fingertips, when Stefan murmured, "We're twenty-two minutes into overtime."

"Overtime?" she said. "I haven't even started the second quarter of play."

"Oh." And then, faintly, he said, "Glad you bought the three-pack."

The phone call came an hour later, when they were dozing in each other's arms, temporarily sated. Katie rolled up and out of bed, grabbed the phone and listened tensely.

"No progress," she said over her shoulder to Stefan. "Thank you, Captain. Listen, does the name Calipatria mean anything to you? Is it a town?"

"Yeah," Captain Menchaca said. "Out by the Salton Sea and the gunnery range, you know? Off Highway 111 on the California side. Why? You got a lead?"

"Yes," she said. "Get on the phone with the California Highway Patrol and ask them to focus their search with the hub at Calipatria, radiating west on 111 and 78. Check the side roads. Any other freeways they can intersect with from there?"

"If they're going south, they could go up to Los Angeles or down to San Diego. Either way."

"We don't know which they'll take," she said. "Cover the whole stretch, if possible. Thanks. I'm on my way."

She hung up and headed for the bathroom. She looked back, blinked, and saw that Stefan was sitting up in bed, watching her.

"Well?" she asked. "Are you showering with me?"

He scrambled out from the tangle of sheets to follow.

They didn't speak until they were in the car; for some reason, Katie felt a kind of serenity between the two of them that had been missing before. An acceptance. Words seemed a little…superfluous just now. They were together. She didn't know how long it would last, but it was hers, and a single spark of brilliance in a day that had grown increasingly dark.

Stefan faded away as she drove, keeping his connection with Teal open, though for shorter periods. Caution or prudence, Katie wasn't sure which, but she hadn't asked him to do it—he'd simply assumed she would want him to. That was a genuine gift to her. If it had a personal cost, he kept her unaware of it, though she thought his face grew paler over time, and he seemed less able to come back to her quickly. That can't be good for him, she thought. The human brain wasn't meant to do that.

They were about half an hour outside of Calipatria when her misgivings proved true. Stefan had quietly faded out, leaving an empty, breathing shell, and returned with the same gasping urgency that she'd seen in the hotel room, and earlier, at the apartment complex. Something wrong. Something badly wrong.

She reached out with her right hand and touched his shoulder, then the beard-rough texture of his cheek. "Stefan? You all right?" He didn't answer her, but he grabbed her hand in his and held it tight, very tight. His eyes were open, staring straight ahead, and as she stole fast glimpses at him from the dark road they were traveling, he seemed out of it, still.

"Stefan?" she asked again. "Can you hear me?"

His hand was shaking, and he hadn't let go.

"I'm going to pull over."

"No." His voice was hoarse, barely recognizable this time as his own. "No, we have to keep going. They were stopped. Two Highway Patrol cars on Highway 78, heading northwest toward I-10."

She'd eased off the gas, but now she pressed down again, feeling a surge of exultation sweep through her like a strong breeze. "See?" She grinned. "I told you. Teamwork."

"They're dead," he said, and closed his eyes to drop

his head back against the headrest. "Oh my God, they're dead. Three cops. The fourth—they left the fourth one dying. You have to get him help, Katie. I don't know if they got a radio message out."

Her joy turned to shock. "You're sure?"

"I saw it." He didn't open his eyes. His thick, dark lashes were wet. "The ones in the van opened up on them point-blank. Two of the officers went down before they even knew what was happening. One of them got off a couple of shots, but—"

"Stefan, give me an exit number, a mile marker, anything!"

He was silent for a few seconds, then said, "I'll try." And then he was gone again. Katie waited tensely, drumming her fingers on the steering wheel, cursing the night and curving road that slowed her down.

"The van's moving again," Stefan said. "They just passed an exit, number seventy-three. I couldn't see the mile markers... Shit!"

Katie looked at him, startled, as Stefan clapped both hands to his nose and fumbled for the box of tissues sitting in the floorboard. Nosebleed. A bad one. He tilted his head back and applied pressure, and Katie cursed silently and reached over to stroke his cheek again, then cupped her hand at the back of his neck. He felt cold again, and damp.

"Don't," she said. "Don't try again. That's enough."

"I'm not leaving her alone," he mumbled around the tissues pressed to his nose. They were soaking through with vivid red. "I can't."

"You're killing yourself!"

"It's a nosebleed, Katie. And you got shot today. Don't talk to me about killing yourself." He sounded shaken and furious and annoyingly stubborn. "They're kids, and I'm not leaving them alone there if I can help it. I have to let her know—"

He was trying to communicate with Teal, not just observe. No wonder he was blowing blood vessels. "Stefan, do you think she can sense you now? When you're there?"

He nodded, exhausted. "I can't talk to her, but she can feel my presence. I'm sure she's trying to send me messages, it's just that I can't—I'm not strong enough. I'm trying."

No wonder they wanted to kill him, Katie thought. He wouldn't give up. She'd known from the beginning that he was persistent, but now she was seeing the steel, and the steel went deep. He was as dangerous to himself as any hired killer, but she couldn't fault him for that— she was too much like that herself.

"Rest for a while," she said. "I'm calling it in."

Cell coverage was patchy, at best, but she managed to get through to Menchaca, who sent word on down line. It was the best they could do. She took the Highway 78 turnoff and edged the FBI-issue sedan well past the legal limits, rocketing northwest toward I-10.

Stefan, whether he wanted to or not, had taken her advice; he'd fallen asleep by the time they came within sight of the flashing police lights. Ambulances were on the scene, and Katie coasted up to the barricades and rolled down her window to show her credentials to the uniformed officer on duty. The intersection was a crime scene, and they'd set up harsh arc lights for the forensic techs. Katie parked on the shoulder, trying to let Stefan sleep as she eased her door shut, and went in search of the on-scene commander. *Please, God, give me some good news,* she thought, and stopped, out of courtesy, at the edge of the brilliantly lit tableau. Two Highway Patrol cruisers, one with both doors open and a bullet-shattered windshield. Three still forms left uncovered to the night air while the crime-scene documenters and techs did their work.

"You're Agent Rush?"

Katie turned to see a tiny dark-haired Hispanic woman standing at her elbow. She was dressed in a well-tailored uniform, had gleaming perfect skin. She extended a delicate hand, which Katie shook. She didn't smile, but then, the situation hardly called for it. "I'm Lieutenant Arellano," she said. "On-scene commander. Thanks for the heads-up. It may save Officer Warren's life."

"I hope so," Katie said sincerely, and felt a breath of relief. He was still alive, at least. "I'm sorry for the loss of the other officers."

Arellano looked even grimmer. "It was a duck shoot, and they shouldn't have been caught like this. They knew they were doing a stop-and-search for extremely dangerous people. Our thoughts are that the captors used the girls for cover and shot from behind them. That would have made it nearly impossible for our guys to return fire."

Sick, and effective. Katie nodded without speaking.

"Got another FBI team on the way," Arellano said. "This isn't just a small event anymore, it's a major manhunt. I've been told to tell you that you're officially relieved."

Katie, who'd turned away, spun toward her, shocked. "That's not possible!"

Arellano shrugged. "Take it up with your boss. I'm just the messenger, but Special Agent Evangelista says come home."

She couldn't do that. *Couldn't.*

"Thank you for passing the message, Lieutenant," she said. "You have the information about the van's current location?"

"Not up to the minute, but we'll head them off."

Katie no longer had any confidence that would be true, but she shook the woman's hand and went back to her car without protest. Protesting wouldn't do any good, and she'd already made her decision.

It might mean her career, but she couldn't explain to Evangelista why she needed to be here. To do this. These girls, they were family to her, and now she was responsible for even more.

Somehow, she'd become responsible for Stefan Blackman, too.

Stefan was awake again. His nose had stopped bleeding, thankfully, but he looked worse than before. His skin had a papery, translucent quality that made Katie even more worried. "Is he alive? The officer?" Stefan asked.

She buckled her seat belt. "Yes. It's touch and go, but he's alive. Stefan, when you saw the shootings—where were Teal and Lena?"

"Right in front," he said. "They were in the doorway, and the kidnappers shot around them. They used them as shields, Katie."

She didn't say anything else, just eased the car into gear and drove on the shoulder around the crime scene, to the access road for the freeway. Traffic should have been light at this no-man's-land hour, but she supposed traffic to and from Los Angeles never really stopped. It took concentration to merge into the sea of fast-moving cars and eighteen wheelers, heading west.

"You're upset," Stefan said.

"Of course I'm upset. There are three dead police officers—"

"Something else. Something personal." He opened weary eyes. "Is it me?"

"No. It's— They're trying to pull me off the case. Send me back home."

"Can't do that," Stefan murmured. "I'd have to train a whole new agent, and besides, I try to make love with only one incredible woman a day. Anything else just looks greedy."

She snorted. "You're unbelievable."

"Bet you say that to all the psychics." His smile faded. "Seriously, Katie, what are you going to do?"

"Take advantage of a loophole," she said. "Even if I wanted to back off, I'd have to go to Los Angeles to get a flight out, right? And since I'm already heading that direction…"

"So staying on the case, that's purely for efficiency."

"Absolutely." She paused for a second, listening to the hiss of tires, the humming vibration of the road. "Look, I can't back off. If I do, they'll never believe you, not in time, and you're the key to keeping track of these perps. They'll get lost fast once they hit the city, and I have to believe they have a way out. Unless they're delivering the girls to a final destination here, they'll be heading for some kind of transportation. I don't think it would be a commercial flight—too hard to get them on board without somebody seeing something, and way too easy for the girls to raise a fuss. Same for any other kind of public transportation. Even a private plane might be tough."

"So you think they're going to hand the girls over to someone else? Why?"

"Let's just say it's a hunch," she said. "And it's a hope. The more hands the girls go through, the better our chances of finding them before they get to where they're going. And the better our chances of catching who's behind this."

Stefan looked sober. "You could try telling your boss all this. Making him understand."

"Stefan, I'm in the middle of it and I'm not sure *I* understand. And let's just say I'm predisposed to believing crazy things are possible."

"Because of the Athena Academy?"

He was *way* too close to the truth, and she didn't answer him. After a few minutes he settled himself more comfortably, sighed, and drifted off into that strange trance state.

He was still gone when the premonition hit her—a hot tingle up her spine, a pressure coming at her from her left, on the driver's side of the car. It was just a second's warning, just enough. She gasped and instantly hit the brakes, twisting the wheel to the right and digging the tires into the gravel shoulder.

The other car almost overshot them, but the two vehicles still hit at a huge force, and Katie's hands were knocked off the steering wheel. The air was full of flying glass, ripping metal. She felt her seat belt snap tight, locking her in place, and instinctively turned her face away from the shattering driver's-side window. Something hit her head with stunning force, and a blip of a thought ran through her mind in the instant before everything went dark:

Not now!

Stefan came back to the world in slow, tortured seconds. He could feel cold air on his face, and then a second later heard the tinkle of shattered glass hitting concrete. In the next heartbeat he felt the hot spark of cuts and bruises, one or two burning especially hot.

He opened his eyes and looked dazedly into the muzzle of a gun.

There was a guy leaning in the window of the car, and he had a gun, and he was aiming it right between Stefan's eyes, and Stefan believed, absolutely, that his life was over.

Time slowed down. He could see every flick of light passing over the other man's face, every glittering spark reflected in his eyes. Every mote of dust in the air between them.

He thought he'd actually see the bullet when it left the chamber. Bullet catch, his speeding brain informed him, but the bullet catch was an illusion, it was a trick, it couldn't possibly be done.

He was dead.

And then he wasn't, because the gunman screamed, staggered and went down, out of sight below the frame of the door. Stefan blinked. None of this seemed to be making sense. Shouldn't they be moving? Driving? How could they be parked on the side of the road...

He realized that the white haze of cracks in front of him was the shattered windshield, and put it slowly together. *Oh. We crashed.*

A bloodied face appeared in the window where the gunman had been, and it panted, "Christ, Stefan, you could at least *duck!*" The door creaked open with a dry shriek of bent metal, and she leaned in to unhook his restraints. "Guess those side air bags really work, eh?"

Katie. His lips shaped her name, but he couldn't get it out past the lump in his throat. She grabbed him by the shoulder and hauled him out of the car. He stumbled over the prone body of the man who'd held the gun—the gun was now in Katie's right hand—and the body didn't move. Still breathing, Stefan saw. But definitely not in the fight.

"What—"

"Shut up for now. Act dazed."

It wasn't an act. He sank down to a sitting position on the gravel, cradling his aching head. His nose was bloody again, and he sniffed and wiped at it ineffectually. Other cars were stopping, including some big-rig trucks, and a crowd was gathering. Someone—a pretty little redhead in shorts and a baby-doll T-shirt—handed him a wet washcloth wrapped around ice cubes, which he pressed to his flooding nose. She asked him if he had any broken bones, and he told her he didn't know, which was perfectly true. Nothing hurt. Everything hurt. He was too confused to begin to diagnose how he felt.

And then he looked at Katie, standing nearby talking to two massive tattooed truckers, and how he felt came into sharp, merciless focus.

They tried to kill us. He knew that was true. Someone had run their car off the road, and when that didn't finish them off, the driver had gotten out to put bullets in their heads.

He was getting kind of used to the idea that someone wanted him dead, but the idea that they had hurt Katie, would *kill* Katie, made something catch fire inside him, something slow burning and dark, thick with rage.

The two truckers finished their discussion with Katie and went around the car, picked up the unconscious trigger man as if he were a plastic bag and carried him off. Stefan didn't wonder where because he was watching as Katie limped toward him. Not much of a limp, just a slight hesitation in her step, a little favoring of her left leg. She had cuts on the left side of her face, probably from broken glass, and a new set of bruises darkening all along the lovely skin of her left arm.

That bastard could have killed her. No, that bastard almost certainly intended to kill her, and whether it happened before or after Stefan was dead probably was just tactics.

"Hey," she said, and reached out to move the ice pack to inspect the state of his face. "Not so bad."

He grabbed the second washcloth the redheaded good Samaritan was offering and pulled Katie down beside him, then began gently sponging the blood away from her face. The cuts weren't as bad as they'd looked—mostly shallow. One came dangerously near her eye.

"Stefan." She grabbed his wrist and took the washcloth from him gently. "I'm okay. We're both okay. Look, the guy had a shot at us, but he didn't get us, all right? We're fine."

He wanted to take her in his arms and protect her from all this, and he knew that was stupid; Katie was the protector, the one trained and ready to take on the bad guys. She'd probably call it male ego, but the impulse was so strong it made him ache.

"You were right," she said suddenly, and looked him straight in the eyes. "I saw it coming. Sometimes, I can see it coming. I think you need to teach me about how to handle that better."

He captured her hand back and kissed the soft skin of her palm, slightly damp from the washcloth. "I will," he promised. "Katie, I have something new on Teal. We need to get moving."

Katie, for answer, pointed to the car. The once-pristine sedan was a wreck, ready for the junkyard, still hissing steam and dripping fluids. "We're not going anywhere without wheels."

"Katie." He held on to her hand and regained her full attention. "*We need to get moving.* They're in Los Angeles. You said it yourself, by the time we get other people convinced that we know what we're talking about, it'll be too late. I think—I think they're handing them off to someone else. Soon."

"We need to wait for the police."

"And if we do, we end up stuck here for another two hours, and they'll be gone. Gone."

She went very still, searching his eyes, communicating things that neither one of them needed words to understand. She nodded. "I'll get us transportation."

"Wait," he said and reached out to pull the would-be assassin's gun from her waistband. She blinked, but didn't try to stop him. Stefan checked the clip, made sure the safety was engaged, and said, "You're an FBI agent. Whatever you've done so far, you can probably talk your way out of it, but fleeing the scene of an accident and stealing a car might be a career setback." He stuck it in the waistband of his own pants, at the back.

"I wasn't going to steal a car!"

"Commandeering? Same thing, only with a badge. Let me handle it. That way, you don't need to explain it later." He stood up, staggered, and braced himself on the redhead's shoulder. She was looking as if she regretted the whole idea, and her big blue eyes were darting around, looking for a quick exit. He gave her an edgy smile. "So. Are you heading to Los Angeles?"

"Yeah…" She drew it out, frowning.

"How does an extra thousand dollars sound to take on two passengers?"

"Stefan!" Katie snapped. "She's not involved in this!"

"Would you like to be?" he asked the redhead and opened his wallet. "I've got about five hundred cash with me, but if you take me to an ATM I'll get the other five when we get to L.A."

The redhead's eyes had lit up like bonfires, but she was still frowning. "You're not, like, killers or anything, are you?"

Would someone actually answer yes to that? "No," he said. "FBI." And he flashed Katie's credentials, which he'd picked from her pocket during the showy removal of the gun.

The redhead looked awestruck. "Cool! I mean, yes, Officer, sure!"

Katie rolled her eyes—even though, with that bump on her forehead, it had to hurt—as the redhead bounced away. "You and women," she said.

Stefan kissed her lightly on her bruised forehead. "One woman, from this day forward," he said. "Come on. Let's catch a ride."

Chapter 10

Katie was acutely aware that she had just broken several laws, not the least of which was leaving the scene of an accident; she phoned Menchaca, whom she was surprised to find was still actually accepting her calls, and explained it as best she could without actually mentioning things like psychic visions.

"Agent." He sighed. "This is not good. I'll talk to the CHP and see what I can work out for you, but they're not going to be happy."

"I'm in hot pursuit of a kidnapper, Captain."

"So you say. I have to say, Katie, the only thing that I see is you cutting a trail of destruction across the desert. If you're planning on ever coming back this way, I'd suggest flying." He paused for a moment; she imagined he was drinking coffee, and wished for a cup herself. "So let me get the facts straight. You were in hot pursuit of the kidnappers along I-10, and you were run off the road by an accomplice, who then tried to shoot you."

"Yes."

"And this accomplice is…"

"Under restraint at the accident scene."

"And your car?"

"I had to leave it." And boy, the Phoenix field office was going to kill her for that. "Engine block was cracked."

She heard a pen tapping on the hard surface of a desk. "This is the last favor for you, *amiga*."

"Last one I'll need," she said. "I promise. Thank you. And if you ever need anything—"

"I'll hold you to that. *Buena suerte*."

She needed all the good luck she could find, and said so before she thanked him again and hung up. Her second call—and pretty nearly her last, she thought as she spotted the glowing red battery bar on her phone— was to the Phoenix field office. It was a twenty-four-hour operation, but the agent who answered directed her to a voice mail, which was fine with her. The less explaining she had to do, the better, at the moment. That done, she called her boss.

Craig Evangelista answered the phone. He sounded wide-awake. "Katie?"

"Sir," she responded. "I got your message."

"Sorry, but you're wanted in here for a full report as quickly as possible. Where are you?"

"On my way to Los Angeles," she said. "About an

hour out. I'll catch an early flight from LAX." She hesitated a second, then continued, "Any word when the task
force is going to be on the ground?"

"They're already in Los Angeles," he said. "Landed
there twenty minutes ago, deplaned and went straight
to the local field office. They're organizing a briefing
now. You should probably go straight there and hand
over whatever intel you have."

"Yes, sir." Another waste of time, unfortunately;
they'd question where she got every piece of information, and they weren't very likely to believe Stefan. Not
until it was too late to do any good. "Thank you."

"Don't thank me, Katie, you've got a hell of an unpleasant few days coming up. I can't imagine OPR is
going to give either one of us much of a break on this."

The Office of Professional Responsibility never did,
really. She said her goodbyes and hung up, turned off
the phone and dropped it into her purse.

Effectively cutting herself off from help—not that,
at this point, help would be forthcoming, except the
kind that would put her on the sidelines and then on a
plane going home.

They were speeding along I-10 in a blue Volkswagen
Beetle, and Katie was in the back—an uncomfortable
position for someone with long legs. She adjusted her
knees, winced, and leaned against the window for a
moment. She wanted to rewind the time, go back to that
blissful hour—or two—in the motel, when it was just
her and Stefan, lost in light. The world was gritty, hard
and unforgiving, and she hated that he was chatting up

the redhead in the front seat, although to be fair he wasn't being more than pleasant. Katie couldn't imagine being as cute or perky as the girl driving the car, whose name, she learned, was Marine. Not Marina... Marine, like the sea.

She was definitely in California now.

"So," Marine was saying, "you're both FBI? Are you working on something exciting? Like terrorists?"

"Terrorists?" Stefan shook his head. "No. But we are looking for a gang of kidnappers. They've got two girls, both a few years younger than you."

"Oh," she said. "That's horrible. So, you have a helicopter, right? Or satellite tracking them or something?"

"Chances of a helicopter picking out one white van in Los Angeles aren't very good," Katie said. "And satellite tracking for kidnappers isn't exactly normal procedure." Although she wondered, now, if it was something that Athena Force—in particular, Allison Gracelyn—couldn't help out with arranging. "Stefan?"

He turned toward her, and she couldn't resist returning his smile, albeit briefly. "You said you had more information about Teal."

His smile faded. "I couldn't figure out what she was doing at first, but I think she's been trying to directly communicate with me for the last couple of times I made contact."

"Still just vision and emotions, right?"

"Right. Sometimes a little sound, but it never makes sense, it's just noise." Stefan shook his head. "She's signing messages. I should have picked up on it, but I thought she was sending them to Lena, not to me. I can't read sign language, but she's trying to tell me something."

"Can you remember the signs?" Katie asked. He concentrated briefly, then began slowly shaping the signs, moving his fingers into each position and holding it until she nodded for him to go on. "That's it?" she asked when he stopped.

"That's all I saw," he said. "Can you translate it?"

"SOS, and her name—Teal—and then *call Athena Academy Glendale Arizona heading for Los Angeles.* Unfortunately, nothing we didn't already know." He looked bitterly disappointed. "It's all right. She may give us more current information in the next contact. If you're willing—"

"Of course," he said quietly. "I can tell you that they're just outside of East Los Angeles, or they were before our crash. I recognized the area."

That was another benefit to having Stefan along, apart from his visions; he had native knowledge of the city, and he'd be quick to recognize landmarks and navigate them closer to the target.

"I have a suggestion," Stefan continued. "You're right about the danger of getting civilians involved in this, and Marine shouldn't be put in the middle."

She nodded for him to continue.

"A fast pit stop at my parents' house. It's on the way. I can pick us up a car, something fast."

"You can't drive and do—what it is you do," she pointed out.

"No, but you're a hell of a driver, Katie." He gave her a sudden, startling flash of a smile. "I'll even trust you with the baby."

"The baby?"

Stefan turned to Marine without answering. "You know how to get to La Habra?"

"Sure," she said. "Is that where you live?" The girl was frankly checking him out. Katie suppressed a hot burst of irritation and gritted her teeth. *Baby?* What the hell was he talking about?

"No," he said cheerfully. "My folks live there. Just get in the neighborhood, and I'll talk you in. There's an ATM on the way. I'll get the rest of your money, and you can drop us at the house."

Marine looked disappointed. Severely. Maybe she'd been hoping that his offer of payment would entail something else, maybe dinner and late-night entertainment. Which Katie wasn't at all sure it wouldn't have, had she not been along for the ride.

"Sure." Marine sighed and shook her long red hair back over her shoulders. "Man, just when my day was getting interesting. Say, you don't have any brothers at home, do you?"

"One," Stefan said. "But he's not at home. He's off saving the world."

Odd comment, Katie thought, but then Marine was asking about Stefan's family, and she was content to listen as he talked about his mother's psychic practice, his father's pet-whisperer talents, the cheerful chaos of his childhood. There was love in what he said, fondness that was impossible to fake. Stefan loved his family very much.

That, unexpectedly, made Katie's heart ache as she remembered the hole left in her by her absent mother. Stefan, damn him, was bringing up all kinds of feelings in her—inconvenient feelings, at an extremely inappropriate time. And she couldn't seem to derail them, no matter what she tried. Something about him made her *want* to feel things, more than she had in many years. He seemed to feel so deeply, so easily, and even though it came with pain—she'd seen that—he accepted it as the price of something good.

She'd never had the courage to do that.

"Tell me about your brother," she said. Stefan, surprised, glanced back at her, then turned to face forward, to the road.

"Angelo. He's a doctor," he said. "The last I heard, he's in Darfur. He's the respectable one of the family. Well, not too respectable, or he'd be content with being a Beverly Hills doctor and raking in carloads of money. He gave that up two years ago, joined Doctors Without Borders, and we get postcards and e-mails from him when he remembers, usually one a month."

"You worry about him," Katie said.

"Of course I do. But he's happy now, and he didn't used to be, so…" Stefan shrugged. "A little pain for us, a good life for him. It's better."

Marine sighed happily. "I have *got* to meet your brother."

Stefan blandly provided Angelo's e-mail address,

caught Katie's eye again, and she didn't have to be psychic to read his thoughts. Why not? Maybe she's perfect for him.

She approved.

After all, he wasn't handing over his own e-mail.

Stefan had another vision. She'd learned to spot it, although he concealed this one pretty well as a catnap with his head pillowed on the window glass. When he came back with a jerk, Katie reached over the seat to put a hand on the back of his neck in a caress, grounding him.

"I've got more," he said after a few moments. His voice sounded wrong—thin and clogged. Katie leaned over the seat. He'd tipped his head back, and he was holding his nose. Blood leaked in a stream into his cupped hand. Katie cursed, grabbed tissues from a box in the backseat and helped him mop up the mess. Stefan kept some pressed to his nose.

"God, Stefan," she murmured with her lips close to his ear. "You can't keep this up."

"I can, for another couple of hours," he said. "Call it a blood donation."

"That's not what I'm worried about. If you're busting up blood vessels in your nose from the pressure, you're bound to be risking some in your brain, too. You could stroke out."

"I won't."

"It wouldn't be a failure of character!"

He gave her a look so full of stubborn resolve that

she wanted to kiss him, nosebleed and all. "I can stroke out when this is over."

Some people, Katie reflected, were just too hard-headed to suffer things like that. He probably had Teflon veins in his brain, anyway. She surrendered. "What's happening?"

"Still in the van. They're cutting through an industrial area, and traffic's pretty heavy. No help to us in identifying a white cargo van there. Could be a thousand of them on the roads. And rush hour is going to start soon."

Rush hour in L.A. was more like rush half day; it began stacking up around 6:30 a.m. and didn't finish until after 9:00 a.m. Traveling west, they'd gained some time, but not enough, and traffic was going to slow them down. Of course, it would slow down the van, too. Hopefully.

"I need two things," Katie said. "A cross street, real time, and your cell phone. Mine's on its last legs."

He handed over his phone. She turned on her own long enough to retrieve Allison Gracelyn's number from it, then shut it down again—she'd missed three incoming calls, all from Craig Evangelista—and programmed the number in Stefan's phone.

"Cross street?" she asked.

"I'll have to go back in," he said. "Teal can't see very well right now. They moved her to the back."

He wasn't saying something important, she could sense it. She put her hand on the back of his neck again, gently. "What happened?"

He just shook his head. "Let's stay focused," he said. "She's okay. She's going to be okay." He sounded as if he more wanted to believe it than actually did, and she felt a chill race through her body at the implications.

"And Lena?" she asked. "Is Lena okay, too?"

"Fine." That, at least, he said without hesitation. "Teal's running interference for her." And it was, without a doubt, costing Teal. And therefore costing Stefan, too. "I have more signs for you."

Marine was watching them curiously, bright-eyed, but she wasn't saying anything. Apparently, she took her role as hired driver seriously. Katie focused on Stefan's right hand as he carefully formed the signs, one after another. The first few were the same as Teal's previous message—she must not have been sure that he was receiving it—and then it branched off. "North Soto, and passing Valley... I don't think you need to go back in. She must have been looking out the windows before you dialed in. That's probably why they pulled her to the back." She had her cross streets, and a hot flicker of excitement started burning in her stomach. She dialed Stefan's cell phone.

"Who's this?" asked a strong contralto voice on the other end. Of course—Allison wouldn't recognize the number, and she'd instantly know that. Being a math whiz allowed her to keep a permanent, instantly accessible database of such things in her head; being an NSA agent imbued her with serious paranoia about unknown phone calls to a very private number.

"It's Katie Rush," Katie said. "I'm on a borrowed phone, sorry, I know that's not a good thing for you. It's an emergency."

Some of the tension left Allison's voice. "Is this about the girls? Lena and Teal?"

"You heard."

"Of course I heard. Everybody's heard. How can I help?"

"A friend of mine had a good idea about using satellite tracking on the van the girls are in," she said. "But you're the only one I can think of with the resources to make that happen. Maybe."

"Can you pinpoint a location and description?"

"North Soto and Valley, Los Angeles. White cargo van."

"Do you have the plate number?"

Katie blinked. "You can match a plate number? From a satellite?"

"Not officially, no."

"Well, unofficially, no, I don't have a plate number. Do you think—"

"Hold on," Allison said, and there was an instant silence that stretched on for a while. They were definitely getting close to Los Angeles—the suburbs were rolling by on either side, stretching off to infinity in rows of strip malls, houses, streams of cars moving either with or against them. The sun wasn't up, but the horizon was growing lighter. Los Angeles was waking up.

"Right," Allison said. "Do you know exactly when the van passed those cross streets?"

"Not exactly, no. We're working with secondhand information."

"Hmm. That's a little more of a puzzle. What kind of time frame are we talking about?"

"Anywhere from five to fifteen minutes ago," Katie said. "That's a guess, but I think it's pretty accurate."

"Narrows things down," Allison said. "I've got several possibilities. One's still traveling in a straight line on the same road, so that's probably our guy, but I've painted the others just in case he got tricky."

"But you can track him?"

"Unless he goes underground—tunnel, parking structure, something like that—or unless he gets outside of the satellite's range, yes. I'd have to retask the satellite to get him back, and that would require some paperwork I don't think you have time for. And I don't have adequate justification for, either." Allison's voice softened. "You doing okay?"

"I'm fine," Katie said. She was, remarkably. Her ribs ached—more after the crash than before, and now she was about ninety percent sure there were hairline fractures—and she was so tired she could feel her whole body trembling with it. She was so tired, in fact, that she no longer craved sleep. "I want to finish this, but I'm pretty low on resources right now."

"Name it and you'll get it."

"Backup when I call for it. There's an FBI task force that just landed, they're at the local field office. I'd call myself, but I'm pretty sure that we might have to waste some time on questions I can't answer now. If you make the call for me, you can cite need-to-know and scary black-box operations."

She expected to hear amusement in Allison's reply, but it surprised her by being completely sober. "I'm not so sure it isn't," she said. "This is no ordinary abduction, Katie. I'm sure you already ruled out sexual predators...."

"Not completely," Katie said grimly. "Let's just say that one of the men holding the girls isn't someone I'd want babysitting."

"But that isn't the real intent behind it. This is a massive operation, Katie. I've been tracking it from this end, and the data flows are strange, to say the least. Favors are being called in at a rate that I can't quite believe, and it's stretching out to a lot of criminal organizations that normally don't interact."

"What do you mean?"

"Let's take Timmons Kent," Allison said. "He's a drug trafficker and dealer. High level. Who does he interact with? To stay where he is, he has to be very careful. It's a closed loop, very small interactive circles. Yet all of a sudden, Timmons is calling people outside of his own organization for favors. This includes the Salomon brothers, who promptly start calling *their* people on the west coast. This van's been defying the odds, Katie. Between you and the state police, not to mention the resources of the FBI, these guys should have been found a half dozen times. Instead, they've been evading the search, and when they're caught, they shoot their way out. Not normal."

Katie remembered her previous conviction, that someone in law enforcement had been providing information. "Insiders," she said.

"Big time. And not small ones, either. I can count at least three data ripples that are significant—"

"Allison, I have no idea what that means."

"It means three people out there in positions to influence and direct the investigation have been compromised," she said. "Bad guys are coming out of the woodwork on this one, and they're blowing the covers of resources they probably worked very hard to get. That means this isn't an ordinary abduction, or even an ordinary ransom kidnapping. This is something else. Something much bigger."

In the front seat, Marine and Stefan were starting to have a hushed conversation of directions to follow, exits to take. Apparently, they were nearing Stefan's family home.

"I don't think that can matter to me right now," Katie said. "My one priority has to be getting these girls back safely. Anything else needs to be another conversation."

"Understood, Katie, and no argument here. But I wanted you to get the big picture—this thing is attracting attention, and it's going to attract even more unless it's resolved quickly. It's in the best interests of the Athena Academy to make sure that happens. So do whatever you can." Allison's tense voice thawed a little. "And take care of yourself."

"Look who's talking," Katie replied.

When she hung up the phone, she erased both number and call record. She didn't have to worry about the provider network; Allison would take care of that as a matter of course. She handed the phone back to Stefan, who was pointing out a sprawling hacienda-style house sitting on a sinful expanse of California real estate behind a wrought-iron fence.

Marine drove them to the gate, and Stefan hopped out to key a number into the data pad attached to a post. The entrance swung open, and Stefan walked up the drive, motioning for Marine to follow with the car.

"Wow," Marine said, marveling as they rolled past a lovely landscaped yard and up to the front walk of the house itself. "I sure hope he *does* have a cute brother."

Katie rolled her eyes and got out of the car as soon as it came to a stop. Stefan was unlocking the front door with a set of keys from his pocket. Marine stayed in the car to await her payment.

"Shouldn't you knock or something?" she asked.

"What? It's my house!"

"It's your parents' house."

"Trust me, if I knocked, they'd never believe it was one of their kids." He flashed her a smile, and she was struck by the thought that his family wasn't exactly going to be thrilled with the condition in which she was delivering their son…bruised, pale, bloodstained and a whole lot the worse for wear. She wasn't in any better shape, of course, but she wasn't their kid.

And obscurely, she *wanted* Stefan's parents to like her.

Stefan swung the door open, barged in and yelled, "Mom! Dad! Anybody home?"

The inside of the house was a pleasant sort of chaos…thick mismatched overlapping rugs, a battered, comfortable sofa next to an antique desk. A chocolate Labrador, sprawled on the red tile hearth, looked up but couldn't be bothered to do more than a vague wag of his tail at the sight of intruders. Photographs everywhere, a dizzying clutter of them—black-and-white, sepia-toned, color. Casual and formal portraits, as well as instant snapshots. One caught her eye—a recent one, by the look of it—of a crowd of people gathered in front of the very house she was standing inside. At least twenty people were in the photograph, and Stefan was in the center of it, laughing, his arm around a slightly taller, thinner, more intense man with shorter hair. Angelo, the doctor brother now in Darfur, most probably. Presumably that was Stefan's father next to them, with a short, stout woman next to him who just *had* to be their mother, because although Katie had thought Stefan probably had his father's smile, she corrected that immediately. There was a certain impudence to the woman's grin that invited you to share a secret joke…exactly like her son's.

She was still taking it all in, the riot of color and fabric and texture, when a voice called from the top of the stairs, "Stefan?" A man's voice, low and smooth. A shadow appeared up there, and then a tall, lanky man with a wild shock of black-and-silver hair was coming down the steps. He didn't bother with the railing, but that was mostly because he had something in his hands…

…and she had no idea what it was, except that it looked like a cross between a rat and a porcupine.

"Hey, Dad," Stefan said. "I'd hug you, but—"

His father looked blank for a second, then looked down at the creature in his hands. "Oh, right." The two men had similar features, though Stefan's weren't as hawklike as his father's. The same eyes, though. "Sorry, Pasha's under the weather. I'm trying to keep her warm."

Pasha, the rat/porcupine, sneezed on cue. Katie blinked. "What *is* that?"

"Hedgehog," both Blackmans said together. Stefan and his father exchanged amused glances, and then the elder seemed to actually *see* his son for the first time.

"My God," he said and put the hedgehog down on the floor, where it proceeded to amble away to explore the corner between a bookcase and a floor lamp. "Kid, you look terrible. What's happening?"

Before Stefan could answer, his father had him in a bear hug. Stefan looked briefly embarrassed, then surrendered to it, patting his dad on the back. "I'm fine, Dad," he said.

His father held him at arm's length. "Yeah?" he asked. "You have a funny way of showing it. Is that blood on your face? Were you in an accident?"

"Yes!" Stefan seized on it immediately. "Yes, an accident on I-10. This is Katie, by the way. She's—" He seemed to struggle briefly for a definition. "She's an FBI agent."

"Oh my God. FBI? Are you in trouble? Are you under arrest?" The elder Blackman turned on her, frowning and fierce. "Did you arrest my son? On what charge?"

"Dad! Dad, I'm not under arrest, okay? Katie's—my—friend." He seemed to want to say more, but he stopped, clearly uncomfortable.

His father backed up a step, glanced at Stefan, then

at her, then at Stefan again. "Oh," he said, and then, weighted with meaning, "*Oh*. Well, I'm sure your mother would say she's a big improvement over the beach bunnies you usually—"

"Dad!" Stefan interrupted, pleading. Katie pressed her lips together to conceal her grin. "Could we not do this right now? Could you embarrass the hell out of me later, maybe?"

"I guess I could." His father turned again toward Katie, and this time, he held out his hand. "Ben Blackman," he said. "Katie—?"

"Rush," she supplied, and shook. Stefan's dad had strong hands, but a gentle, controlled grip. "Katie Rush. And I am an FBI agent. Stefan's—helping me on a case."

"Helping you?" Ben's eyebrows rose in thick black-and-silver arches. "So the two of you, you're not…" He left the implication to hover in the air.

"I didn't say that," she said, perfectly calmly, although there was a deep current of hysterical laughter inside, under a seething river of impatience. "We can discuss all this later, as Stefan said. For now, though, we're in a hurry."

"A hurry."

"Dad, you're repeating things," Stefan said, in the tone of a son who's said it too many times. "Yes. A hurry. I need to borrow Angelo's car."

"Which one?"

"What's the fastest one?"

Ben looked simultaneously amused and horrified. "You're not taking his baby!"

Stefan was already headed for a key rack hanging on the wall near a large open arched doorway leading into a wood-floored kitchen. More keys than a dealership, Katie thought, and Stefan sorted through them and held up a set. "Yep," he said. "I'm taking the Jag."

"Angelo's going to kill you if you scratch the paint."

"I know, Dad. He's told me a dozen times already." Stefan juggled the keys, hand to hand, looking at Katie. "I'd like to change my shirt. Five minutes?"

She nodded. Stefan climbed the stairs, leaving her alone with his father, the Labrador and the hedgehog, Pasha, who was busily rooting around in the corner.

Ben retrieved the strange little animal, holding it gently in both hands and stroking its head. It seemed to relax in his large square hands, clearly content, closing its beady little black eyes and snuggling in. Ben gave it a distracted smile, but he was watching Katie with shrewd, kind eyes. "You're sure my son's not in trouble."

"Not from me, sir," she said. "He's been—great." She wasn't one to open up to strangers, but there was something about Ben Blackman that made her want to continue talking. "He's got a lot of courage, your son. You should know that. He could have just put in a phone call and gone about his business, but he put himself out to help some kids in trouble. That's special."

"Yes," Ben said softly. "It is. He is. Katie—can I call you Katie?—my son's got a great heart, but he's always been a little—" He shrugged. "Blown by the wind. Couldn't keep him home, he was always out wandering. If ever a kid had gypsy blood, it's Stefan."

He was trying to warn her. She recognized that, and was both flattered and offended—for Stefan more than herself.

"I think he knows what he's doing, sir," she said. "I've seen him do things today that I wouldn't have had the courage to try."

Ben gazed at her, thinking something that shadowed those big dark eyes. "He's never lacked for courage," he said. "Just conviction."

"I think he's found that," she said.

"Looks like he found more than just that."

She shrugged and smiled. "I can't speak for Stefan's feelings."

"What about yours?"

She *never* talked about her feelings. "Are you asking about my intentions toward your son?"

He laughed. "I'm old-fashioned, kiddo, but I'm not *that* old-fashioned. I just wonder what's pulling the two of you together. You don't look like you have that much in common."

Heavy footsteps on the stairs. Stefan hadn't taken five minutes, he'd taken only two, and there were still drops of water caught in his curling hair. He was buttoning up a clean shirt of dark blue silk. He'd changed to a fresh pair of jeans, too.

Katie felt obscenely grubby, suddenly.

"More in common than you think," Stefan said, as calmly as if he caught his dad talking about his relationships every day—which maybe he did. Katie had no idea how normal families dealt with this stuff. Hers had never been a model to follow. "Katie's a precog."

"No!" Ben's eyes widened. "You're kidding."

"I hope he is," she said. "What's a precog?"

"Precognitive," Ben said before Stefan could get the word out. Stefan, behind his back, looked exasperated, and continued buttoning his shirt. "Means you sense or see things before they happen. Stefan's always been more an empath than anything else. His mother's precognitive, though."

He said it as if it were factual, as straightforward as saying that Stefan's mother had brown eyes or jogged every morning. Okay, Katie thought, here's where things get strange. And then she had to mentally shake herself. *You're on the trail of two supernaturally gifted girls abducted by drug dealers, tracking them with the help of a gypsy psychic. And this is where things get strange?*

"Dad, great, but we really have to get going now," Stefan said and moved around to face him. "Thanks for the car."

"Hey, that's between you and your brother. It's a good thing he's halfway around the world, or he'd be coming after you to make you sign some kind of waiver. In blood."

"Say goodbye, Dad."

"Goodbye, Katie. I have a good feeling about you," Ben said. The hedgehog in his hands yawned, displaying a perfect pink tongue, and sneezed again. "Come back soon, will you?"

Stefan kissed him on the cheek. "Yeah, thanks for saying that to *me*, Dad."

"You come back whatever I say," Ben said. There was

so much love in his eyes when he looked at his son that it almost brought tears to Katie's eyes. "Stefan."

"Yes?" He fussed with the cuffs of his shirt, not looking up.

"Come back soon. And come back safe."

Stefan looked up into his eyes, and there it was, that same glow of affection, devotion, connection. Katie realized that she'd never felt that, not really. Not since her mother's disappearance. She had to swallow a lump in her throat.

Without a change in that adoring expression, Stefan asked, "Can I borrow five hundred dollars?"

The elder Blackman's eyes went wider. "Excuse me?"

"The girl outside in the car. I owe her some money. Services rendered."

"What did she do for you for five hundred? No, don't answer that, I'd only have to tell your mother about it later, and I'd rather have plausible denial." Ben seemed to have second thoughts. "Wait… If it was worth five hundred, maybe you should invite her in…"

"*Dad!* She gave us a ride, I promised her some cash. Please? I'll get some out of my bank later and drop it by."

Ben sighed and handed Katie the hedgehog. She took it, too startled to do anything else, and was fascinated by the warmth of it, the way it turned to look at her, then settled down into the cup of her hands. Cute, she thought. And then she thought, I haven't got time for cute. But it was too late to protest because Ben was already crossing the room, swinging aside a painting on the wall and keying in numbers on a safe. He extracted a bundle of bills, removed some and closed it up.

"Dad must like you," Stefan commented in an undertone. "He never lets anybody hold Pasha."

His father handed him the money and retrieved the hedgehog. "Actually, I never let anybody see me open the safe," he said. "Pasha loves everyone. But you looked like you could use a little animal relaxation therapy. Even a few seconds' worth."

"Animal relaxation…"

"Dad's specialty," Stefan said, counting the bills. "Well, he does vet work, mostly, and he trains animals, too, kind of got a Dog Whisperer thing going—"

"I do not! What I do is completely different!"

"Whatever, Dad. He has a program where he takes animals in for sick kids, seniors, even into prisons. Animal relaxation therapy."

"It helps," Ben said simply. "Maybe sometime you can go with me, see the effect it has on people. It's pretty dramatic."

"Dad, we really have to—"

"Go." Ben nodded. "Yes. I know. I'll tell your mother you said hello. She's out with one of her clients."

"Which one?"

"The blond one."

Stefan grinned and stage-whispered, "We're top secret around here about clients. But her initials are Cameron Diaz."

"Wrong," his dad called from behind them.

"Or maybe Uma Thurman." Stefan guided Katie out

the door. She looked back, once, to see Ben Blackman still standing there, the hedgehog nestled contentedly in his hands, watching them go with a frown of concern on his face.

"I'll watch out for him," she promised.

And he nodded. "I believe you will, Katie."

Stefan shut the door behind them, jogged down the steps and leaned in to hand Marine the money. A conversation ensued, which Katie watched closely, and then Marine backed up her Volkswagen and drove off with a cheery wave. The iron gates swung open for her, then closed.

Stefan came back up and took Katie's hand, then kissed her. It was a gentle, sweet kiss, and she leaned into him to savor it, just for a second.

"What was that for?" she asked. Stefan smiled.

"For not laughing at my crazy family," he said. "Come on. Jag's in the garage. And because of my current vision disability, you get the pleasure of driving."

Once the family hacienda gates had closed behind them, Katie felt the pressure close in again. The Jaguar was clean, and looked fast. She knew little about cars, but she knew what she liked, and she liked this one. It was forest-green, very sleek, with a finish like glass. The interior wasn't roomy, but it was comfortable.

"Your brother likes cars," she said. There had been quite a selection under tarps in the garage, which was actually more of a converted stable, or part of one.... The other half had still housed horses. She shifted gears, and the Jaguar leaped forward with a low growl, pressing her back in her seat.

"No, my brother is insane over cars," Stefan corrected. "Those are just the ones he couldn't stand to part with. He sold off about twenty, I think. Gave the money to charity a couple of years ago. This one's his favorite—a 1968 XJ6."

"Is that good?"

"Very good." He watched as she shifted gears again, and the engine practically purred. "Very fast. And Dad's right, we'd better not scratch it or it's my ass."

He didn't seem that worried, though.... Not worried enough to ask her to slow down. The Jaguar continued to pick up speed, rocketing down the deserted street until they reached an intersection. Katie sent him an inquiring look.

"West," he said.

"You're sure?"

"Sure enough."

The Jaguar's speed didn't serve them particularly well, given the traffic, but its maneuverability did, and they made very good time darting in and out of traffic. Katie's Indy-style driving earned them more than a few honks and finger-flips, but she didn't take it personally. When Stefan's cell phone rang and he took it out, she said, "That may be for me."

"For you?" He checked the number and shrugged. "No ID."

"That's for me."

Katie thumbed the phone on and identified herself.

As she'd expected, the person on the other end was Allison Gracelyn. "I've got the van," she said. "Real-time tracking."

"Where?"

"They stopped off at a warehouse, but I didn't spot any girls being unloaded, just a couple of guys getting out, going inside, then coming back. They're on South Hill Street, at the intersection with East Third. I'll give you turn-by-turn for as long as I can."

"As long as you can?"

"I've got exactly twenty minutes before the station-keeping cycle cuts the signal for your part of the world. I can't retask it, not without serious questions, and besides, I'm piggybacking on top of another investigation that's very important. So we're going to have to do the best we can. Do you have any backup plan?"

Katie glanced at Stefan. "Yes."

"Keep it warmed up. Okay, they're turning…East Fourth, heading northwest."

"I'm handing you off to Stefan," Katie said and gave him the phone. "Relay what she says. And tell me how to get to East Fourth Street."

"Forget the side streets. You said northwest, right? Take the 101."

He talked her through to the freeway, a gigantic behemoth of concrete that shimmered with cars. Katie tried not to think about how many traffic laws she was breaking as she dodged through the traffic, speeding by on the shoulder and breakdown lanes whenever possible. Stefan clung to the door handle and looked several times

as though he was going to say something—probably
"Slow down!"—but then he kept his silence, listening
to whatever Allison was saying on the phone.

"They're on 110," he said. "Heading south. Take the
turnoff, it should be about five more miles ahead."

Five miles took too long; traffic jammed to a stop,
and all Katie's maneuvering couldn't levitate the Jaguar
over the blockage. The Angelinos around her seemed
accustomed to it; they yawned, drank coffee, read newspapers, brushed their hair.... She was ready to scream.
She grabbed the phone from Stefan. "Allison, did you
give it to the task force?"

"Already done," Allison said. "They should have air
support heading out there, too. Don't break your neck,
Katie. They're on top of it."

But there was something wrong; Katie could simply
feel it. It wasn't just the frustration of being away from
the takedown, although that was undoubtedly eating a
hole in her stomach; this had to do with other things.
Things that she couldn't define or explain.

Something was *wrong*.

"Chopper's in the air," Allison said. "They're arranging for a roadblock, but they want to let the van get off
the freeway first before they close in. Too many variables on a crowded freeway."

"Allison—"

"I have to put you on hold, Katie." Dead air. She
growled in frustration and pitched the phone back to
Stefan, who fielded it neatly.

"What?"

"That van. It doesn't feel right."

"What doesn't?"

"I don't know." Katie shook her head impatiently. "I hate to ask, but…is it possible you could…?"

"Plug in?" Stefan finished, so quietly she could barely hear the words. "I can try."

She heard the resolve in it, and the dread he couldn't quite conceal. She reached over and grabbed his left hand with her right and squeezed it tightly.

"I need you to get to her, but stay with me. Don't let her drag you all the way, okay? I need you to relay to me what's happening, minute by minute. You can do that, right?"

"I don't know."

"Please try."

He nodded, then took in a couple of deep breaths, leaned his head back against the seat, and closed his eyes. For a few seconds he looked tense with concentration, and then she felt a tremor go through him.

His hand went slack in hers.

"Stefan?" No answer. He was gone. But that was what she *didn't* want.… She had no idea how long he'd be gone, and even though he might come back with information, that was of no help to her in real time. She squeezed his hand again, sharply. "Stefan! I need you to talk to me! *Talk to me!*"

He groaned, a deep and primal sound of pain that shivered her skin into goose bumps. She couldn't stop; there wasn't any place to pull over, and she had no idea if they'd be able to gain ground again if she gave it up now. She had to concentrate on driving, too. What she was doing, weaving in and out of traffic like this, was horrifyingly risky, even though she was trained for it. Any lapse in her concentration could put them in an accident, cost innocent lives.

"Stefan!" She almost screamed his name, and squeezed so hard that she felt daggers of pain stab through her own fingers. "Stefan, you *talk to me! Now!*"

"Not in the van," he whispered. He sounded so faint, so far away, but he was talking. She caught her breath, and it felt like a sob. "They're not in the van. Switched somehow. Don't know how."

When the van had stopped, probably. The bastards had concealed what they were doing from the satellites. *They'd known,* or at least, they'd suspected that someone might be watching. "Stefan, tell me where they are! Tell me what you see!"

Long silence this time, but she could tell he wasn't gone, not all the way gone. He was fighting to stay with her, and it physically hurt him.… She felt the tremors going through his body. Teal's gift was strong, maybe *too* strong; she had no experience in controlling it, and Stefan was trying to hold her off.

I'm asking too much. Too much. But she couldn't ask any less, not and live with herself.

"Truck. Some kind of truck. Two small windows in the back."

"A delivery truck?"

"Can't see. It's dark." She risked a glance. Stefan's eyes were still closed, but there were tears leaking from beneath the lids, and he struggled for breath. And words. "She's on her knees, handcuffed. Lena's—Lena's face-down on the floor. They have a gun pointed at Lena's head. I think—they're threatening to kill her. Making Teal do what they want. She's angry, Katie, she's so angry…."

"Focus on what she's seeing. Anything, *anything!*"

Stefan shook his head, a violent convulsion more than a controlled motion, and then opened his mouth and gasped. His back arched in agony.

"Oh God—Stefan! Stefan, talk to me!" She kept saying his name because some part of her knew it helped, it helped him remember who he was, where he was. "What's happening?"

"Fighting. Fighting them." His eyes flew open, and they looked strange, so strange that for a moment she couldn't figure out why. Then it hit her with chilling force…. His pupils were widely dilated, as if he was in a pitch-black environment, but he was in full sunlight in the car. *Teal* was in the dark.

His body was mimicking whatever was happening to her. This was what Stefan had been afraid of, she realized; feeling so intensely, being hurt and being helpless to prevent it.

"What's going on? Stefan!"

His pupils suddenly contracted, and he screamed. It shocked her so badly that she let go of him, grabbed the wheel, jammed the clutch and brake and slewed the Jaguar to a gravel-spewing stop in the breakdown lane. She jammed it into Park, unbuckled her seat belt and grabbed his shoulders to hold him down as he thrashed. He was completely out of control, and he was stronger than she'd expected. She managed to lean her weight on him to keep him from hurting himself too badly, and then suddenly he collapsed into the seat, breathlessly making a sound that was halfway between a whimper and a moan.

"Stefan!" Katie grabbed his head in both hands and forced his eyes to meet hers. He looked dazed and horrified. "Stefan, please talk to me. Come back. Talk to me."

"Can't," he gasped. His face was going dirty-pale, and as she watched, a trickle of red dripped from his nose. He didn't seem to feel it, even when the trickle became a flood. Katie had come prepared this time; she'd grabbed chamois cloths from Angelo's extravagant car-care rack in the stables, and she hurriedly took one and folded it to catch the blood flow. "Oh God, Katie, I can't."

"You are. You're talking to me. Just stay with me, tell me whatever you see, okay?"

"Can't," he said again, and for a second his dazed eyes locked on hers. "Can't shut it off. She's scared. Drowning."

Teal was clinging to the link, trying to send information at what must have been overwhelming strength. And he could neither shut it off and save himself, nor fall into it completely and give in.

Katie was his only lifeline.

"Just tell me what happened," she said, putting her lips close to his ear, trying to keep her voice calm and gentle. "Please. Please try."

He gasped it out, voice thick and wet behind the bloody towel pressed to his nose. "She—took out the one with the gun on—Lena—kicked open one of the doors—but—couldn't jump—going too fast—sun too bright—"

"She saw where they were?"

"Sepulveda. Passing Sepulveda. On the 110."

"How far ahead of us?"

"Don't know."

"Stefan, I just passed—" What the hell was that? "The 405. How far ahead of us?"

He was almost sobbing with effort. There was sweat on his face now, and sweat darkening his silk shirt. "Ten miles, maybe. Don't know, Katie, please. Just drive. They hurt her."

"Teal? They hurt Teal? How badly?"

He shook his head again. "Taser."

Oh Christ. He'd stuck with Teal during *that?* No wonder he'd screamed. Katie checked his nosebleed; it was lessening again, but he'd lost a hell of a lot of blood over the past few hours. *You're killing him, Katie. You're killing him, and it's not fair.*

As if he heard her thoughts, he said, "It wasn't your choice, Katie. It was mine. Whatever happens."

"I know," she whispered, and stroked his forehead and hair. "I know, honey. Let go now."

"Can't. She won't—"

Stefan's eyes went entirely blank, and he went slack. Gone.

She'd lost him completely. He was with Teal now.

Katie wiped tears from her cheeks, strapped herself

back in and peeled out hard to merge back into the constant traffic. She drove like a demon now, totally focused on the goal. The Jaguar blew through open spaces, braked and drafted like a race car. It didn't like the rougher pavement of the breakdown lane, but she controlled its tendency to shimmy and kept moving ahead, always ahead.

It took ten more minutes before she spotted a sign up ahead. Sepulveda Boulevard.

The truck had passed Sepulveda ten minutes ago. She was catching up. She *had* to be catching up.

Because everybody else was looking for the wrong damn van.

Chapter 11

The world was pain, a constant red haze of it, and Stefan wanted to just turn away from it, burrow into the darkness and hide. Katie's voice had been like a drill in his head, all the questions, *questions,* and it had been so hard to answer from where he was.

He could see his body behind him, slack and empty in the passenger seat of Angelo's cherished Jaguar. He could see Katie, gorgeous sweet Katie, glorious in her fury and resolve as she steered the car in and out of traffic. *Oh, Katie, I don't want to leave you.* He wanted to tell her that, but words were gone now, and he was being pulled inexorably away, into the red haze, into the world where Teal was trapped.

Fall, or jump. He couldn't hang on any longer. It was ripping him apart to try.

Stefan let go and dived into the mind of a seventeen-year-old girl. A girl with more power than he could really comprehend, but still just a kid, a scared and angry kid. A hurt kid, now, thanks to the vicious Taser jab her guards had administered to keep her in line.

Teal was lying on the floor, next to Lena Poole, who had raised her blond-and-purple head to stare at her friend. *Are you okay?* Stefan couldn't hear the words, except as a distant buzz, but he could read her lips in the dim light. *Teal?*

First Katie, now Lena. Stefan supposed Teal looked as dazed and frightening as he had earlier. Whatever Teal answered, it brought a flash of relief to Lena's face, relief that was immediately overshadowed by fear as a big hand buried itself in her hair and dragged the girl upward. At the same time, Teal received similar treatment. Stefan felt the red-hot pull as Teal was jerked up to her knees. Her hands were still restrained behind her, but her legs were free. She was in bare feet, and the truck's floor felt cold and gritty.

Flashes of light illuminated things inside the truck. Nothing that would help him identify it, but he saw the faces of the kidnappers. They'd taken off the masks, maybe because of the warmth of the van, maybe because they no longer cared whether or not the girls saw them.

Teal made sure to look at the faces, and Stefan looked through her eyes. The first man was tanned and very hard-looking, with a shaved head and a tattoo of a roaring lion on the right side of his bare dome. He was the one with the Taser, and he seemed to enjoy his work;

Stefan hated the way the man's eyes slid over Teal. He could feel the girl's disgust, as if she'd been covered in slime and was unable to wash it off.

The second kidnapper was a woman, and the instant Teal's eyes fixed on her, Stefan felt a pure, hot spurt of fury go through her. This was personal, he sensed; this was her betrayer. He hadn't gotten a clear look at her before, but Teal stared at her now, surely deliberately, to give him a chance to etch the woman into memory. *Sheila Prichard.* The woman who'd tried to blow them up with a booby trap in her apartment, who now loaded a clip into an automatic pistol with cool competence. There was nothing but contempt in her eyes.

The third was another man, shorter and stockier than the bald man. He had a mess of brown sun-streaked hair and a golden-tanned face. A surfer, Stefan thought; he had the look, and the cat-quick reflexes. There were two others, but they were in the cab of the truck and visible only as dim shadows in the narrow sliding window.

Five adults, for two young girls. An elaborate plan, clearly nearing fruition from the attitude of the three holding the girls hostage. They all looked tense, silent, and anticipating something big.

Maybe the final handoff. Because Stefan no longer had any doubt that this was only the beginning of their plan; the girls were going to be transferred to someone else, or some other place. A plane, a boat…something capable of getting beyond U.S. jurisdiction, because these shadowy masterminds, whoever they were, must have known that the FBI was hot on the trail, much less Katie's mysterious government friends.

But *why?* What did they want? It was clear that they didn't just want money, or they'd have already demanded it. The number of people they'd killed to get this far meant that money wasn't the point.

The girls were the point.

Lena's lips were moving again, but the angle was bad; Stefan couldn't see her clearly enough to read the words. Whatever they were, Sheila leaned over to put her face very close to Lena's, and he read her lips clearly enough: *They want you both.* There was more, and he thought she said, *spoiled little bitches,* which matched the vindictive contempt and the cruel light in her eyes.

Someone was calling his name. He felt tired, very tired—Teal was weakening, too. She swayed, but the surfer holding her by the hair yanked on it to keep her upright and still.

Not far now, the bald one said to Sheila, and she nodded. Such a pretty girl. A waste of beautiful skin.

Stefan felt himself slipping and struggled to hold on. He needed to know *where.* He had to know. Katie was depending on him. He thought Teal knew he was in trouble; he could sense her trying to push him back, let him go, but he fought to hang on now. To stay with her.

Look out the window, he tried to send his thoughts to her, but he knew she wasn't getting the messages. She couldn't, just as he couldn't access her thoughts or hear her words. *Dammit, I know this town! I just need one look, just one…*

Without warning, Teal yanked her head forward, pulling the surfer off balance, and then slammed him back into the side of the truck with her body weight. The second he let go she lunged toward the doors, and fetched up against them with a bruising impact.

She pressed her cheek to the glass, and Stefan got his look. Just one.

Thank you. He didn't know if she could feel his weary gratitude, but he knew that she felt his withdrawal from her. He felt the pulse of fear.

They were going to hurt her again, and there was nothing he could do to prevent it. He had to believe that Teal and Lena were important to their captors—critically important. They wouldn't damage them permanently....

But it was a hell of a risk to take with a child's life. He felt sick with the weight of it.

He drifted back into his body and was instantly crushed by weariness, an aching hot fire in his muscles as if his body had been put on the rack while he was away. He felt weak, horribly weak, and when he moved to take away the cloth smothering him he saw that it was soaked with blood.

"Stefan?" Katie's voice. It sounded as if it was coming from a long, long way. Even the touch—the back of her hand gently laid on his cheek—seemed more like a dream than reality. "God, don't do that again. Please. I'm begging you, don't."

He swallowed and tasted blood, sniffed and wiped the worst of the mess from his face. His shirt wouldn't show the blood that much, thankfully, and he didn't think he'd bled all over Angelo's vintage seats. He found a plastic trash bag in the glove compartment—Angelo was always careful about such things—and crammed the bloody chamois inside.

"They're at the port," he said.

"The airport?"

"No, the harbor. Port of Los Angeles. They're heading for Terminal Island." Stefan forced his eyes to stay open, even though he desperately wanted—needed—to sleep. "Stay on the 110, then merge onto 47. They're somewhere right off the freeway, heading south on North Harbor. They're close, Katie. *We're* close."

The world was unraveling at the edges, his vision closing slowly off. "Katie," he said, and felt her hand on his face again. "Katie, I can't—"

He skidded away, into the dark, and for the first time in what seemed like an eternity, he didn't feel any pain.

Katie, alarmed, pressed her fingers to Stefan's neck and tried to concentrate on detecting a pulse while she kept most of her attention on combat driving down the L.A. freeway. That was getting easier—apparently, traffic had either loosened up its stranglehold or she was just getting better at it, but there was free airspace between cars now, things were moving at nearly half posted speed, and she was taking full advantage of it.

She felt a faint, fast throb against the pad of her fingertips, and let out a slow, relieved sigh. She'd thought, when he'd relaxed like that, that he'd slid back over to Teal, out of body, but then she'd realized that this didn't look like his other trances.

This was unconsciousness. His mind and body had finally rebelled against the abuse.

Katie slid her hand down his arm in a silent caress, then put it back on the Jaguar's gearshift as she downshifted to Third and powered around a slow-lumbering semi. Her brain was working faster than ever, examining and cataloging every panel truck she spotted. None of them—and all of them—matched so far. She wasn't going to find them this way.

Stefan said that the truck had been on North Harbor, at the Port of Los Angeles. It was too big, too nonspecific, and too hot a crisis for her to continue to Lone Ranger her way through this.

I'm sorry. I'm sorry, girls. She'd wanted to do this for them—for Kayla—for the school. She'd wanted to be there and protect them, but in the end, it was all about getting them back, not whose hands were on the job.

Katie slowed the Jaguar, drifted through lanes of traffic, and pulled off the 110 to a side street, found a parking lot and put the lovely automobile in Park.

Then she reached across and retrieved the cell phone from the floor where Stefan had dropped it.

Her first call was to Allison Gracelyn. Her second was to Alex Forsythe. Her third was to the FBI Los Angeles field office, and that one took a while because she had to establish her bona fides and convince the agents there to put her in touch with the task force. It seemed to take forever, but she knew that was subjective; they moved as fast as they could, given the circumstances. The task force had a lot to process right now.

She didn't mention Stefan, or psychic visions, but she did tell them she had impeccable information that the van they were preparing for takedown was a decoy, and she described, as best she could, what they should be looking for. In the end, she wasn't sure that the agent in charge, Salazar—she'd worked with him once before on a missing persons case—was completely convinced, but her reputation alone was enough to make him commit resources. They'd pursue both courses, she was sure…the decoy van, and the truck heading for the port.

Nothing else useful she could do. She risked Stefan's health, and maybe his life, if she continued to push him for information. It's out of your hands, she told herself. It's being handled. It's all right to let it go.

She never let anything go. It was a character flaw, but there wasn't anything she could do about it; even when she'd had to walk away from cases, she always kept copies, boxes of files for reference, and she would periodically go back and review them, start to finish, to be sure she hadn't missed any leads. Cold cases got hot, that was a definitive fact.

But this… This ached in ways that other cases hadn't. It was family. It was personal. And she was so *close!*

Katie Rush folded up the phone, stared out into the blinding Los Angeles morning, and thought about failure. She'd failed before…. Failed to find people in time, and seen the bitter aftermath. Failed to close cases at all. Even failed herself, once or twice, with bad relationships and worse habits.

But she'd never failed her sisters from Athena Academy. Never.

And you won't, she promised herself. *You never will.*

It wouldn't hurt to just *go* to the Port. All she had was a vague description and North Harbor Road, after all. The chances of her actually finding anything were small to infinitesimal.

Stefan needs a doctor.

Stefan would agree with her about going to the port, too.

The voice in her head had no real answer for that.

Katie leaned across, checked Stefan and cleaned his face as best she could. He still looked pale and felt chilly despite the warm L.A. sun. His pulse continued to beat steadily, and his eyes moved rapidly behind his lids...dreaming, maybe.

"Sleep," she whispered and pressed another kiss to his forehead. "You've earned it."

She started the Jaguar and eased it back into gear, heading for the entrance to the freeway and the port.

Stefan didn't want to wake up because it hurt. All over. First, his head: Post-vision hangover didn't cover it. It felt like a real hangover, one induced by several bottles of Everclear and a punch from a world champion boxer. He tried to open his eyes, but the light was searing, and the swirl of color made him instantly sick.

"Shit," he whispered, and leaned forward to brace his elbows on his knees, face in his hands. "Katie?"

Her hand, gentle and warm on the back of his neck. "Right here," she said. "I'm right here."

He felt road vibration, and his brain slowly put the pieces together. They were still in the car, then, still on the trail...and it wasn't over. Some part of him screamed in pain at the thought, but he ignored it. He'd do what he had to do, and deal with the consequences later.

"I told you, right?" His voice sounded hoarse and unsteady, and he worked to make it normal again. "About the truck? About the port?"

"North Harbor Road," she assured him. "We're three minutes from the exit. I called the task force—I'm hoping they'll be there ahead of us, or at least get the Port Police mobilized."

"But they don't have a description. Not of the truck."

She was quiet for a few seconds, but her hand stayed on him, steadying him. Reassuring him, without words, that he was still here and still wanted.

"It doesn't matter," she said. "If we have to stop and search every truck, we will. They're not getting away, Stefan. Not this time."

Whistling past the graveyard, he thought. He sat back and forced his eyes to open and stay open, and braced himself as his mind came to terms with the world beyond his skin again. There. Not so bad. Bright and blinding, yes, but he could deal with it. It was no worse than the champagne hangover after the last development deal with Paramount, right?

"If you're so sure," he asked, "why are we still going that way?"

"Because when they get Lena and Teal back, I think we should be there. I think *you* should be there." Katie turned and glanced at him, and he was struck by the emotion in her lovely eyes. She looked tired, stressed, but there was a glow in her that even the current circumstances couldn't dim. "You're a hero, Stefan."

He wanted to deny that because he knew deep down it wasn't true.… He'd gone out to Arizona in the first place partly for altruistic reasons, sure, but also because he'd just been interested. And then there had been Katie…and Katie was a powerful inducement all on her own. Heroes didn't need bribes.

But, shamefully, he wanted her to keep on thinking it, even if it wasn't true. The feeling it gave him was indescribable.

"When this is over," he said, "I'm going to take you away, Katie Rush. Someplace tropical, where bikinis are formal wear and a full meal is a mai tai and a banana. And I'm going to make you forget every moment in your life that's ever hurt you."

He had no idea what prompted him to say it. It wasn't calculated; it wasn't smooth; it came out rough and unprepared but from the heart. Her eyes widened, and she shot him another very fast glimpse.

There was a whole world in that look. A universe.

"I'll hold you to that," Katie said, very softly.

He held out his hand. She took it, and the warmth and strength of her fingers made something wounded in him begin to heal.

"Then let's finish this," he said. "Because I can't wait to see you in a bikini."

"You've seen me in less," she reminded him.

"Not in the last hour. I think it should be a rule that I see you naked every hour."

She lost her smile, and her gaze fixed straight ahead. "We're getting close," she said. "Stefan, promise me you won't let Teal drag you in again. Promise me."

Because she was afraid that now, if they were cornered, Teal could be hurt badly, maybe killed. She was afraid that might hurt him, too, maybe fatally…and he couldn't be sure of anything, at this point. His physical reactions were getting worse, and clearly Teal didn't know, or couldn't control the effect she was having on him.

Then you have to control it. After all, he was the adult.

"I can't promise," he said. "She may need me."

Katie's eyes glittered briefly, but she didn't look at him again, and she reclaimed her hand from his to handle the shifting duties. The rest of the drive—and it was short and fast—passed in tense silence. He kept his mind still, listening for any hint that Teal might be trying to send to him, but he felt and heard nothing.

Maybe they'd finally knocked the girls out. He wondered why they hadn't done it earlier.

"I have to make a guess," Katie said. "Would they go to the public-access areas, or do they have some kind of private shipping ready for the girls?"

"It's not much of a guess, is it?"

"No," she said. "The way these bastards planned things, they wouldn't take the risk of bringing the girls through any public areas. Lena and Teal are too resourceful, and Lena in particular is too recognizable. So we look at commercial shipping."

"That's a problem. There's about eight million containers that come and go from this port every year. Right now, there are probably at least twelve thousand containers sitting on the docks."

"But how many of them are outbound?"

Stefan thought about it. "Less than half that many. If I had to guess, I'd say between three and four thousand."

"But that's shipping containers. How many ships?"

He shrugged. "Couple of hundred in docks right now, probably. Rule out the cruise ships and other passenger vessels and you're looking at maybe a hundred to a hundred and fifty cargo and commercial vessels." She shot him a look that clearly asked how he knew. Stefan smiled. "Didn't my father tell you I was a born gypsy? I've spent most of my life on the streets. You pick up all kinds of knowledge. That's courtesy of some dock work I did a few years ago."

"Dock work," she repeated. "You?"

He shrugged. "I was researching some ideas for a new network show, and I had to try it out. Tough guys down there, but they have good hearts."

Stefan sensed that he'd once again tilted her perceptions of him off-center. He smiled again, this time to himself. Keep surprising her, he told himself. She can't resist a mystery.

And he wanted to keep her interested in him, wanted that in ways he'd never wanted a woman before. Not just physically, but in his soul.

"Bridge coming up," she said.

"Go over the bridge. It'll dump you out on Seaside."

"Where do I go from there?"

"Katie—" He hesitated for a second, then said, "Follow your instincts. I told my dad you were a precog, and I meant it. You've been right at every step—more right than anybody else. It's time to let yourself believe in your own abilities. Have faith in yourself."

"I'm *not* psychic, Stefan!"

"Then how did you know? How did you know they'd switched the girls out of the van? Your friend on the phone said there was no evidence the girls had been moved at all, everyone else agreed, but you *knew,* Katie. Didn't you?"

Her knuckles whitened on the Jaguar's leather-wrapped steering wheel. "It was a guess."

"Then guess now. But don't doubt yourself. Just do it."

She didn't say a word in response. The Jaguar rocketed over the Vincent Thomas Bridge, over the iron-gray waters of the Main Channel, and Stefan caught sight of helicopters above. Police helicopters, two of them. He pointed, and Katie nodded, lips compressed into a straight line.

"Right or left?" she asked as they exited from the bridge, and Seaside stretched across in front of the hood of the car. "Stefan! Right or left!"

He folded his arms. "You decide."

She glared at him, then whipped the steering to the right. "I have no idea what's this way."

"Just keep following your instincts. Trust me, Katie. I know you can do it."

She was utterly furious with him, but she drove

without argument, following the curve of the road and ending again on Seaside Street. The entire area was commercial, some of it taken up by old cannery factories, many still operational. The smell of the docks hit Stefan with a vengeance, and he tried to remember anything that could have been helpful.

There was no sign of the FBI this direction. The police helicopters were hovering over a spot at least half a mile distant.

"They've got the wrong truck," he said. "We're on our own."

"Maybe I'm the one who's completely wrong!"

"No," Stefan said with absolute certainty. "You're not wrong. Trust yourself. Trust *me*."

She muttered something about gypsy psychics and their high opinions of themselves, which made him smile, and suddenly braked and downshifted the car to a crawl. Her head snapped around to look at a completely nondescript warehouse behind a closed and locked chain-link fence.

"Stefan," she said slowly. "I think—can you reach Teal? See if we're close?"

He closed his eyes and opened up, opened fully, and felt a tentative brush against his mind.

Teal. She was awake—drugged, scared, sick, but awake. The vision he got from her was a confusing blur, but enough. Just enough.

Stefan opened his eyes and said, "We're here. They're inside the warehouse. There's a ship docking outside. They're going to load the girls onboard."

Katie stopped, handed Stefan the cell phone and said, "Stay in the car." She reached under her jacket and removed her pistol, checked the clip and safety, and made sure that her extra clips were ready to hand. "Call the Port Police and the FBI—the task force is the last call, so just redial. Get backup here as soon as possible. Tell them I have a visual on the girls."

"Wait, Katie—"

"Stefan." She already had the car door open. Even though she was physically next to him, she was already in the warehouse in every other way. "Every second counts. I won't put myself at risk, but I have to do this."

"Let me—"

"No. *Stay.*"

She slammed the door. Stefan cursed and opened his passenger-side door, got out and stood there as Katie vaulted athletically up the chain-link fence, expertly climbing and avoiding the razor wire at the top. She dropped down lightly on the other side, pulled her service weapon and ghosted away into the shadows.

Stefan's fingers located the slender picklocks sewn into the cuffs of his silk shirt. Habit, but he never went anywhere without them.... Street magic was preparation meeting opportunity, and he was always prepared.

The lock on the gate took seconds.

He was no precog—he was happy to leave that to his mother—but there had been something not quite right about the vision he'd had from Teal. Something she'd only glimpsed, something he hadn't properly interpreted.

He had to warn Katie, once it came clear.

* * *

Katie eased around the corner of the rust-and-aluminum warehouse, listening to the constant din of the port in the background.... Shrill beeps for loading equipment in operation, deep booming basso ship horns, metal banging on metal, and under it all, the constant hushing rush of the sea. Too much information. Too easy for something to be hidden.

There was a door at the side, partly ajar. She stopped when she saw it, frowning. In her experience, bad guys were more paranoid than good guys, and with better reasons. Leaving a door open at a critical moment like this? A very bad sign...for her.

She no longer doubted that she was in the right place. Her entire nervous system was sparking warnings to her. Beyond the warehouse, on the water, she saw a boat riding the waves at anchor, docked in close. Time was running out, if Stefan was right. If *she* was right.

She pulled back silently from the invitingly open door and retreated, went around the other side and found some grimy windows offering a dim view of the interior. Junk, mostly—a few wrecked boats being scavenged for parts, nameless pieces of rusted metal and pipe.

But near the open back sliding door, a cluster of people, and two kneeling figures.

It was her first physical look at the hostages, and her heart kicked into high gear, hammering her pulse in her temples. *Save them. You have to save them.* But the odds were bad, and getting worse; three armed HTs that she could see, and at least two more, according to Stefan's visions, who were missing from view. Not counting the crew of the ship, who almost certainly would be armed and wouldn't hesitate to shoot.

One agent alone wasn't going to be enough. She'd have to wait for backup.

She was starting to retreat when she spotted the broken window. It was in the junkyard part of the warehouse, and it gaped and flapped gently in the chilly sea breeze. She stared at it for a few seconds, then moved silently up to check the access. It looked clear, and it would give her a better vantage point; she'd be able to cover the other agents who arrived.

Getting through the window was a challenge, not so much for the awkward angle but the need for absolute silence. She managed, holding her breath at even the slightest scrape of glass under her feet, and counted to ten before she moved, very carefully, deeper into the shadows.

There was still no sign of the other two hostage takers that Stefan had seen in the visions.... Maybe they'd dropped off, or maybe they had other duties elsewhere. It was only the three silhouetted in the far end of the warehouse, and the two kneeling girls. Katie took a position behind a rusting ship's prow, a massive piece of metal, and checked her firing angles. I can take them, she thought, and felt the back of her neck tighten up. It was against all her training, all her instincts to act alone, but it might also be necessary.

She took aim, but before she could fire, someone grabbed her bodily from behind, lifted her and flung her to the gritty concrete floor. She hit hard, rolled and tried to bring up her gun, but no further assault followed; the figure backed off and dived for the ground himself.

Stefan. He'd tackled her, and she'd been about to—

About to get her head blown off, apparently. A hail of gunfire erupted an instant later, sparking hot from the iron hull she'd been intending to use for cover…and the bullets were coming from *behind* her.

She'd been taken. Badly.

"Trap," Stefan gasped, and inched closer for cover. A bullet pinged off of a giant metal flywheel not a foot away, and he went flat and motionless.

"I see that!" Katie retorted. She got the flywheel between her and the incoming fire, waited for a lull, and lunged up to fire where she'd seen muzzle flashes in the dark. Two hits, she was sure, from the muffled screams. Nonfatal, obviously. More fire came her way, and she ducked and put herself between Stefan and the bullets, acutely aware that this time she was without the protection of a vest. "Did you get through? Call for backup?"

"I had to warn you!"

"I'll take that as a *no*," she said grimly. "Call now."

He did. She continued to fire, putting every round where she wanted it into the dark, until finally the bullets stopped coming her way.

She crab-crawled to look around the iron hull, which blocked her view of the back dock. As she'd expected, the girls were gone. So were the hostage-takers.

"Backup's coming," Stefan said. He was still down

on the floor where she'd pushed him, phone clutched in his hand.

"Good. Stay there. I mean it."

Katie made a zigzag pattern from cover to cover, heading for the spots she'd mentally marked as hostiles; she found the first man, turned him over and felt for a pulse. Nothing. He'd bled out from a hit to his femoral artery. The second one was dead, as well—a lucky head shot; he hadn't felt a thing, most likely.

The third was gone, as well, but the fourth was still struggling for breath. He was a thin black man, just a kid really, bone-hard but scared beneath it, and he was dying.

Katie removed his weapon first, safetied her own, and then put pressure on his chest wound. "Stefan!" she yelled. "Ambulance, *now!*" Frankly, she didn't care just now about the man's life—adrenaline made you selfish that way—but she did care that he was a potential source of information. "Get over here and put pressure on this!"

He was there in seconds. She grabbed his hands and pressed them down, showing him how, then darted away again, using cover all the way to the back doors that opened on to the dock.

The ship was already well away. She aimed, but there were no clear targets, and firing blind could hurt the girls as much as their captors.

The name on it was the *Ramona Lou.* She committed it to memory, gazed after it for a long, furious second, then turned and went back into the warehouse.

Stefan was talking to the prisoner in that low, soothing voice of his, but he stopped as she approached and looked up. The question on his face was clear. She shook her head grimly, and the light died in his eyes.

"The FBI is on the way," Stephen said. "His name is Lial. Lial Davenport. I know him."

"You *what?*" she asked sharply.

"I know him. He's GD—Gangster Disciples. They're probably all GD. Hired guns. I told you, I spend a lot of time on the streets, not just in Venice. I know most of the gang leaders, one way or another."

So someone—probably Timmons Kent, again—had hired the Gangster Disciples to take out anyone who tried to stop the HTs from shipping the girls out of the country. The open door had been a trap, but so had the open window. It was a killing field, and if Stefan hadn't knocked her out of the way...

Stefan chose that moment to look up at her.

"You should have called for backup," she said. "Those girls were more important than my life."

He froze for a second, then said, "I had to make a choice. I made it."

"You were wrong. And now those girls are gone. And God help us if we lose that ship."

"I can contact Teal—"

"They know!" Katie shouted it at him, almost screamed it in her fury and black frustration. "They know about you, Stefan, that's why they tried to take you out twice already. Now they're manipulating your visions. They used you to get us here, to try to kill us. You're a liability to the investigation now!"

He looked away, down at the boy whose life was in

his hands. "I'm not apologizing for saving you," he said. "You are worth saving, Katie."

Not right now, she wasn't. She didn't want to be. She'd failed.

Chapter 12

Stefan couldn't tell what she was thinking, and he didn't have time to find out; the FBI descended like a plague of jacketed locusts on the scene, swarmed over the place, demanded credentials and explanations from Katie and finally allowed the paramedics access to attend to Lial, who was still—barely—alive. Stefan collapsed wearily back against a rusty piece of marine junk and stared at the blood on his hands. Literal, figurative… It didn't really matter. It was all just…too much.

"Here." A female voice, but not Katie's; he looked up to see a fresh-faced young woman wearing an FBI jacket and flak vest holding out a handful of moist towelettes. "You're Stefan, right? Stefan Blackman?"

The FBI never asked about your identity without already knowing the answer, Stefan thought. He nodded, but didn't speak. There were plenty of people in view, and a dull roar of noise and bright harsh photography flashes, but no sign of Katie.

He missed her.

"Hi. Rachel Evans," she said, and didn't offer to shake hands, but then he was still wiping his down and trying to clean the blood away "You were—assisting Special Agent Rush?"

"She told me to wait in the car," he said.

"I see." She lowered herself into a crouch, coming to eye level with him; she was older than he'd thought at first glance, with fine lines around her china-blue eyes. It was her hair that made her look twenty, he decided. Strawberry-blond, worn long and straight, with an old-fashioned headband to hold it back from her face. She was probably closer to thirty. "May I ask why you didn't follow the agent's instructions?"

"She was—she was walking into a trap." He finished scrubbing his hands and balled up the moist cloths; Evans silently held out her hand, accepted them and sealed them in a plastic bag that she put in her pocket. Either that was out of concern for the crime scene, or she'd just collected evidence. He had no idea which.

"And you knew this how, Mr. Blackman?"

He didn't know what Katie was saying, but she probably wasn't telling them about his visions. "I saw Lial. The wounded kid. I know him."

"You know him," she repeated. "I see. In what context?"

"I'm a street magician. I meet all kinds of people. Lial's

in the GD, the Gangster Disciples. I knew when I saw him here, out of his territory, there was something wrong."

Evans stared at him, unblinking. "Street magician."

This will go a lot faster if you don't repeat everything I say, he thought, but he was just able to stop himself from saying it aloud. "Like David Blaine, Criss Angel…?"

She had no idea, clearly. He usually got some kind of *aha!* off that, but she just continued to watch him without a flicker of expression.

"In Los Angeles."

"In and around. I spend a lot of time in Venice Beach."

That finally got a reaction; Evans took a notebook out of her pocket and made a note. About Venice Beach? Was that a hotbed of terrorists these days? "And how did you become acquainted with Special Agent Rush?" she asked.

It went downhill from there. He tried to avoid mentioning the visions, but at a certain point it was obvious he was avoiding something, and if there was one thing Evans seemed to be really good at, it was homing in on whatever he was trying to conceal. Before long the whole unlikely story was in front of her, and she'd stopped taking notes. He couldn't tell if she was just frozen in disbelief, or had decided the whole story was too far-fetched to bother documenting it.

When he was finished—and it took another hour of questioning, from Evans and then from another agent, clearly her senior—Stefan asked to make phone calls—denied—and then asked to see Katie. Also denied. Finally, word came down that Katie was on her way to see him, and for the first time he felt a surge of hope.

Until he saw her.

It was like looking at a stranger. She saw him, but she didn't *see* him…. It was as if everything that they'd been through in the past twenty-four hours hadn't happened at all.

As if the two of them had never met before.

"Katie," he murmured, and heard the pain in his voice. She didn't react to that at all.

"I've asked that you be released for now," she said. "They're going to investigate further to find out your links to the Gangster Disciples…."

"My *what?*"

"…and you shouldn't leave town. I called your dad. He's coming to pick you up. Your car's being impounded. It'll be examined for forensic evidence."

"Forensic evidence of what, Katie? And you know it's not my car. It's Angelo's car. He'll kill me if you take it apart."

She didn't answer him, not directly. "I know that you meant well, Stefan. I know that you intended to help me, and maybe you even believe that you did, but the end result is that those girls are missing, and I lost my chance to save them. And if I'd been on my own, this wouldn't have happened."

"Yeah," he said and got to his feet to face her. "Yeah, you're right about that. It wouldn't have happened because you wouldn't have been able to so much as trace the van out of Phoenix, much less come this close. Katie—"

"I have to go," she said. "I need to work."

She turned her back on him, and walked away. He

clenched his fists, saw a red haze settle over everything, and deliberately breathed in and out until it faded. He had a gypsy temper, as well as a gypsy instinct for wandering. What the hell was *that*, she needed to work? They'd been working, both of them, trusting each other, depending on each other…and now…

Now she was an FBI agent, he was some street-corner palm reader, barely a step up from a three-card-monty dealer. A palm reader with gang ties, and who the hell knew what else they suspected. Maybe it wasn't Katie, not completely, but she was willing to let it happen to him.

She was willing to *walk away*.

"Katie!" he called. She kept on walking. "You really think I won't embarrass you in public if I have to?"

She wheeled around and came back at him, fast. He held his ground, meeting her angry dark eyes steadily.

"You wouldn't dare," she said. Her tone was low and viciously intense.

"I don't want to," Stefan agreed, "but I'm not letting you just dump me like this. Katie, whatever happens, I want to see you. I *need* to see you. Remember that."

"Remember this," she snapped back. "If those girls die and I find out that you had anything, *anything* to do with delaying me along the way, God help you, Stefan. We're done now."

And then she was gone, and he was standing alone in a roomful of people, all of them staring at him with identical, chilly expressions that conveyed their doubts more than words could. He knew he should be worried for himself—an FBI investigation wasn't anything to shrug off—but mostly, he was just worried about Katie Rush.

She'd cut the bond between them so brutally that he wondered how, and when, she'd start to bleed.

And who'd be there for her when she did.

It was the hardest thing she'd ever done, walking away from Stefan. He'd looked so alone there, and so...*disappointed* in her. But surely he had to understand how she felt. Looking at him reminded her bitterly and agonizingly of the past day, of the girls on their knees, silhouetted in the doorway, of Stefan's grim determination to do whatever it took to save them.

She'd let him down. She'd let herself down. And now they were both at risk. She had to distance herself from him, and try to avoid pulling him down with her. They were going to crucify her, no question, and she fully deserved it.

Stefan...Stefan deserved to go back to his life. She'd hurt him, badly, at the end, but that was better. It was just better that he give up and go back to the beach, back to the pretty tanned girls and the uncomplicated fun they represented. He didn't belong in her world, and she definitely didn't belong in his.

Still, what she'd said to him had caught her by surprise. She'd simply meant to say whatever was necessary to push him away, but that had been...bitter. She hadn't known she was so angry until it had boiled out of her, and that had been wrong, directing it at him. Stefan had never tried to hurt her.

Two task force agents were waiting for her outside; she glanced over at the forest-green Jaguar—Angelo's car—that they were loading onto a flatbed truck for processing at the local field office. That was a waste of time, she knew, but it hadn't been prudent to argue about it. She was out on a small enough limb as it was.

Still, Stefan was right: Angelo *was* going to kill him about the car.

"Agent Rush," a woman said. She had long reddish hair, held back with a simple headband. It gave her an innocent look that probably played well with the men she interrogated. "Agent Evans. We're your ride to the field office. Hop in."

"I'd like to wait," Katie said.

"For what, exactly?" The female agent crossed her arms, studying Katie like a particularly interesting potential suspect.

"For word on the boat."

"Agent Rush, whatever word comes down, you're not going anywhere near that boat, and you know that already. You abused your authority in conducting this investigation without authorization. You recklessly endangered civilians. Your failure to follow procedures might have killed these girls. So you tell me again…what is it you're waiting for?" Agent Evans's blue eyes seemed much too shrewd for that young face. "Maybe you just want one last look at your personal psychic network."

Katie drilled her with a look that wiped the smile from her lips. "I want to make sure he gets picked up by his family," she said. "I damn sure don't want him here."

"Afraid he's going to have some kind of psychic fit and tell us all about how the girls are on their way to Venus with Captain Kirk and E.T.?" Evans had concealed her contempt when interrogating Stefan; she was a professional, after all. But she didn't have to do it now, and Katie felt sick for Stefan all over again. If he'd been honest with her—and she still couldn't be one hundred percent sure of that, after his actions at the warehouse—then he didn't deserve the ridicule he was going to endure. *He was telling the truth. I know it. I feel it.* But she couldn't prove it, and in the end, proof was the only thing that really mattered.

And if there was any way that the task force could discredit Stefan, they would. It wasn't quite policy, but it was unwritten law…. The last thing anyone wanted was to give credence to psychics, because law enforcement would be overrun with would-be seers, mystics and frauds. Not to mention victims, and the families of victims. It would be a free-for-all.

She had no idea if he knew what he was in for, and she ached to tell him, but Agent Evans's all-too-discerning eyes were looking for anything that might be construed as unprofessional.

Wait until she finds out about the room at the truck stop. Because Katie no longer had any illusions about that; it would come out, sooner or later, and whatever credibility she had—or Stefan had—would be ruined.

But for now, all she wanted was to see Stefan safely away from all this. He'd still be at the mercy of the visions, but maybe he could find a way to cut them off, now that she wasn't driving him to continue to endure them. Maybe he could find a way to save himself.

As if she'd conjured him up like stage magic, he appeared in the doorway of the warehouse. He looked around, saw her, and for once, he didn't smile. He just looked…tired.

It could have been, some part of her insisted. *You could have had something fine.*

Maybe. And maybe it would have turned toxic on her, like her memories of her mother, like her first two long-term relationships.

This way, she didn't have the agony of knowing.

Stefan's father pulled up in a battered old Ford Explorer—the original model, before there was any such fad as sport-utility vehicles. Ben jumped down, charged over to his son and embraced him with unreserved relief.

Katie blinked back tears and said, "I'm ready to go."

Stefan was still watching when she got into the back of the black federal-issue sedan, and was driven away.

Katie was assured, over and over, with varying degrees of impatience, that the situation was under control. In fact, the task force had been all over tracking the ship; they'd debated intercepting it with coast guard cutters, but it had demonstrated some surprising speed, and had been joined by at least two other ships along the way…gunboats, probably.

So they tracked the ships, while preparing a tactical strike team, and Katie sat on the sidelines, answering questions, repeating her story over and over to an ever-changing array of faces, none of whom appeared sympathetic. No sign of Stefan, but then, she didn't expect they'd allow her to see him again. It was likely they'd go to him, rather than bringing him in, anyway. The last thing they wanted was to risk a reporter's interest at seeing a member of the famous Blackman clan being brought into the field office.

Eventually, they gave her a cot in a closed office and let her sleep. She barely remembered lying down before darkness swept her out and away, a tide she couldn't fight. Her last thought was more of a tactile illusion; she remembered Stefan's warmth, curled against her in their sweet, stolen hours. Remembered his voice whispering her name like a magic spell.

She woke up with a start. Her cell phone was ringing. She fumbled with it and sat up, fighting back disorientation, and checked the display.

It was flashing Low Batt.

"Hello?"

"Katie!" Stefan's voice, rubbed raw by a bad connection. "I don't care what you think, but I need to see you, talk to you, please—it's Teal. It's about—"

The battery failed, catastrophically, and took Stefan's ghostly voice with it. Katie banged it against the desk. She reached for the desk's phone, but hesitated. All calls into and out of the office would be monitored, as a matter of course, and she wasn't sure that she wanted anyone else to hear what he had to say.

She pressed a hand to her aching head and tried to

think. According to her watch, it was just a little after six at night; the task force should have had their tactical response well underway by now, she thought. Katie stood, wincing at the ache in her muscles but most especially in her bruised and probably still cracked ribs, and tried some tentative stretches to avoid hobbling like an old woman in front of her peers.

When she opened the office door, she heard the shouting. That was deeply troubling. Shouting just did not happen, not in the FBI offices, and this sounded just one or two Marines short of a full-scale war.

She followed the uproar down the hall to the open door of a situation room, where Rachel Evans stood toe-to-toe with a burly senior agent—one who probably remembered the Hoover days—and was engaging in a full-volume frank exchange. Katie leaned against the wall, eyebrows raised, and folded her arms. She edged closer to one of the youngest field agents, who looked on with the fascination of the uninvolved.

"What's going on?" she asked. He barely glanced at her, just enough to verify her badge was valid, and then riveted his gaze back on the main event.

"Evans is getting reamed," he said. "Tactical assault just reported in. The gunboats fought back, major ordnance, and there were casualties."

Oh God. "The girls?"

"No," he said. "No girls onboard. There was some monkey business with the tracking system, they lost contact with the boats for about half an hour, but nobody thought there was anything to worry about because they

were still on the projected course and speed when
telemetry came back. Now they think there was a
seaplane that landed, picked up the girls, and took off."

"Took off for where?" Katie asked.

He shrugged. "Nobody's saying. That's why Evans
is getting reamed. It was her operation."

Katie honestly wanted to feel sorry for her, but the
image of Evans sneering at Stefan stood in the way.
What goes around…

She pushed away from the wall, yawned, and said,
"Hey, is there coffee?"

The agent nodded next door. Katie strolled that direction, looked back, and found that nobody was
watching her. Why would they be? She wasn't a suspect;
at worst, she was a screw-up who'd be thrown out of the
FBI for conduct unbecoming, and they had other things
to worry about, namely the mess that had just landed on
the FBI's doorstep.

She picked up a disposable cup of coffee and kept
walking, took the elevator downstairs, and calmly left
the building.

The Los Angeles evening was cool and dry, and she
sipped coffee while she walked a block to where a
cabbie sat behind the wheel, reading his paper.

"Where to, lady?" he asked and looked at her in the
rearview mirror. If he found anything odd about her—
her generally ragged appearance, the bruises, the still-
fresh cuts on her cheek—he shrugged it off.

She gave him the address of Stefan's family hacienda.

* * *

Stefan was lying on the couch, staring at the ceiling and trying not to think too much about anything, when his mother delivered him a gin and tonic and words of advice. "You should get cleaned up," she said and planted a kiss on his forehead. "You look like hell, peanut." His mother had come home just after he'd been retrieved from the debacle at the port; she'd arrived in a rush, clearly knowing there was something wrong even if she hadn't foreseen the specifics. That was one thing about his childhood that had been maddening: Mom always knew. Good, bad, indifferent, Mom always knew about his day before he did.

"In a while," he said. He accepted the G and T—she made great G and T—and sipped it while his mother perched in an armchair a few feet away. She'd changed from her pantsuit to a multicolored silk caftan, very *Sunset Boulevard* with her turban. He sometimes thought she dressed like that just to play up the stereotypes.

"You'll want to do it now," his mom said, inspecting the front page of the evening newspaper. She tsk-tsked over the state of the city section, then turned toward the national news. That rated two separate clucks of her tongue.

"Why?" He sipped. Fire and ice, the perfect combination. Stefan didn't often imbibe—alcohol interfered with reflexes, and reflexes were his life's blood—but today seemed like it deserved to be an exception.

"Because your friend is coming," his mother said calmly, and raised her perfectly shaped eyebrows at the look on his face. "Yes. *That* one."

"Mom, she's at the FBI field office. She's not—"

"You called, yes?"

"I'm not even sure she heard me. We had a bad connection."

"The two of you? No such thing." His mother dismissed the subject and went back to her newspaper, crossing her legs and dangling a jeweled slipper from one red-nailed big toe. "Do you want me to tell you what I see?"

"No!" Stefan sat up, sucked down the rest of the gin and tonic, and stood up. He was already heading for the stairs, unbuttoning his shirt, when he heard his mother's chuckle. She loved doing that to him, he knew. And he fell for it, every single time. She wouldn't have told him anything. He wasn't absolutely sure that she actually *knew*.

But just the possibility of it was enough to get him moving, as she'd no doubt planned.

Stefan always kept a few things at home in the closet of the room he'd once shared with Angelo—shirts, pants, a couple of battered pairs of shoes that had seen their best days, even for a street-addicted wanderer. He stripped completely, had a two-minute shower—his specialty, which had always made him a favorite in a house of people who seemed to take hours to wash their hands—and slipped into an ancient pair of blue jeans, comfortably threadbare, with a gray T-shirt. He left his feet bare, thinking, *I'm not going anywhere.* He had no doubt that Katie would categorically refuse to be seen anywhere with him. He couldn't blame her, not really. She had a reputation and a career to protect.

He was leaning on the bathroom counter, staring at his bloodshot eyes in the mirror and wondering what to say to her when the doorbell rang downstairs. A sigh worked its way up from deep inside him. As always, Mom was right.

Stefan took his time coming downstairs, and stopped four steps into his descent because he could see Katie standing in the entry hall. She looked…different. No longer exhausted, no longer beaten, the way she'd seemed at the warehouse.

Most importantly, no longer angry.

She was talking with Dad, and smiling at him—not just the strained, polite smile she'd shown before, but something real.

And then, as if she'd felt his eyes on her, she looked up, and the smile was for him.

"Careful," Stefan said. "I might think you still like me."

"Come here," Katie said and held out her hand. He padded down the steps, never taking his gaze from hers, and came right into her space, close enough to feel her warmth. Their fingers tangled together, warm and sweet, and he leaned forward to place a kiss just so, at the sensitive juncture of her ear and her neck.

"I thought you hated me," he murmured.

"I do," she murmured back, but there was a catch in her voice, a breathless thrill that roused something dangerous inside him. "But you called me, remember?"

"Oh, get a room," Stefan's dad said, but he was smiling, and his eyes were kind. "I was just telling Katie that you've been resting most of the day, but there was this vision—"

"Dad. I can tell it myself." Stefan sighed. His dad held up his hands in surrender and went into the kitchen. Mom had already gone there, but then she always knew the right move. Part of her gift.

Which left him, and Katie. Up close, she looked worn and tired, and badly in need of a shower; he thought she was the most lovely thing he'd ever seen, and thought about telling her so.

Instead, he told her about his vision.

"Teal reached out," he said, settling Katie on the sofa and fetching her the extra gin and tonic his mother had conveniently mixed and left on the counter. "I think that last time we were in contact, she learned something about how and when to send information. She definitely wasn't overwhelming this time, and she communicated a lot in a very short burst. She isn't on the ship anymore. I don't know how that happened, but—"

"Seaplane," Katie said. "But more significantly, somebody with access took down the surveillance long enough for the plane to land, board the girls and take off without being detected. And that means somebody at high levels inside of the FBI, or another government organization with access. That's why I came, Stefan. The game's rigged. The FBI isn't going to find these kids because key people have been bought, or suborned in some way, and there's no way I can prove it in a court of law. Even if I could, it wouldn't help get Teal and Lena back safely. God, I hate this. Every time we get close, some other evil surprise pops out, and it's worse than the last. Bad enough when they had somebody inside the Academy, but then the cops, and now the FBI…" Katie shook her head and scraped her hair back from her weary face. "There's got to be a way."

"Maybe there is," Stefan said. "That's why I called. I think from the level of control Teal had this last time that I can stay with her and still relay information to you, too. It's a real breakthrough."

Katie blinked, clearly surprised. "But—you're sure? I don't want you to risk—"

"I think Teal realized she was hurting me. She backed off the power, and we've got a clear lock now. It's like a door, I can open it when I need to. If you want me to." He searched her face, fascinated by the colors sparking in her eyes, the sweetness hiding in the corners of her smile. "Do you? Want me?"

"Yes," she said. "I want."

He'd drawn closer to her, somehow, although it hadn't been a conscious decision, and now their lips were touching, a ghost kiss, teasing and torturous. "Want," he repeated. "You mean, you want me for my information."

"Yes," Katie murmured, so quietly it was more of a tremor of her lips than a word. "Maybe not…exclusively for the information."

He let himself off the leash, just a bit, and the kiss deepened and sweetened. Her lips felt ripe and damp under his, and he couldn't believe that he'd ever thought about letting her walk away from him.

"Teal's plane," he said, and kissed his way down the side of her neck, paying special attention to every place that made her shiver. "It's still in the air."

"Meaning?" Her hands were in his hair now, combing through curls, and it felt so unbelievably good. She slid her palm around the back of his neck, that special, gentle caress he remembered from the car, when he'd been so lost and alone.

"Meaning that we have some time before she can tell us anything more. She's looking at cloud cover."

"Ah," Katie breathed. "Cloud cover. Ah!" That last was more of a gasp, and he grinned against the soft skin of her neck and continued to explore. "Wait. *Wait.* Stefan—your parents—"

Oh, *ouch.* Cold water. He pulled back, remembering where he was…on Dad's favorite couch, with Mom's patented G and Ts frosting on the coffee table in front of them. Parents fifteen feet away, in the kitchen. Or maybe spying even closer.

"Upstairs," he said.

Katie clung to some last shred of professional dignity. "Just until you get more intel about the plane," she said. "Then I have to go."

"I won't stop you," he said.

"Good," she said, and gripped his hand tightly, pulling him to his feet. "Then let's see what's upstairs. If there's a shower, I'm yours."

Stefan brushed his lips by her ear. "You're mine anyway, Katie."

She smiled. "We'll see."

Katie was drifting off to sleep, cradling warm and clean and tingling against the smooth warm skin of

Stefan's bare chest. He stroked his fingers up and down her spine, and if she hadn't believed he was a magician before, that light, constant caress convinced her. Only magic could possibly feel that good.

She was so closely tuned to him that when his fingers stuttered, hesitated and then resumed their rhythm, she opened her eyes and said, "Teal?"

Stefan nodded. "Her plane's landing." Silence. She sat up slowly, watching him, and got out of bed to put on her bra and panties. Stefan had ransacked the family's storage to find some clothes left by—he said— a female cousin; Katie generously overflowed the bra, but the blue jeans were almost a perfect fit. One of Stefan's silk shirts completed her change. She buttoned it quickly, watching him as he lay quietly, staring up at the ceiling. There was a difference now in the visions, no question about it; he was still drifting, but it was a controlled drift, not a tornado pulling him apart.

He blinked, put his arm behind his head, and focused on her. "You're already dressed. Disappointing."

"Where are they?"

"What are you going to do, Katie? Go off on your own? Alone?"

"That's what I have to do," she said. "Not as an FBI agent. As a private citizen. You tell me what you know, and I'll take it from there."

He looked thoughtful, and then he said, "No."

She stopped in the act of tucking in his shirt. "What?"

"I said no," he repeated and sat up. He began to dress while he talked. "You're not going alone, Katie, and that's not even up for discussion. You'll need me along, and apart from that, you're going to need to access FBI files for me, so I need you, too."

She didn't answer. He pulled on his jeans and T-shirt, retrieved a battered pair of running shoes and socks from beneath the bed.

"You're not asking why," he said.

"Because I'm afraid you're going to say something that I'll regret." *Don't break my heart, Stefan. Not now, not after you made me feel so much.*

He finished with his shoes and sat, hands dangling limply between his knees. Not looking at her. "They're in Colombia," he said. "I got a good look at some of the men who came to look the girls over. I can identify them for you, if the FBI has pictures. So you need to show me the files."

She sank down on the bed beside him, trying to get a good look at his face. "Is she—are they all right?"

"Yes." He sighed and scrubbed his face with his hands. "Every time I think they're not, somebody backs off, or gets backed off. I think these girls are important. Too important to risk damaging. At least, somebody thinks so. That's all that's keeping them safe, Katie. If they find out differently…"

If they found out differently, he'd be trapped in Teal's visions, unable to escape. Like before. Living a nightmare of an especially horrible kind.

She put the back of her hand against his beard-rough cheek. "Colombia," she said. "I'd better check flights."

This time, Stefan looked up. "You won't have to," he said. "Mom will let us borrow the plane."

She frankly laughed in shock. "The *plane?* Stefan, we can't take some Cessna to—"

"It's a Learjet," he said. "Gift from a grateful client. Not in our name, it's leased through a blind corporation, so it can't be traced back to the family. We only use it about twice a year, but it's always available. Now, do you want to show me some photographs? Because Colombia's a big country, and it'd be nice to know exactly where we were going before I tell the pilot."

He wasn't wrong, but there was no way she could waltz Stefan into the FBI field office and log on to the system; remote access was out of the question, too, considering just how angry her bosses were likely to be when this was over. Instead, Katie commandeered the broadband connection upstairs and logged into AA.gov, and sent a coded instant message to Allison Gracelyn. Allison was at her desk, as always; a few exchanges, and windows began opening on Katie's desktop. The NSA, Allison's playground, had access to just about anything it wanted, on any system that counted, including the FBI's files. Katie pulled up the Colombian files, which were—of course—dominated by drug cartels. She began paging through photographs, working quickly, as Stefan pulled up a chair next to her. Nothing in the Cali cartel files sparked recognition from him. She moved on to the Medellin files, but again, nothing.

The instant she pulled up the first page of the Tumaco photographs, Stefan grabbed her arm. "Him," he said and nodded at the man on the screen.

"Juan Mercado Tulio. You're sure you saw him? Teal saw him?"

"Definitely."

Mercado was middle-aged, fit, with the hard look and shallow, sharklike eyes necessary to his profession. Katie was only vaguely familiar with him, but she scanned his file quickly for the high points. "He's one of the top three narcotic kingpins in Colombia," she said. "His organization's almost as ruthless and wide-spread as the Cali cartel, but more focused. He's been implicated in a lot of deaths, including DEA agents, judges, prosecutors—you name it. She rubbed her forehead, thinking. "He's the reason Timmons Kent was involved, and why Kent put his network and contacts at risk. What Mercado wants, he gets."

"And he wants the girls. Why?"

"I honestly have no idea."

"Because they're like you?" Stefan asked. "Teal's got one of the strongest psychic abilities I've ever seen. I don't know about Lena, but these kids are exceptional, and somebody knows it. Somebody wants it."

"Mercado? Doesn't track. If he wants something, he just buys it. This feels like some kind of strong-arm pressure to me. Mercado had to step out into the lime-light to bring this off, and that is not his style. I think someone else is pulling his strings."

"Which means maybe the girls won't be there for long," Stefan said. "Maybe it's just another way station…"

His eyes went blank again, this time for longer than

before. When he came back, he bowed his head for a moment. His voice sounded unsteady.

"The other guy," he said. "Keep looking. I want this guy's name."

Katie paged down through the file until Stefan made a sound—not an affirmation, more of a low, vicious growl. She looked at him in surprise, but he was staring at the screen. She hadn't thought she'd ever seen that look on his face, but in that moment, she realized that Stefan Blackman, one of the gentlest men she'd ever met, was also capable of violence. Cold, calculated violence, and it was directed at Rudolpho Mercado Ruiz.

"Juan Mercado's son," she said. "He's only twenty-five, but he's making a name for himself as a total bastard. His father's grooming him as his heir, but Rudolpho is unpredictable."

"Steroids will do that," Stefan said. God, he sounded cold now, cold and hard and genuinely chilling. "Turn little paranoid men into big, paranoid men with muscles."

In the photograph, Rudolpho Mercado looked frightening enough.... Big, overbuilt, with a clear vicious light in his eyes.

"What did you see?" Katie asked.

"Teal saw," Stefan said flatly. "He wanted to make a point to the girls that he wasn't going to put up with any crap. So he dragged one of the servants out of the kitchen and beat her. I don't know if she's dead. They took her away."

"Oh Christ," Katie whispered. "I'm sorry."

Stefan continued to stare at the photograph. "Katie.

I know it's crazy, but what if there's a way to get to the girls? To at least try?"

"In the middle of a drug lord's compound? There isn't a way. There wouldn't be a way if we had the Army Rangers parachuting in at our backs."

"Trust me," Stefan said. "I think there might be. What do you know about tigers?"

It was a two-part self-working trick, driven less by any difficult stage magic than simple gullibility; Stefan had worked with the cage before, but not often, because he preferred up-close magic to stage. But in his early days, when he'd thought every magician needed to put on a David Copperfield show, he'd invested in some elaborate set pieces, including a pretty fair lady-and-tiger.

And he still had it, in the barn, under the tarps next to the space where Angelo's Jaguar should have been parked.

"I don't understand," Katie said, frowning, as he pulled the canvas down to reveal the plain-looking iron-barred cage. "It's a cage. So?"

"You're looking in the wrong place," Stefan said and pointed. Of course, she looked, and the second she looked, he stepped behind the illusion, and when she turned her head back, he was…gone.

He walked out from the other side of the cage, circled behind her and tapped her on the shoulder. She whirled, mouth opening in astonishment.

"It's not just a cage," he said. "It's a way to get Teal and Lena out. Trust me. I can make people disappear. I do it for a living."

"But—" Katie was struggling to get her head around things. "What kind of excuse is there to get this cage into their compound?"

"Simple. You didn't read the file?"

"I skimmed it!"

He smiled. "Juan Mercado Tulio likes to collect exotic animals. He especially likes tigers. And this cage was built for a tiger illusion, so it's exactly like the best transportation cages ever made, unless you know where to look. And the job of an illusionist is to make sure you don't know where to look." Stefan raised his left hand, shot his cuff back and wiggled his fingers. When he was sure she was looking there, he performed a little sleight of hand, palming and then displaying the key to the cage in his right. "Mercado's bringing in a new tiger tomorrow. It was in the FBI file. Nothing more natural than bringing in a backup cage, too. All we have to do is get it close and park it near the compound, close to an exit. You go in, get the girls, get them out the gate, and I hide them in plain sight."

"That's crazy!" Katie blurted. She looked scandalized. And maybe a little intrigued.

"That's show business. It beats bringing in squads of guys with automatic weapons and staging a pitched battle." He snapped a queen of hearts out of the air and handed it to her. "Come on. You love me right now, don't you?"

He strongly suspected she would have, graphically, if they hadn't been in a hurry.

Chapter 13

It took surprisingly little time to organize things; Katie was used to bureaucracy, where requisitioning a paper clip took two weeks. Stefan had a cartage firm at the hacienda in an hour, the plane fueled and ready in two, and they were wheels up before midnight. It was about an eight-hour flight, and she was surprised to find that although she usually found flying confining, the Learjet felt…restful. Maybe it was that she spent the hours curled next to Stefan, planning and drilling until they fell asleep with the folders spread open between them.

She woke up to the thin, pastel light of dawn filtering in through the cabin windows, and found Stefan already awake. He smiled. *"Como está, querida?"* he asked, in what sounded like—to her admittedly inexpert ear—flawlessly fluent Spanish.

"You speak Spanish."

"I told you, I work the streets all over Los Angeles," Stefan said, switching back to English. "My Spanish is better than my Mandarin, but I'm working on it." His smile faded. "Katie, I don't like you going in alone. I was hoping you'd get someone else to come with you. Your friend Alex, maybe."

"You're cute when you're overprotective," she said. "Besides, I can't involve her in this. I've left her with all of the information we put together in case things go wrong. She'll be able to follow up from back home. It's not much safer there, not considering who we're dealing with here, but she'll have more resources."

"It's just that…you're a cop, not some kind of commando."

"I'm an FBI agent with tactical training. I've been sent in undercover before, and I've had to sneak into bad guys' hideouts before, too. Trust me." She said it with a confidence she really didn't—couldn't—feel. There was a vast gulf between a midnight raid on a kidnapper's hideout with the resources of the FBI and a tactical team at your back, and walking into the tiger's cage of a foreign country and a drug lord known for torturing and killing DEA agents.

And if she felt that way, there was no possibility she could fail to make her best attempt to get two young girls out of there. She knew Stefan felt the same—more so, since he'd seen through Teal's eyes just how vicious her captors could be.

"Are they awake?" she asked. "The girls?"

Stefan's eyes flickered briefly, going blank, then warm and alive once more. "They're awake," he said. "While you were out, something happened."

She tensed, pulling herself upright away from comfort. "What?"

"It's strange. I'm not sure I can explain it. Teal's always alert to her surroundings, and she's quick to take advantage if she can, but…they left her unguarded. Not for long, but long enough. She made a break for it, and she almost made it."

"Did they hurt her?"

He avoided answering that, and from the grim set of his lips, she thought about what had happened in the car. Tasers. It was the easiest way to control the girls. "She's fast, Katie, she's amazingly fast. I think they wanted to see just how fast. I think they wanted a demonstration."

"Oh God," Katie said. "Proof of concept, for the buyers."

"She gave them a show, if that was what they wanted. I can't name any Olympic sprinter who could have crossed that courtyard in the time she did, even with her hands tied behind her." He shifted, clearly uncomfortable. "The thing is, I'm almost sure I saw a video camera in a window. I think they were taping her. It was a setup, and Teal fell for it."

Katie made a frustrated sound low in her throat. "You're sure you can't send them a message? Let them know we're coming for them? It'd be an enormous help if they had some sense we were on the way."

"I've been trying, but no. It's a one-way pipe, from

Teal to me. She's sensing my presence, but nothing else. I've been sending as much as I can, but there's no sign she's picked up anything at all."

"Then we'll improvise," Katie said and stood up to stretch. "How much time?"

"We'll be on the ground in half an hour." He still looked grim and far away, lost in the memory of Teal's near-escape. "Not soon enough."

This was part of what she loved in him—the darkness, as well as the light. The desire to protect, to save, to risk everything for others.

She kissed him. He was surprised, but his lips warmed under hers, and he cupped her face in one hand and drew her closer to him with the other. She shifted over to sit on his lap and put her arms around his neck. God, he tasted good, and felt even better. *I could touch him forever,* she thought, and moaned into his open mouth when his all-too-clever hands roamed under the silk shirt.

He said her name, but it was muffled against her skin, and then he hit a seat control with one deft, clever motion, and then they were falling backward as the chair reclined. Oh, better, much better.

"How long did you say?" she asked again, voice shaking.

"Thirty minutes to landing," he said, and concentrated on unbuttoning her shirt. "But I don't think we're that far away from where I want to be right now."

They landed at the local airport in thirty-three minutes, and deplaned fast. Stefan had arranged for local transportation for the tiger cage—a shiny, nearly new flatbed truck. He saw it loaded aboard, making adjustments to the position with minute accuracy, and then gave Katie the thumbs-up.

"This had better work," Katie said, "because if it doesn't, we'll never leave Colombia alive."

"I know." Stefan didn't look up from his intense inspection of the cage's mechanism. "I told the pilot to stay ready, that when we come, we'll be coming fast."

"Stefan...you don't have to do this. I won't think any less of you."

"I would." He evidently found everything to his satisfaction, rose from his crouch on the bed of the truck and hopped lightly down. "Right. Time to go. You know where I'll be."

"I know," she said, and kissed him, light and quick this time. "That's a deposit. You can collect on the way home."

"Is that an opportunity to make a joke about interest?"

She smiled and walked away. She didn't look back as the truck's engine coughed and caught. She didn't know if he waved at her, or watched her, because when she finally turned, the truck was disappearing behind the hangar, and she'd missed her chance.

"Be safe," she told him. "I can't lose you now."

The airport was a study in odd contrasts. There were Americans present—several of them—sitting at tables, reading newspapers, looking bored. American contractors. And out on the tarmac, brand-new planes...spray planes. Katie had read the file on the way down to Tumaco, but she hadn't quite believed how open and obvious the business was here. U.S. pilots were shuttled here every few weeks, put in those brand-new crop dusters, and sent out to spray pesticides over Juan Mercado Tulio's vast coca crop. Most of them never left the airport during their trips, except when they flew. A Western-style hotel had been built for them right on the edge of the property, complete with a swimming pool and an ocean view. They never saw Colombia, except when flying over it and dumping their cargoes.

No doubt some of the pilots also flew cocaine out, too, back to the U.S.

Katie went to the main terminal and out through the front entrance. Tumaco was a hellhole of poverty and corruption; the street outside the airport was a rutted dirt road, and it was probably the best the place had to offer. Beggars were everywhere, as were filthy, gaunt children offering services as guides, porters or anything else a corrupt visitor might want to buy.

The place made the worst slums Katie had been through look like middle-class housing, and for the first time, she doubted that they were going to be able to pull this off at all.

She relaxed a little after the first few minutes. Nobody looked at her for long; Stefan's skill at disguising her was standing the test. She was dressed in blue jeans and a locally made embroidered shirt, just another peasant woman in the crowd. She had pulled her hair back into a severe bun; it emphasized the sharpness of her face, turned her American features into something more ambiguous. Her skin was already dark enough to

pass for a native, if one with more *Norte Americano* in
her veins than Maya—there were women on the streets
similar enough in skin tone to be cousins.

Katie walked. It would have been faster to get there
in a cab, but peasants walked. The morning was hot for
February, but not blistering yet. The humidity was, of
course, high; on the west side of Tumaco, the Pacific
stretched out in a wide glittering net, and the thick sub-
tropical growth rolled right up almost to the water's
edge. Tumaco wasn't a tourist destination, despite the
lovely views. It was far too dangerous a place.

Most of the people walking with her on the road
were heading to the same place: the Mercado estate. It
was a vast sprawl of a place, and she'd studied the aerial
photographs and gotten as close a pinpoint on the girls'
locations as possible from Stefan just after landing. She
knew which gate to enter—luckily, it was a common
entry and exit point for the kitchen staff and gardeners—
and at least generally where the girls might be found.

It was time to put her true training into play—not the
FBI training, which had served her well all these years,
but the skills granted to her by nature, and honed by the
Athena Academy.

It was an unusual gift, one she'd spent years concentrating on suppressing: Katie Rush could make herself
invisible. Not physically…she still registered on film
and surveillance. But in a strange way, she could simply
make herself *not there* to direct observers. It took time
and concentration now—it had been a protective skill,
when she'd been younger, something for when she'd

been vulnerable. It would have made her a spectacular assassin. It could, and did, make her a very effective FBI infiltrator.

Now, she made herself a colorless, faceless peon, no more interesting than the dun-colored beetle trundling along the roadside. She put work into it, well aware that it was her only hope of getting inside the compound, and tensed as the road curved, and she saw up ahead the first of Mercado's guard posts. There were no papers—most of the peasants in Tumaco didn't have any, and couldn't read or write—but the guards were locals, and they'd recognize strangers. They sat or stood in shaded enclosures, sipping drinks and watching the passing parade with flat, snake-cold eyes. Katie kept her eyes down, and kept the image of that trundling brown beetle in her mind. *I'm nothing. I'm beneath notice.*

None of them so much as glanced her way.

Katie breathed in deeply, then out, when she was past their sight. The back of her neck ached from tension, and the thin cotton shirt was already soaking with sweat. *It's only going to get worse from here.*

She resumed her concentration, and kept moving steadily toward the girls.

Stefan's luck was holding. Juan Mercado Tulio's compound had more exotic and dangerous animals than the average zoo, and as a consequence, the sight of cages arriving were nothing special. Stefan had taken pains to make himself look grubby and working class, and his story—told ad nauseum to anyone who wanted to listen—was that he was to wait with the cage for the tiger importer to arrive, that he'd already been waiting for days without sleep, that his sick wife needed him home…in short, whining. Even among the paranoid, whiners were annoying, to be avoided if at all possible. His truck driver, who was the biggest risk, left in disgust after an hour of sitting parked outside of the gates, gone off to a cantina for a morning drink or three. He might have done it anyway, but Stefan thought that a nonstop monologue about Stefan's imaginary *bruja* of a wife and his pack of unpleasant children probably contributed to the man's hasty departure.

The guards had come and gone, not much interested in the cage, which appeared to be entirely empty. They'd thoroughly investigated the truck, which was completely innocent, and had interrogated Stefan himself for five minutes before being driven off, as well.

Now, he sat silently in the cab of the truck, eyes half-shut, and waited for Teal to open the channel. It was something to do, something to keep himself from thinking about the hideous danger Katie was walking into. *We also serve who only sit and wait….*

He didn't want to sit and wait, but he was sensible enough to know that he'd get her killed if he interfered. Katie had skills he couldn't fathom. He had to let her use them.

The connection to Teal opened with a clarity and urgency he hadn't felt since she'd started to control the strength of her sendings, and Stefan felt himself slipping dangerously toward trance state. *No. I need to stay focused. Stay alert.*

Teal was being hustled down a stucco hallway with a tile floor, then out into the blinding morning sunlight. Stefan felt the morning's heat on her skin, and she twisted to look behind her. Lena was also being taken out. Both girls were bound and gagged. They'd taken extra precautions—two huge guards per girl, one guiding, one armed with a Taser.

The girls were being moved. Not just inside of Mercado's compound, but to a large black Hummer parked in the center of the white-stoned courtyard—the same courtyard Teal had raced across earlier in her bid to escape. Teal fought when they pushed her into the SUV, and Stefan's fists clenched hard in impotent anger as Teal watched her friend receive the same rough treatment.

Why move the girls? Why now? Was it because of what they'd seen when Teal had demonstrated her abilities? It didn't really matter; if the girls were being taken from the compound, the plan was destroyed.

Time to improvise.

Stefan slid over to the driver's side of the truck. His driver had taken the keys, but hot-wiring was nothing new to him—a necessary street-survival skill in his youth. Stefan started the truck, idled it for a few seconds until the door slammed shut on Teal, locking her in the Hummer, and then he eased his flatbed into Reverse and pulled it back out of the road and onto a rutted path.

Three minutes later, the SUV glided past him, kicking up rocks and dust, heading into Tumaco. Stefan jumped down from the cab of the truck, stuck his hands in his pockets and strolled toward the compound gates. He asked for water from the guards and was told to go away; he grinned, just another fool, and shrugged. "That's all right," he said in Spanish. "I can pay." He pulled two cold cervezas from thin air and held them out. Cheap local beer, but beer nevertheless.

The guard laughed. "What you need water for?"

"My wife brews the beer. I'd rather drink the water."

More laughter. They'd already heard about his wife. The guards weren't fools, though; one took the beer, flipped the cap, and handed it back to Stefan. "Drink it," he said, and when Stefan hesitated, cocked the lever on the automatic pistol strapped casually around his chest. "Drink it, amigo."

Stefan obligingly downed it, and gagged. It was foul, all right. The guard grinned and tossed him a bottle of chilled water. "Here," he said. "You earned it. Where'd you learn that?"

"This?" Stefan produced another beer out of no-where. "Eh. It's nothing. My uncle taught me."

Magic fascinated everyone, from the smallest child to the most cynical bastards. Stefan continued to do sleight of hand. He was out of beers, so he moved on to cards, using a worn American deck with Budweiser advertising on the back. He gathered attention, which was what he wanted. It took about three minutes for someone with higher rank in the cynical bastard department to arrive and tell him to get lost; he promptly folded up his deck, handed over his last beer and went back to the truck.

He'd done everything he could to get Katie's attention, short of yelling her name, but she could have been anywhere, could have been still somewhere on the road and unaware....

The passenger-side door opened, surprising him. He hadn't seen anyone walking up.

Katie climbed inside. "What the hell are you doing?" she asked furiously. Her eyes were more green than brown now, blazing with fury. "You stand out in the open and do *magic tricks?* Do you understand the kind of risks—?"

"We have to go," he said, and started the truck. "They moved the girls out five minutes ago."

Katie's mouth shut with a snap, then opened. "Where?"

"Teal can't see through the tinting. They're in a big black Hummer, and they were heading into Tumaco. Can't be that hard to find."

Katie was no longer angry. Stefan bumped the flatbed out onto the road and roared toward Tumaco, not caring about the delicate machinery of the cage itself, or anything, except finding the girls before they lost them again.

And...they were back at the airport.

"Funny," Stefan said sourly, and eased the truck into Park on the street in front of the terminal. "We could have just waited. All that work for nothing."

The Hummer was visible behind the fence, sitting on the tarmac next to a gleaming Learjet—it dwarfed the more modest private plane they'd flown to get here. This one was a Learjet on steroids, Katie thought. Of course, Juan Mercado Tulio would have only the biggest and the best.

"We'll have to leave the cage," she said. "Too much time to load it again."

Stefan looked briefly pained, but he nodded. "I'll get to the plane and get it ready for takeoff."

"We're going to be moving fast," Katie said. "Tell the pilot that once the girls are onboard, we don't stop. We don't stop for anything." Once they were in U.S. airspace, she could get Allison to give them an escort fighter, but the danger was between Colombia and the U.S. And in taking off at all. "Go, Stefan. Hurry."

He nodded and slipped out of the truck, heading for the side gate of the airport. It was secured with a shiny new lock, but she didn't expect that would slow him down.

Katie gathered her shadows around her, concentrating hard on being nothing. She had no idea what it would look like to someone actually watching her do it, but in her own mind she simply began to fade…slowly…away.

Until she was invisible.

She walked into the terminal, past unseeing security, past armed guards, out to the tarmac.

The Hummer was five hundred feet away, glimmering in the sun like polished onyx. It was surrounded by armed men, all facing outward and scanning for trouble. She took a second to order her mind, then kept walking.

You don't see me. You see nothing at all but a dull brown beetle making its way across the concrete. Nothing.

She was fifty feet away, with a gun in her hand, when the Hummer's back door was opened and Lena Poole was yanked out onto the ground.

Katie felt a hot rush of anguish. *So close, we're so close...* Lena's eyes skipped right over her, then suddenly came back and widened. *She can see me.* If Lena could, it was only a matter of time before the guards saw through the illusion, too. Katie pointed to her right, toward the hangar where Stefan's plane was powering up its engines.

Lena nodded.

Teal was fighting extraction from the SUV—a critical lapse in security, as Lena's guard loosened his grip to reach inside to help.

Lena exploded into motion, racing toward Katie and the plane beyond. Katie went smoothly to one knee, braced herself, and began firing. Three guards went down, and then Teal appeared in the doorway of the SUV, held as a shield with the muzzle of a gun sticking out from under her arm.

This is what they did before, Katie recognized coldly. When they killed the cops on the road.

Teal was too tall to shoot around, and whoever was behind her was well covered. Katie knew she'd lost the element of surprise; she couldn't recover invisibility once the illusion was broken, and the rattle of gunfire would bring all kinds of trouble down on them, anyway. She had seconds to act.

"Hey, Sheila!" she called. "Christine Evans says your typing sucks!"

It was a guess, but an educated one; the hand holding the gun was too small to belong to one of the male guards. She got a flicker of motion behind Teal, as the other woman—the one who'd wormed her way into a position of trust with the students and faculty at the Athena Academy—revealed herself for just a second, long enough to take a surprised look.

It was enough. Katie didn't miss.

Sheila Richards Stanley's body thumped back inside the Hummer, and the gun tumbled down to the floorboards. Teal jumped down from the truck, took a step toward Katie…

…and then stopped. Something like realization spread across her face.

And then, resignation.

"Teal!" Katie yelled. "Come on! Hurry!"

People were starting to react. At the Learjet behind the Hummer, a graying middle-aged man with a hawk-sharp face appeared in the hatch, and Katie recognized him instantly. Juan Mercado Tulio. An overbulked younger man crowded in next to him and pushed by to clatter down the steps—his son, Rudolpho, the one who liked to beat women.

There was a third man in the doorway—about Juan's age, with close-cropped brown hair and a neatly trimmed goatee. Caucasian. Katie didn't recognize him.

"Teal!" she yelled again. "Teal, come on, we've got to move *now!*"

The girl took another step toward her, and their eyes met.

And Katie saw Teal's fingers blur into motion, fast sign language, just as a guard reached her and dragged her backward toward the waiting plane.

Katie retreated—had to retreat—as the steroid-swollen hulk coming down from the plane sprayed a hail of automatic fire in her direction. He was a terrible shot, but he didn't have to be good to kill her. Just persistent.

Juan yelled at his son in Spanish, and Rudolpho stopped shooting. They must have realized that it put Teal in danger.

Teal's sign language had said, *Can't go now, have to find out more, you go with Lena.*

God, Teal was *choosing* to stay.

More bullets bounced Katie's way, driving her back. The guards were arriving, and they had an angle on her that wouldn't endanger Teal. She had seconds to live.

"Teal, come on! Run! You have to!" Katie shouted, even as she fired at the guards and retreated across the open tarmac. Behind her, Stefan's Learjet was powering up, and she could hear him shouting something, but it was lost over the roar and gunfire.

Something hot grazed her thigh. Katie controlled her flinch and dropped two more gunmen, steadily retreating and facing the enemy the whole way.

Teal didn't—wouldn't—follow. She stood there, watching, until two guards closed in on her and began dragging her toward the other plane, where Juan, his son and the other man waited at the top of the stairs.

"Teal!" Stefan yelled. "Teal, come on!" He was on the ground now, out of the plane. Katie cursed and kept firing until her gun ran dry, grabbed a second clip and changed it on the fly.

"Stefan, *get in the jet!*" She was twenty feet away. Less.

Instead, Stefan came *toward her.* Staring toward Teal, oblivious to his own danger.

"Stefan!" she screamed, and in that moment she knew he was right, she was precognitive. For all the good it did.

She saw the bullet strike him in slow motion, low in the chest, and then explode out of his back in a spray of blood.

Stefan staggered, mouth opening, and went down to his knees. He looked confused as he tried to get up, as if his brain simply wouldn't admit what had happened.

Katie screamed, emptied her clip toward the plane, grabbed Stefan with one hand and towed him toward the steps. She had to drop her gun to get him up into the fuselage.

"Go!" she yelled to the pilot, who was standing in the cockpit opening, looking frozen. He threw himself into the seat and flipped switches. "Oh God, no, Stefan—"

Katie sobbed, but she didn't let it stop her. She grabbed the steps, yanked them up and closed and locked the hatch. Bullets were rattling on the skin of the plane, and it was entirely possible they were all going to die here, all of them, but it was out of her hands now and *Stefan was bleeding*....

Lena was sitting in one of the leather seats, eyes wide, looking terrified. Katie barely registered her presence as she threw herself to her knees next to Stefan and rolled him over to take a look at the wound in his back.

It wasn't gushing, so he had no torn arteries, but it was bleeding badly. Katie stripped off her peasant blouse, wadded it up and jammed it into the wound, pressing as hard as her shaking muscles would allow.

"Don't," she panted. "Don't you die on me, Stefan. Don't you dare die on me now."

His eyes were open, but she wasn't sure he could see her. Her tears fell on his face as she rolled him onto his back, pinning the makeshift bandage in place, and applied pressure to the bullet wound in the front. He was still breathing. There was still hope.

There had to be hope.

"Teal," he said, in a pale thread of a voice. Katie choked back another sob and put her hand on his cheek.

"It's all right," she said. "We have Lena. She's safe."

"Teal," he said again, and his eyes drifted shut. "She stayed. She wants to be a hero."

Katie hung on to him against gravity and the world as the plane hurtled down the runway and into the air.

Chapter 14

The only sounds in the hospital room in Los Angeles were the sounds of machines. Stefan's chest rose and fell, draped in white. Katie pillowed her head on her crossed arms and tried to sleep, but despite an extreme amount of weariness, she couldn't close her eyes.

She had the feeling he was an illusion, that the second she looked away, he'd disappear and she'd be left with nothing but tears.

Somehow, he'd hung on during the flight; they'd put down in El Paso, and Stefan had been rushed into surgery. It had taken days before he was strong enough to transfer via helicopter here, to Cedars-Sinai. She hadn't left his side. Neither had Lena Poole, until the FBI had arrived to debrief her, then return her to her family.

Katie missed Lena. The girl had brought warmth

with her, a kind of constant cheer that left the world feeling a bit colder in her absence.

Small victories, seeing Lena cradled in her mother's arms.

Small tragedies, seeing Teal's family without that comfort.

The FBI had come and gone. Katie hadn't paid much attention really; she already knew that she was likely to be censured, at the very least, and she had no argument with it. She'd done what was necessary at every turn, and so had Stefan.

And Stefan had paid the real price.

"Katie."

She raised her head. Ben Blackman was standing there, holding out a cup; she registered the warm, nutty aroma of coffee. Another product of Colombia, like the bullet that had torn through Stefan's chest, narrowly missing the tangle of arteries, nicking his right lung but miraculously avoiding any of a dozen fatal bounces.

Stefan's spine was intact, and so was his heart. Hers was near to breaking, though, at the look in his father's eyes.

"I'm sorry, sir," she said, and stood up slowly. "I'm so sorry. I broke my word to you."

Ben put the coffee down and opened his arms. Katie stepped into his embrace, sucked in a deep, uncontrolled breath, and tried—failed—not to cry. It felt good, being forgiven so freely. She didn't deserve the grace.

"My son loves you," Ben said, and moved her back to look into her tear-streaked face. "You do know that, don't you?"

"He barely knows me."

"He knows you better than you know yourself, Katie. And you didn't break your word. My son's still here." He kissed her gently on the cheek and let her go. He walked to the bed and took Stefan's limp hand in his. "I know you can hear me, son. I love you." He smoothed Stefan's tangled hair back. "Angelo sends his love. He even forgives you for the car, but he says you have to pay him back. So you have to wake up. It's a really big loan."

Katie covered her mouth with her hands, tears sparking again. Stefan hadn't moved or spoken since that terrible moment on the plane, and the doctors weren't sure whether or not there had been brain damage from the blood loss. *He could wake up five minutes from now, or next year, they'd said. He could be fine, or he could be severely impaired. The brain is delicate. We'll just have to see.*

She half expected him to open his eyes, but Stefan just continued to sleep, limp and pale, fed by tubes.

When Stefan's mother came in, Katie retreated, heartsick. She walked down the hall for air, got coffee she couldn't taste and didn't want, and paced. There were a hundred dramas unfolding around her, but she couldn't care about any of them at the moment.

Teal wanted to stay. Stefan hadn't explained that, and she *couldn't* explain it. It wasn't possible for Teal to have been brainwashed so quickly, was it? Lena hadn't hesitated to take the opportunity to run, but Teal… *Teal wanted to stay.* Because Teal understood how deep this thing went.

Teal was offering herself as a secret agent, already on the inside.

Katie gnawed on a thumbnail already bloody with the habit, and was turning the problem over and over in her mind when she heard familiar voices. She hadn't realized what she was doing, but she'd been gathering herself in again, making herself small, and as a result, the three women standing just a few feet away hadn't spotted her.

Allison, Kayla and Alex. They didn't know she could hear them.

"—Spider files," Alex said. "Rainy's daughter Lynn helped break the code. Looks like Arachne wants those files destroyed, whatever the cost."

"Arachne?" Kayla asked and frowned.

"You probably know her as A, but it's the same woman," Allison said. "Lynn and Kim Valenti from the NSA did a superb job getting as far as they did. Those files are unbelievably difficult to crack. Even as much as they've done, there's still a lot more we can't read yet."

Alex nodded, arms folded. "Let's leave that for another day. What about Morgan? Is he coming?"

"Can't," Allison said. "NSA's got him on another job, but he knows what happened. He tried to get free, but things were too tenuous where he was. He knows Katie's in some trouble, and he's prepared to help sort it out. I think it's going to be up to Athena Force to pull some strings, though. She went way over the line for us."

Morgan? Katie's brother was barely a presence in her life, these days; his job was his life, and even though she'd been through hell, he wasn't likely to declare an emergency and fly to her side unless she'd been the one hooked up to machines. Still, it was nice to know he'd thought about it. She'd always thought of her family as more polite strangers than real support, but maybe...

She was still thinking about Morgan, and family, when Allison suddenly looked her way, eyes wide. The other two women stepped back, equally surprised and off balance. "Katie," Alex said, recovering her poise first. "I didn't see you there. How's Stefan?"

"The same." She managed a quick smile. Kayla murmured something polite and left; Alex went with her, casting a puzzled glance at Allison, who shook her head and took a seat next to Katie. After her initial start of surprise, Allison looked self-contained, and if she was feeling sympathy for Katie's suffering, she didn't show it.

"How is he, really?" Allison asked.

"Still in a coma," Katie said. "What are you doing here?"

"Business," Allison said. "To do with you, actually. I need to show you something."

Katie nodded and sank down into one of the hard leather chairs against the wall. Allison perched next to her, reached into her bag and pulled out a small color PDA. "There was a reporter at the airport in Tumaco, taking some unauthorized footage of the drug traffic. For obvious reasons, he didn't want to be identified, but he tried to peddle the video of the shootout to the media. The Colombian authorities confiscated it, and we got a copy. We went over the footage frame by frame, and we found something."

"What?"

Allison hit a button, and a blurred still image appeared on the screen, a close-up of the Caucasian who'd been on the plane with Tulio and his son. Brown hair and goatee, light-colored eyes.

"I don't know him," Katie said. "Why? What's so important?"

"His name is Dr. Jeremy Loschetter," Allison said, "and we think he's behind the abduction."

"What kind of doctor?"

"Medical researcher. He used to be involved with, of all things, a fertility clinic in New Mexico."

Katie was tired, and it took her sluggish brain a few seconds to catch up. "Zuni, New Mexico?"

"That's the one." Allison looked gratified. "You understand."

"So Teal and Lena—they weren't random. They were chosen deliberately—harvested."

"We think so. It would explain what you told us about the videotaping of Teal's abilities. They did something similar to Lena, too—took video of her lifting heavy objects. Apparently, Lena bench-presses like an NFL linebacker." Allison fell silent for a few seconds, clearly debating something, and then said, "There are things I can't tell you, Katie. Things it wouldn't be safe for you to know. But the point is that the secrets of Athena Academy are coming out, and we should all consider ourselves potential targets now. Especially those of us with—"

"Abilities," Katie supplied. "Like Teal."

"Like Teal," Allison agreed. "Like Lena. Although all of us, to a lesser extent. We don't know what he wants, but he wants it badly enough not to care about the cost in human lives. I just wanted you forewarned, Katie. Watch out for yourself. You're one of the best investigators I've ever seen—if you can find out anything about Loschetter, contact me immediately."

"I will," Katie said. Allison cleared the image from the PDA and put it away. "Do you want to see Stefan?"

Allison busied herself with the straps on her purse. "I'd love to, but I can't. I'm on a schedule. But believe me, I wish him the best. And you." She pulled in a breath and looked up. "When Stefan wakes up, I'm going to need to talk to him about his connection with Teal. I'm going to have to try to take advantage of that."

"You can't. You don't know what it costs him."

"I can't *not* do it. She's still in danger, and it's up to us—all of us—to see that we get her back safely. I'm going to need you to understand that."

"Understand? Well, understand *this,* Ally, you're going to get him killed. I saw him walk out into the path of a bullet because he cared too much about that girl. He's not one of us. It's not even his fight!"

"It's yours," Allison said, and her eyebrows raised slightly. "From the little I've heard about him, evidently that makes it his fight, too. Think about it, Katie. Are you really going to walk away from this girl now? Do you think he will?"

She couldn't answer that question. Even trying to

made her want to hit something. Allison, sensitive to her anger, quietly gathered her things and walked away. Katie hated it, but Allison was right. Stefan wouldn't quit, if he had any way of being useful. And neither would she, however much she hated putting him at risk.

A group of people passed in front of her, chattering and happy; they were escorting a young girl in a wheelchair who had a huge flower arrangement on her lap, trailing a heart-shaped balloon. Katie stared at it blankly for a long moment, then felt a jolt of surprise.

Funny, she hadn't realized it was St. Valentine's Day.

Waking up was a real disappointment for Stefan because the one person he'd wanted to see most of all when he opened his eyes…wasn't there.

"Kiddo," his father said, leaning forward in the chair near the bed. His smile was enough to melt a glacier. "I knew you could hear me. Welcome back."

Stefan's mother stood up and kissed him on both cheeks, wet smacks that were theatrical enough to almost conceal the glitter of tears on her round cheeks. She hated to cry, his mother; she claimed it gave her wrinkles.

She had never looked more beautiful to him…until she hit him lightly on the cheek. "That's for scaring your mother," she said. "I told you, didn't I? I told you I was seeing darkness. Why don't you ever listen to me?"

"Mom," he complained, and struggled to sit up. That was a bad idea, and he decided that maybe lying flat was a better one. Yes, much better. His head felt clouded and luminous at once…. Good painkillers, he was guessing.

Once they wore off, he probably would be a lot less cheerful. "How long …" Because his muscles felt lax and weak, and he had a bad moment wondering if months had passed, or years, and maybe that was why Katie wasn't here…

Or something worse. Maybe after he'd gone out, she'd been hit….

"Five days," his father supplied. "You had surgery five days ago. I know you like to sleep, but this was getting ridiculous." He was still smiling, but there were tears in his eyes. "Doctors say you're going to be fine."

"Yeah, they always say that," Stefan said, and decided to give sitting up a second try. It took more effort than scaling Everest, but he managed it. "Katie…"

His father immediately looked contrite. "She left about an hour ago. Here, she said to give you this."

It was a red envelope with his name scrawled on the front in a bold, sprawling cursive. Stefan opened it and pulled out…a Valentine. It was brisk and unsentimental—very Katie—and the verse was routine. He fixed on the words she'd written beneath.

In case you wake up before the day's over, Happy Valentine's Day. I'll see you soon.

That was it. No *I love you* or *I want to spend my life with you.* This was…businesslike.

He remembered her walking away from him at the warehouse, and felt the day grow colder.

And colder still when he remembered Teal, standing motionless on the airport tarmac, refusing to come with them. His head was aching and blurred with the drugs, but he felt no sign of her presence. If she was trying to send, he was no longer receiving. Maybe that would change, but he couldn't know when, or how.

All he knew was that he'd failed, and if it was bitter for him, it had to be worse for Katie. Maybe that was why she'd left him. Too sharp a reminder of what she hadn't managed to do.

Lena. Lena's safe. That was something, a spot of warmth in a frozen landscape.

His father was watching him, frowning, but Stefan turned his head away, put the Valentine down on the table beside the bed, and said, "I think I need some time."

His parents exchanged looks. "Of course, peanut," his mother said, and kissed him again, then laid her warm hand on his cheek. "Don't be sad."

He closed his eyes and tried to breathe against a knot in his chest that had nothing to do with stitches, or bullet holes.

"Hey."

He opened his eyes with a start because he'd been sure—absolutely *sure*—that there had been nobody else in the room. But there was Katie Rush, sitting in the armchair across from him, with a gigantic cup with a spill-proof lid.

"Coffee," she said, and lifted it. "It's still hot. Your mother gave me a heads-up prediction on when you'd be waking."

He felt the cold dissolve in the warmth of her smile. He eased cautiously up on the pillows and took the coffee from her, sipped, and his eyes almost crossed in ecstasy. His body had been five days without caffeine. It was like giving a starving man Godiva chocolate.

He reached over and picked up the Valentine. "You said *see you soon.*"

"Well, this is soon," she said.

"You going to tell me how you did that?"

"Did what?"

"Hid in plain sight?"

Katie's smile was pure brilliance. "I thought magicians never revealed their secrets."

"For you? I'll make an exception."

He put the card down and captured her hand in his. Warm, strong fingers that trembled slightly; her pulse was racing, and he dreamily measured it with his fingertips on her wrist. "I love you," he said and closed his eyes. "I thought I'd better tell you now, because you're going to be angry."

"About what?"

"I'm going to keep looking," he said. "And when Teal contacts me, I'm not going to shut her out. No discussion, Katie. I have to be there for her when she needs me."

Her fingers pressed tighter on his. "No argument, Stefan. And by the way, I love you, too."

"I know," he said. "I'm psychic."

Not psychic enough to anticipate the emotion in the kiss that followed…but more than human enough to revel in it.

* * * * *

REQUEST YOUR FREE BOOKS!

2 FREE NOVELS PLUS 2 FREE GIFTS!

Silhouette® Romantic

SUSPENSE

Sparked by Danger, Fueled by Passion!

YES! Please send me 2 FREE Silhouette® Romantic Suspense novels and my 2 FREE gifts. After receiving them, if I don't wish to receive any more books, I can return the shipping statement marked "cancel." If I don't cancel, I will receive 4 brand-new novels every month and be billed just $4.24 per book in the U.S., or $4.99 per book in Canada, plus 25¢ shipping and handling per book plus applicable taxes, if any*. That's a savings of at least 15% off the cover price! I understand that accepting the 2 free books and gifts places me under no obligation to buy anything. I can always return a shipment and cancel at any time. Even if I never buy another book from Silhouette, the two free books and gifts are mine to keep forever.

240 SDN EEX6 340 SDN EEYJ

Name	(PLEASE PRINT)

Address	Apt. #

City	State/Prov.	Zip/Postal Code

Signature (if under 18, a parent or guardian must sign)

Mail to the **Silhouette Reader Service™**:
IN U.S.A.: P.O. Box 1867, Buffalo, NY 14240-1867
IN CANADA: P.O. Box 609, Fort Erie, Ontario L2A 5X3

Not valid to current Silhouette Intimate Moments subscribers.

Want to try two free books from another line?
Call 1-800-873-8635 or visit www.morefreebooks.com.

* Terms and prices subject to change without notice. NY residents add applicable sales tax. Canadian residents will be charged applicable provincial taxes and GST. This offer is limited to one order per household. All orders subject to approval. Credit or debit balances in a customer's account(s) may be offset by any other outstanding balance owed by or to the customer. Please allow 4 to 6 weeks for delivery.

Your Privacy: Silhouette is committed to protecting your privacy. Our Privacy Policy is available online at www.eHarlequin.com or upon request from the Reader Service. From time to time we make our lists of customers available to reputable firms who may have a product or service of interest to you. If you would prefer we not share your name and address, please check here. ☐

HARLEQUIN®

Mediterranean NIGHTS™

Experience glamour, elegance, mystery and revenge aboard the high seas....

Coming in September 2007...

BREAKING ALL THE RULES

by

Marisa Carroll

Aboard the cruise ship *Alexandra's Dream* for some R & R, sports journalist Lola Sandler is surprised to spot pro-golfer Eric Lashman. Years after walking away from the pro circuit with no explanation to the public, Eric now finds himself teaching aboard a cruise ship.

Lola smells a career-making exposé... but their developing relationship may force her to make a difficult choice.

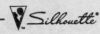

SPECIAL EDITION™

Look for

BACHELOR NO MORE

by *Victoria Pade*

Jared Perry finds more than he's looking for when he and Mara Pratt work together to clear Celeste Perry's name. Celeste is Jared's grandmother and is being investigated as an accomplice to a robbery, after she abandoned her husband and two sons. But are they prepared for what they discover?

Northbridge Nuptials

Available September wherever you buy books.

nocturne™

KISS ME DEADLY

by

MICHELE HAUF

When vampire Nikolaus Drake swears
vengeance on the witch who almost killed
him, a misdirected love spell causes him
instead to fall in love with his enemy—
Ravin Crosse. Now as the spell courses
through him, Nikolaus must choose
between loyalty to his tribe and the
forbidden desires of his heart....

*Available September
wherever books are sold.*

SN61771